BROKEN TRUST

MICHAELA GREY

1

—————

"You can't leave me." Dominic briefly considered going to his knees to beg but discarded the idea. She'd probably just laugh at him. "I'm serious, Cory, you *can't.* Please, *please* don't leave me. We'll figure this out."

Cory straightened from tidying her desk with a grunt of pain and pressed one hand to her swollen stomach as she tucked dark red hair behind her ear with the other. "Dom, honey, I can't have the baby in your office."

"I'll get you a recliner," Dominic said. "A—a nurse on duty at all times. An ambulance standing by to rush you to the hospital when you go into labor. *Cory—*"

Cory turned to him at the naked desperation in his voice. Dominic swallowed hard as sympathy flickered across her face.

"You'll be fine," she said gently. She crossed the room to pull him into a hug, going up on tiptoe to wrap her arms around his neck. "I found the perfect replacement," she said against his ear.

"She won't be as good as you," Dominic muttered, hugging her back. "She won't know what I like to eat for lunch and that I'm allergic to pine nuts and to not let Denise corner me when I come out of my office or how I take my coffee. She won't be *you*. Are you sure you can't stay?"

"First of all, that was pretty sexist of you, assuming my replacement's a woman," Cory said. "Second, do *you* want to be the one to tell my wife that I'm not taking maternity leave like I promised?"

Dominic flinched. Melissa was the most beautiful woman Dominic had ever met, and the most terrifying. Six feet tall, with perfect skin and a shaved head, she looked like she'd be right at home leading warriors into battle. Instead, she ran the bakery downstairs in his lobby, and her croissants were the stuff of legend.

Dominic sighed and shook his head.

"That's what I thought," Cory said. She patted his hand. "It's just six months. And you have only yourself to blame for having such excellent health insurance and benefits for your employees." She grunted again, pressing her palm to her stomach. "Little one's getting restless. I think she's hungry."

"I'll get you something," Dominic said instantly. "What do you want?"

"The usual," Cory said as she sank into her chair and Dominic picked up the phone to call the cafeteria. He placed the order—an extra large turkey sandwich with warm pear compote on sourdough bread for Cory and roast beef for himself, cola for her and pomegranate soda for him—before turning back.

Cory smiled up at him. "I'm fine," she said before he could ask. "Baby's just antsy to come out. Can't say that I blame her."

Dominic perched a hip on the edge of her desk and ran his hands through his hair with a sigh.

"Hey, I have an idea," Cory said. "While I'm gone, why don't you see about finding yourself a boyfriend?"

Dominic stiffened. "We've been over this."

Cory cocked her head. "You're lonely, Dom. You can't tell me you're not. You need someone."

"I don't—" Dominic scowled and stood up. "You know I'm not good at that shit." He crossed to the window and gazed down at the traffic twenty-seven stories below. He turned to face her and rested his shoulder blades against the glass.

"There's no way you don't get hit on every time you go outside," Cory said, gesturing at him.

Dominic shrugged. With his height and the tousled brown hair that fell in soft, glossy curls to his shoulders and eyes that had been described by various journalists as "pale gray like a winter dawn," "hard and glinting like steel," and—his personal favorite —"piercing silver orbs, sure to make women everywhere swoon," he knew he caught and held attention. Didn't mean he liked it.

"That's why I stay inside," he muttered. "I don't like people hitting on me. I don't like people flirting with me—I never know what to say, or what they want."

"You, honey," Cory said, suddenly sympathetic. "They want you."

"But I don't want *them*," Dominic said. "I've never—"

"I know," Cory interrupted. "Even in college, you were like this. Remember that time I set you up on the blind date?"

Dominic scowled. "He spent the entire night

making innuendos, half of which I didn't even get. And he was handsy."

Cory's eyes were kind. "But he was hot, right?"

"Well… yeah." Dominic hunched his shoulders. "But I didn't want to have sex with him." He looked up. "He called me frigid."

"Yeah, and I snuck into his room and replaced his toothpaste with diaper rash cream." Cory giggled as Dominic fought the laugh.

"We're off-topic, anyway," Dominic said. "What if I give you a raise?"

Cory glanced at him. "How much of a raise?" She held up a hand before he could answer, though. "No. Nope. I promised Mel. She'll kill us both if I break that promise. You're just going to have to do without me."

"I can't, that's the whole point!" Someone knocked, and Dominic jerked. He closed his eyes briefly, praying Cory hadn't noticed but knowing she had, and crossed the room to answer the door. He accepted the basket with a nod of thanks and turned back.

"I hired the best assistant possible," Cory said. "He's got glowing reviews from every employer he's been with, he's responsible for several practices stream-lining procedures in a couple of those positions, he's basically going to do my job with one hand tied behind his back."

"It *is* a guy?" Dominic said. His stomach sank as he handed Cory her sandwich and dropped into the chair on the other side of the desk with his own.

Cory took a huge bite and moaned happily. When she'd swallowed, she nodded. "His name is Farid. And don't worry, I've left him detailed notes on what you'll need and expect, and how to run interference for you. It's gonna be fine."

"I want to see him."

"Of course you do," Cory said. She swiveled her monitor so he could see it.

Farid Qadir, Dominic read. A man about his age gazed solemnly at him, almond-shaped dark eyes startling in their intensity. His nose was big and his lips were pressed together, but Dominic couldn't stop looking at his eyes.

Cory sighed. "God, he's pretty."

Dominic twitched, recalled to himself. "If you're matchmaking, Cor, I swear to God—"

"I'm not!" Cory protested. "Look at his credentials, Dom, he might be better qualified than me."

"Than I," Dominic mumbled, but obeyed. His eyebrows rose as he read down the list. "He worked at Lockheed Martin?"

"And they begged him to stay, but he missed Seattle and his family, apparently," Cory said. She propped her chin on her hand and pointed. "He's got glowing references, too, see?"

"Well, if Jean-Baptiste recommended him, I definitely don't want him," Dominic said. He looked at the picture again, memorizing the shape of Farid's eyes. "Tell him we don't need him, I'll be fine without you."

Cory laughed out loud and nearly dropped her sandwich. "Bitch, please. You can't get *dressed* without me. You're just bitter because Jean-Baptiste made a pass at you."

"No, I'm bitter because he told the press we slept together after I turned him down," Dominic snapped. He set his sandwich on the desk and shoved his hair out of his face. "When does he get here?"

"Tomorrow," Cory said. "That way I'll have two weeks to train him and make sure he's up to speed on your, ah… eccentricities, shall we say?"

Dominic switched his glare to her. "I'm not eccentric!"

"Oh, because normal people are virgins at twenty-seven?"

"Fuck you."

Cory grinned. "That's kind of the problem, isn't it?"

"At least I don't macramé," Dominic tossed back.

"Hey, macramé is very relaxing, and people love it as gifts!" Cory snapped.

"Macramé this," Dominic muttered, startling Cory into laughter. The anxious knot under his breastbone eased, and he took another bite.

He glanced up as a thought occurred to him. "You're not leaving for good, right? You *will* be coming back when the maternity leave is over?"

"Of course I will," Cory said soothingly. "Can you see me as a stay-at-home mom?" She pitched her voice up half an octave. "Little Junior is gluten and soy and sugar free. Why isn't *your* child on a paleo diet? Did you know that vaccines cause autism? Everyone, L.L. Bean is having a sale on children's clothing!" She shuddered. "No fucking way. The best thing for everyone is me going back to work. Melissa will be keeping the baby with her at the bakery."

"No one sane says autism is caused by vaccines these days," Dominic said absently. He'd had an idea for a new code, and his fingers twitched as he sorted through the pieces in his mind.

"Oh, get back to work," Cory said. "You've already forgotten I'm here."

Dominic strode for his office.

***

He waved Cory away when she put her head in to tell him she was leaving for the day, still deep in code, but caught a glimpse of her indulgent smile as she shut the door.

This was good, he knew. It was going to turn the operating system upside down and inside out, if he could just get the code to *align*—

He fell asleep at his desk somewhere around 3:00 a.m., head pillowed on his arm.

***

Cory woke him the next morning, and Dominic nearly fell off his chair when she touched his shoulder.

"What time is it?" he demanded.

"Nearly nine," Cory said. She looked tired, Dominic realized, and guilt stabbed him. "Farid is here. I want you to meet him."

The guilt faded, replaced by anxiety, and Dominic pulled away.

"I'm busy," he said.

Cory rolled her eyes. "You're always busy when you don't want to do something I need you to do."

"I mean it," Dominic insisted. "I have to get this program written. Just… show him around the office."

"Don't tell me how to do my job," Cory said. "And now it's time for you to meet him."

"No." Dominic slouched in his chair and folded his arms.

"You do realize that acting like a toddler won't

actually make the problem go away, right?" Cory inquired.

Dominic looked up at her and quickly away, but it was too late.

"Oh, honey," Cory said. She took his chin in her cool fingers and turned his head toward her. Dominic closed his eyes, the anxiety battering the inside of his skull until he thought vaguely he might shake apart, crumble into tiny pieces on the carpet, and leaned forward until he could rest his cheek against her round stomach.

"I can't—" He hated this part, the tailspin feeling of his life spiraling out of his control no matter how wildly he grasped at it, tried to glue it back together.

"Yes you can," Cory interrupted. "God, Dom, I'm so sorry, I wish I hadn't done this. Melissa could have carried the baby, then I'd have only been gone a few weeks. Look, I'll come back sooner, okay? I won't take the whole six months."

"*No*," Dominic said, jerking away as horror flooded him. He stood and took her hands. "No, Cor, I'm being selfish and stupid. You wanted this, you *deserve* this. I'm—I'm glad I can give it to you, okay?"

Cory freed a hand and wiped her eyes. "Stupid pregnancy hormones. So will you meet him?"

Dominic sighed. "Yes." His cell phone rang before he could move toward the door, and he answered absently, not looking at the number. "This is Dominic."

"I didn't think you'd take my call!" The voice was breezy, cheerful, as if the last time Dominic had heard it, its owner hadn't been telling Dominic how frigid he was, how he'd never find love because he didn't know how to relax, that Dominic should thank him for sticking around as long as he had.

Dominic stood very still, and alarm flashed across Cory's face.

"What do you want, Lance?" A distant part of Dominic was proud his voice stayed even as horror replaced the alarm on Cory's expression. Low voices floated in from her office, but she stayed where she was, watching Dominic.

"Is that any way to say hello?" Lance chided. "Maybe I just called to catch up with you, see how you're doing."

"I'm fine, and you never do anything unless it benefits you in some way," Dominic said through his teeth. "So what do you want?"

"I hear Cory's leaving," Lance said smoothly. "Who's taking over while she's gone?"

Dominic lowered the phone and covered the speaker. "I've got this. Go deal with—whatever that is."

Cory hesitated, and Dominic shooed her toward the door. He brought the phone back to his ear.

"That's not news," he said.

Lance's laugh was low and rich, phantom sticky caramel dripping onto Dominic's skin and making him twitch. "Mm, no, but who's replacing her is, isn't he?"

Dominic clenched his jaw. "Really none of your business."

"I'm a reporter," Lance reminded him. "Everything is my business. Even you." His voice dropped. "*Especially* you."

"Not anymore," Dominic ground out.

"Don't let him fall for you," Lance said, malice heavy in the words. "He won't thank you for it."

Dominic stiffened. "I—" Shame scoured his chest and clogged his throat. "I never meant—"

"Whatever," Lance said briskly. "I wanted to see if I could get an interview with your new assistant. I'm doing a piece on 'the power behind the thrones,' as it were, and I want to talk to him about working for Lockheed Martin and the differences between there and here. I knew Cory wouldn't take my call, and I don't have his number, so here I am."

"It's his first day," Dominic managed through his teeth. "There's not much he can tell you just yet."

"I'm sure he knows more than you think," Lance said, and the patronizing note in his voice made Dominic's hackles stand on end. "Give him the phone, there's a good boy."

Dominic stiffened. "No," he said flatly. "What's more, you are banned from the premises, and I'm going to alert every employee that no one is to give you his phone number. You want an interview with him, you're going to have to figure out another way."

He hung up and went straight for his private bathroom, where he dropped the phone into the toilet just as it began to ring again. It gave a forlorn gurgle and stopped ringing, and Dominic tugged his sleeves down and spun. Time to meet the person who would never be as good as Cory.

He stalked through the double doors into Cory's fishbowl office to see a slim man in a perfectly tailored suit gazing with mild curiosity around the room as he sat in the chair by the window.

He rose when Dominic burst in and held out a hand.

"Mr. Spector, it's very nice to finally meet you."

Dominic looked at the outstretched hand and back up into Farid's face until Farid's eyebrows lifted, and he dropped his hand.

"I need a new phone," Dominic said to Cory, still looking at Farid.

"You couldn't just block the number?" Cory said, but she was already pulling out her own phone and tapping on it.

"I'm very busy," Dominic said to Farid. "I didn't want you here. Your job is to be invisible, got it?"

Farid's eyebrows went higher. "You're the one who advertised for a temporary assistant, are you not?"

"Doesn't mean I want you," Dominic snapped.

Farid narrowed his eyes and opened his mouth, but Cory stepped between them before he could speak. "Enough posturing, boys. Farid, I'm the one who advertised for you, not him. Dom, Farid is very impressed with the size of your dick. Now go back to work and let me train him."

Dominic snapped his mouth shut, stymied, as amusement sparked in the liquid depths of Farid's eyes.

Finding nothing witty to say, he spun on his heel and stalked back to his office.

He couldn't concentrate, though, and after an hour, he ground his teeth and shoved away from the desk. Maybe a change of scenery and some cinnamon tea would shake something loose.

Dominic slipped out the side door so Cory wouldn't see him and strode down the hall to the break room. He froze in the doorway when he realized Farid was there, talking to Denise. Neither noticed him, and Dominic held his breath.

"—her replacement? Well, aren't we lucky! Tell me, Farid, can you sing?"

Dominic deliberated. Should he rescue him?

Farid tilted his head. "I—what?"

"Sing," Denise repeated. "It's a fairly simple question. Can you carry a tune?"

"Not if my life depended on it," Farid said. The kettle whistled, and he turned it off and poured it over the teabags as Denise clicked her tongue in disappointment.

"So the hunt for a new karaoke superstar continues," she sighed.

Farid laughed, and Dominic hated the sound, warm and rich. "You couldn't pay me enough to get me up on a stage anyway," he said. "Sorry. Maybe you should ask Dominic."

Oh, he did not just do that.

"Ask Dominic what?" he said from the doorway.

Denise turned and pounced on him. "Dominic darling, can you sing?"

Farid stirred the tea as it steeped and didn't look in their direction.

Dominic smiled at Denise. She was predatory and intense, but somehow she didn't set off the alarm bells in his head. Maybe because she knew she didn't have a chance with him, and her posturing was just that—for show. "My shower's never complained, but that's the only place I sing."

Denise clicked her tongue again. "I was just telling Farid here that we need someone for karaoke night. Wouldn't you like to join us?"

Dominic couldn't help his laugh at that, and he didn't miss the way Farid's shoulders tightened.

"Don't you have actual work to do, Denise?"

Denise sighed. "I'm not letting this go," she warned.

The door shut behind her, and Dominic was alone with Farid. Farid's back was turned, his head bent as he stirred whatever was in the mugs in front of him.

Dominic shoved his hands in his pockets and took a step nearer, irritation pushing him to speak. "In future, kindly avoid volunteering me out for karaoke or anything else that involves people."

Farid didn't turn.

"It's not your place to sign me up for the office brunch or karaoke or the fucking party that Olivia and Ryan down in R&D throw every month. I want to be left alone. And if you can't get that, you might as well leave now."

Farid's shoulders were bunched with tension, but he still said nothing.

Dominic moved closer. "I don't like people. So part of your job will be keeping them away from me."

"Is there anyone you do like?" Farid interrupted. He turned, irritation simmering in his dark, slanted eyes and his full lips compressed.

"I like Cory," Dominic said. "That's about it."

"Message received," Farid snapped. "No people. Can I go?"

Dominic narrowed his eyes. "What's your problem?"

"I don't have a problem," Farid said, but his mouth was tight, and anger simmered in the taut lines of his shoulders.

"Yes you do," Dominic said. He didn't know why

he was pressing, but he couldn't seem to stop himself. "You have a problem with *me*, don't you?"

"My *problem* is know-it-all employers who think their way is the only way and no one else is able to do their job," Farid said. "You rich techies are all alike. You think because you can code, you know the secrets to the universe. Arm candy hanging off you, magazines and papers begging to interview. But without people like me and Cory, you wouldn't be able to get anything done." He took a step forward, and Dominic flinched back before he could stop himself.

"You are way out of line," he managed, but his voice wobbled, and he snapped his mouth shut.

Farid arched a brow and closed the distance between them. "So fire me," he said, dangerously quiet. "But good luck finding a better assistant with *half* my skills before Cory leaves."

He was a good three inches shorter than Dominic, slimly built with fine boned wrists and a delicate throat. His eyelashes were obscenely thick, his eyes dark and unreadable, and a jolt of… *something* fizzed through Dominic's stomach.

He took a quick step back, yanking his coat sleeves down, and spun on his heel. He was fleeing the field of battle, he knew, but he didn't care. Farid's low, triumphant laugh followed him as he bolted from the room.

2

———

DOMINIC HOLED up back in his office after that. He locked the doors between him and Cory and refused to answer when she knocked, burying himself in code and trying not to think about Farid's mouth or his long, long fingers straightening his tie, or the way he made Dominic feel like he was balancing on a seesaw, an inch from toppling.

His replacement phone rang incessantly until Dominic turned it off and went back to his monitors.

"*Dominic.*" Cory's voice was muffled through the door, and Dominic blinked as he lifted his head and checked the time. He'd been hidden away for three hours, he realized. "Just tell me you're okay, dammit."

Dominic cleared his throat. "I'm fine, Cor. Just… please leave me alone."

"I'm going home," Cory said. "But not until I know you're not going to do anything stupid without me."

Dominic closed his eyes. "I won't." He hesitated. "Is—" He closed his mouth. He wouldn't ask.

"Farid will be going home in a minute too," Cory said. "Are you sure you're okay?"

"I really am," Dominic managed. "Just… busy."

Cory sighed. "Have a good evening, Dom. See you in the morning."

DOMINIC WAITED another half an hour before emerging cautiously from his office. There'd been no sound or movement, surely he was alone—he nearly jumped out of his skin at the sight of Farid, sitting in the chair with his feet crossed neatly at the ankles.

"Why are you still *here?*" Dominic sputtered.

Farid rose and smoothed his jacket. He looked as perfectly put together as he had that morning, and Dominic was suddenly, sharply aware that he'd spilled something on his shirt and his hair hadn't been brushed all day.

"I need to speak to you," Farid said. "And since it was clear you weren't receiving visitors, I decided to wait."

Dominic hunched his shoulders. "What do you want, then?" He sounded abrupt, but he wasn't going to soften it. He lifted his chin and looked down his nose at Farid, who seemed unperturbed.

"I need to apologize," Farid said calmly.

Dominic stared.

"I spoke out of turn, out of line," Farid continued. "I was rude to you. You're my employer, and I should have showed you more respect. You'd be perfectly within your rights to fire me."

"I should," Dominic snapped.

Farid nodded. "I can be cleared out and gone in

the next ten minutes. Thank you for giving me this opportunity."

"*Wait*," Dominic blurted, and Farid stopped.

Dominic fidgeted.

"I'm not—I'm not handling Cory leaving well," he finally said. "It's… it's not your fault."

Farid said nothing, and Dominic ducked his head.

"You can stay," he said.

Farid just nodded, once, and left on silent feet.

Alone in the office, Dominic stared at the wall for a minute. Then he dug out his phone and called his head of security.

"Lily Annapurna," a brisk voice said.

"Lily, I need you to do something for me."

CORY AND FARID were at her desk when Dominic got in the next morning. He stepped through the door, and they stopped their animated conversation and stared at him.

"Um," Dominic said. "Good morning. Why are you looking at me like that?"

"You have breakfast on your cheek," Cory said. She made as if to move and sank back into her chair with a pained noise. "Farid, can you get it for me?"

"I'm a grown man," Dominic said as Farid rose. He swiped at his face, glaring Farid back. "I can take care of it myself."

Cory looked closer. "Nope. Still there. Farid?"

Farid's lips twitched, and he stepped in. Dominic held his breath as Farid reached up and wiped something off his cheek, his fingers quick and gentle.

"Better," he pronounced.

"Can I go do actual work now?" Dominic asked.

"Sure," Cory said. "Go play with code while I show Farid how to run your empire. Oh, call Lily. Press interview at noon!"

Dominic escaped into his office and grabbed his desk phone.

"Lily Annapurna."

"It's me," Dominic said.

"Hey boss, so I did what you asked."

"And?"

He could almost see Lily's shrug. She was probably sitting in her desk chair with her heavy boots slung on the desktop, picking at her peeling red nail polish, the phone pinned between her shoulder and ear as she chewed a wad of gum.

"He went shopping. Got a lot of groceries, more than one person can eat."

"He's got family," Dominic said, remembering the employment packet.

"Right. Well, he took a call in the store, to someone named San, I think, but I couldn't get close enough to hear details. He sounded happy to talk to him, that's all I can tell you there."

Dominic glanced out the window to where Farid's dark head was close to Cory's bright red one as she pointed something out on the monitor.

"Then what?"

"Then he went home, and from what I could see through the kitchen window, he and a really pretty girl who looks just like him—"

"His sister," Dominic said.

"Right—they cooked dinner together. That was it. Need me to stay on him?"

Dominic considered. "For now. And only shadow

him when he's alone. If he's with me or Cory, he's fine."

"You got it." Lily cracked her gum and hung up.

AFTER A FEW MINUTES, Cory and Farid got up and left. Alone, Dominic stared at his computer.

"Why do you hate me?" he asked it.

The code glowed rainbow on black unhelpfully and didn't answer.

Dominic sighed and shoved his hands through his hair, wincing as he hit a tangle.

He only vaguely heard when Cory and Farid came back, hung up on ironing out one particularly tricky bit that refused to develop the way he wanted it to.

When the door opened and light flooded the room, he yelped and covered his eyes. "What the fuck?"

"Press interview," Farid said. "Remember?"

Dominic dropped his hands and glared at him. "Busy."

Farid raised his eyebrows. "Tell that to the reporter in Cory's office."

Dominic stood, frustration and fury a red-hot writhing ball in his stomach. "She can wait."

"Well, you are the boss, but it's also probably not a good idea to piss her off too much," Farid pointed out.

Dominic blew a breath out. He wanted to snarl, to lash out, but there was no point. Farid wasn't the source of his frustration, other than having a mouth Dominic couldn't stop looking at.

"Cory tells me there are clothes in the closet,"

Farid said. "It looks like you spilled salsa on that shirt, so you might want to change."

"It was marinara," Dominic muttered, but he stalked to the bathroom and slammed the door.

He made as much noise as possible as he changed, avoided the hairbrush, and emerged in clean clothes, still glowering at Farid, who seemed unmoved.

"Five minutes," Farid said. "Did you brush your hair?"

Dominic ran his hands over it and shook his head. "I don't like brushing it," he mumbled.

Farid waited, an eyebrow raised, until Dominic sighed and clarified.

"It hurts, okay?" he snapped. "I don't like the way it pulls on my scalp."

Farid gestured at Dominic's untucked shirt. "Tuck it in," he said, and stepped in close. "And don't move."

Dominic froze in place as Farid raised his hands. "What—what are you doing?"

"Fixing your hair," Farid said. He began gently untangling the snarls one at a time as Dominic watched him from inches away.

He held his breath as Farid combed through to Dominic's scalp until every strand was tangle-free and falling in soft waves to his shoulders. Farid's hands were gentle and precise, unsnarling each knot without pulling on Dominic's head once. He smelled like expensive cologne, warm and woodsy with a hint of spice.

"There," he said when he was satisfied, and stepped back. Dominic didn't move, frozen in place. "Do you want me to tuck your shirt in too?"

Dominic shook himself. "I can do it." He shoved

his shirt haphazardly into his pants, and Farid made a disapproving noise.

"Honestly, I see why Cory was worried." He tugged on Dominic's shirt until the placket was aligned with the zipper of his pants and then began tucking it in evenly all the way around. His fingers skimmed Dominic's hipbone, and Dominic stiffened, catching his breath.

He took a step away, twisting out of Farid's reach. "I'm not completely helpless."

"At least let me do your cuffs," Farid said. He waited as Dominic fought an internal battle and finally sighed and put his wrist in Farid's outstretched hand.

Farid bent over the cuff and did it up in deft, practiced movements as Dominic watched his dark head.

When Farid was done, he took a step back and surveyed his work. "Not bad," he said. "Almost presentable."

"Fuck you," Dominic retorted.

A knock on the door forestalled Farid's response, and he went to answer it as Dominic ran his hands through his hair again, pulling his professional persona up and into place.

"Don't mess up my handiwork," Farid warned. He opened the door to Cory and a diminutive reporter with avid eyes behind glasses half the size of her face, and red, frizzy hair only partially tamed by the sloppy braids she'd put it in.

"Dominic, you remember Nadine Lacoste from *Wired*," Cory said.

Dominic took Nadine's hand and smiled at her. "Great to see you again, Nadine."

"I'm so glad you could meet me," Nadine said breathlessly. "I know how *busy* you are." She caught sight of Farid, off to the side. "And who might this be? A boyfriend? Have you finally moved on from Lance?"

An uncomfortable silence fell, and Dominic cleared his throat. "This is Farid, Cory's replacement while she's on maternity leave and most definitely *not* my boyfriend."

Nadine's face fell, and she fiddled with her notebook as if unsure what to do with her hands.

"The press room is ready for you," Cory said smoothly. "If you'd like to follow me?" She led the way out of the office and down the hall, standing aside at the door to let Dominic and Nadine go through.

The interview itself was the usual boring pap Dominic was used to, and he answered on autopilot, leaning back in his chair with his legs crossed, playing with his cufflink as Nadine went through her questions.

When she was done, though, she closed her notebook and fixed him with a bright gaze. "So, Dominic. How are things for you personally?"

Dominic stiffened. "Things are fine, thank you."

Nadine cocked her head, tucking a curl behind her ear. "No new boyfriends on the horizon for you?"

Dominic stood and straightened his jacket. "Right now I'm just focusing on work. Time for my personal life once the new products are rolled out."

Nadine stood too, but the gleam in her eye said she wasn't done yet. "I have a friend you'd *love*, he's handsome and sweet and talented—you two would look great together." She laughed. "Of course, he's also smart, so maybe you wouldn't be interested." Her smile invited him to join in the joke, but Dominic just stared at her.

"Thanks for coming in," he said through his teeth. "Michelle in the lobby will validate your parking."

He made sure she was safely on the elevator to the ground floor before he spun and stormed for his office.

Farid was alone in the front when Dominic burst through, and he stood instantly, concern knitting his brow.

Dominic made for his office, fists clenched, aware that Farid was trailing after him but still too angry to speak.

Farid stopped in the open doorway as Dominic stood in the middle of the room, hands opening and closing, seething. He wanted to lash out, hit something, leave a mark—

"Did she make a pass at you?" Farid asked.

Dominic spun. Farid didn't move, eyebrows raised.

"No," Dominic gritted out between clenched teeth. "She knows I don't… swing that way."

"Then what's got you so angry?"

Dominic ran his hands through his hair, making it stand on end, and Farid winced. "She implied I'm only attracted to brainless gold-diggers," Dominic hissed. "That I only want someone who'll look good on my arm but has nothing to offer."

"I take it from your anger that that's not the case," Farid said quietly.

"Of course it's not!" Dominic shouted. He sagged, fight leaving him abruptly. "I thought… I thought Lance was different. But he was just like the rest." He glanced up. "Why am I telling you? You don't care."

"That's not true," Farid said.

"Sure," Dominic sneered. "You're *paid* to care. Go away. Tell Cory I want her when she gets back." He turned away, and Farid closed the door quietly.

But when Cory got back, it was to tell him she had to go home early, that false labor pains were so bad she couldn't stand up straight, and Dominic forgot his upset in calling her car and making sure she got into it safely.

BACK UPSTAIRS, he sat in his own chair and stared through the glass at the back of Farid's sleek head, bent as he worked at the computer.

Dominic had work to do, meetings to attend, code to write. So why couldn't he stop thinking about Farid's hands as they did up his cufflinks?

He wanted—Dominic rubbed his face. Lance had pushed him, teased him when Dominic had said he wasn't ready for sex.

"What, are you frigid?" His voice was light, affectionately mocking, and Dominic ducked his head.

"I just… don't want to rush things," he said.

Lance rolled his eyes but sat on the couch beside him, taking Dominic's hand. "So we won't rush things."

Dominic glanced up. Lance smiled at him, green eyes still amused, a sardonic twist to his mouth.

"Are you sure?" Dominic asked.

Lance shrugged, lifting Dominic's hand to his lips and kissing it gently. "You're worth the wait, baby."

But he hadn't been worth the wait after all. Dominic winced at the memory of Lance complaining about his blue balls, how any 'normal' person would have put out by then, and finally the shouting, the accusations. *"You're not really gay at all, are you? You're just pretending, for the publicity!"*

The venom in his words had shocked Dominic into silence, and he'd said nothing as Lance packed the few things he'd managed to sneak into Dominic's apartment and stormed out.

He'd gone to the tabloids the next day.

———

FARID OPENED THE DOOR, and Dominic flinched. Farid narrowed his eyes but he just said, "I was about to order lunch. Can I get something for you?"

"Yeah," Dominic said, mustering his thoughts. "I —the usual, please. Shit, you don't know what that is, um, the—"

"I know what your usual is," Farid interrupted. "Roast beef on ciabatta, with aged white cheddar, baby spinach, and a pomegranate soda, right?"

Dominic nodded, stunned, and Farid smiled at him. It lit his dark eyes and left Dominic breathless, but Farid didn't seem to notice.

"I'll call it in now," he said, and disappeared.

3

———

"So I'm sure you've done your homework on what we do here," Cory said, typing as she talked. Her eyes never stopped, roving over reports, calendars, meeting minutes, keeping everything calculated to the perfect degree.

Farid nodded. "Facial recognition software. You guys got a pretty sweet deal with the Department of Defense not too long ago, right?"

"Yep," Cory said. "We stayed independent for a long time, but they finally offered us more money than we could really ignore, along with promising to stay out of the way of Dom's creative process. Even so, they're big on breathing down our necks, so it'll be up to you to keep them away from Dom."

"Who's their primary point of contact?"

"Luanne Elias," Cory said. "She's pretty chill, but don't let her talk to Dominic more than once a week, she stresses him out."

Farid made a note.

"Specter is used across a variety of apps, from

Snapchat to Grindr and a whole bunch in between. The government uses it for tracking terrorist suspects, facial recognition at events/fundraisers/shareholder meetings, etc., tracking large purchases of suspicious products even in cash."

"Isn't that an invasion of privacy?"

"Users agree to it in the terms of service," Cory said.

"Which no one ever reads," Farid pointed out.

Cory sighed. "We're aware of the ways it could be abused, which is why Dom's been so adamant about who uses it and how. It's not perfect but we've done the best we can to protect our customers."

"What about competitors?"

"LineWire is our closest competitor. Cubits is next closest but not really much of a threat." Cory typed in a website, and LineWire's home page appeared. It was sleek, minimalist, but not as elegant as Dominic's, Farid thought. "They're smaller, hungry, but their CEO, Lila Rathbone, seems to be a decent person. Well, as decent a person as a CEO can be."

"Did you just insult Dominic?" Farid asked, fighting a smile.

Cory lifted her nose. "Dom's the exception pretty much always. Anyway, Lila's nice, from what I know of her. I don't trust her any farther than I could throw her, though. If she can get a leg up on us, you can bet she will. So the facial recog is the big thing, but Dom has a few other toys he's working on." She pulled up another website.

"The first is Phantom. It's a driving app. Way better than the current ones on the market—more responsive but less prone to accidentally dial 911 just because the driver bumped the curb. It's due for rollout in three months. It's a pretty nifty gadget—Dom will probably show it to you at some point. You'll need to know the talking points in case of rogue reporters, so I've prepared a spec sheet on it." She pointed with one scarlet nail.

Farid picked it up and studied it as Cory continued.

"The other is Wraith. This is Dom's baby, his pride and joy, and what he's currently working on. It's fighting him tooth and nail, so when he snaps, remember he's mad at himself, and don't take it personally."

"Noted."

"Also try to get him out of the office occasionally, would you? Even just down to R&D or the bakery would be good, something to get him moving. He gets stuck in a rut and he starts spinning his wheels and then he loses his shit and no one's having any fun."

Farid nodded and made a note. "So what *is* Wraith?"

"It's an operating system, and it's going to blow the socks off the current market offerings. It's faster, cleaner, and more powerful—or it will be once Dom's got it up and running." Cory handed over another piece of paper. "Specs on it too. It rolls out a month after Phantom, so you'll be handling the launchings of both."

Farid shuffled it into place in his binder.

Cory eyed him. "Don't lose your temper with him."

"I won't," Farid said.

"I mean it," Cory said. "He's neurotic enough as it is, and he's got some shit in his past that he may or may not want to tell you about, but if you raise your voice at him, you'll make things so much worse."

Guilt wormed through Farid's stomach at the memory of their standoff in the break room, but he just nodded again. "I'll keep my cool."

"He's a good guy," Cory said suddenly. "He's so stressed right now, and I know he's not coming off in the best light, but try not to judge him too harshly until you get to know him, okay?"

"I won't," Farid said again. "I'll take good care of him, I promise."

Cory rubbed her stomach and nodded, swiveling back to the computer. "Oh, team-building day next month. I rented an amusement park. Dom's going to fight you—don't let him get out of attending."

"You rented an entire amusement park?"

"Dom doesn't like strangers or paparazzi, so it seemed the best idea. He'll throw a fit on the day, but when he digs his heels in, remind him what happened senior year of college."

Farid regarded her. "You've been watching out for him for a long time."

"He's like my little brother," Cory said. "You know what family's like."

"Yeah," Farid said. "I do."

THE NEXT WEEK went smoothly enough, the days merging together and Dominic sleeping at the office more than once, staying late in Research and Development to play with the gadgets and work on kinks in the code.

Lily called him with daily updates.

"Went straight home. Cooked dinner again and washed the dishes after. How is he single?"

The next day she reported that he'd gone grocery shopping with his sister.

"They bought chipotle barbeque potato chips. Who *eats* those?"

"I do," Dominic said, smiling faintly. Cory was telling a story to Farid in the front office, her arms waving as she elaborated. Farid's back was to the glass, and Dominic wanted to know, suddenly, how he was reacting to the story.

Lily grunted. "Fine, you both have questionable taste."

That weekend, she called him again. "He's going to the airport, I think. Should I follow him?"

"Yes," Dominic said instantly. "Put it on the company credit card and tell me everything when you get back."

She called the next evening. "We're in Vancouver. The Canadian one, so it's a good thing I had my passport."

"What the hell is he doing in Vancouver?"

"He went to a bar called The Honeytrap, right off the plane."

Dominic did a quick search on his computer, and his eyebrows rose. "A bar offering a unique BDSM experience? What the hell?"

"He met someone, a smokin' hot Indian dude. There was lots of hugging, and another guy came over and got in on it. Kissed Farid right on the mouth."

Something squirmed in the pit of Dominic's stomach. "Are they… together?"

"Nah," Lily said cheerfully. "In fact, pretty sure the

Indian guy and the kisser are dating. They were all over each other after they sat down."

"So what happened?"

"They talked," Lily said. "I couldn't get close enough to hear. For a while, apparently they had a lot of topics to cover. I spent my time flirting with my server, who was hella fine but I think dating the bartender. And then Farid left and went to a hotel."

The next day, she called with the news that he'd been to the Honeytrap again.

"He and the one guy talked for maybe an hour. That other guy was actually my server this time. His name is Fox, he's an asshole but ridiculously charming, and he likes to talk. Told me all about his boyfriend, Sanyam, the best Dom the Honeytrap's ever had. How people fly across the country for the chance to be dominated by him. So I asked him who that was with Sanyam, and Fox said Farid was a friend of theirs, that they'd known each other for ages, but Farid didn't get to come visit very often anymore."

Dominic's skin prickled. "So Farid's… into that, uh… scene?"

"Apparently," Lily said. "Fox said he's a Dom too, but not professionally. Oh, and another dude—more of a kid, really, came by at one point, and I think he tried to hook up with Farid."

Something squirmed in the pit of Dominic's belly. "What did Farid do?"

"Sent him on his merry," Lily said cheerfully. "Kid was barely legal, in any case. But our boy just had another drink, and then Fox's shift ended and, uh…."

"What?" Anxiety churned in Dominic's head. "What happened?"

"He, Fox, and Sanyam all three went in the back.

They were still there when the place closed, and I had to leave, but I'll give you three guesses what they were doing, and the first two don't count."

Dominic stared sightlessly out his window, struggling to process.

"Boss?"

"Yeah," Dominic said, shaking himself. "So he's home now?"

"Yep, left the next morning. I waited and took the flight after him so we weren't on the same plane, but looks like he went straight back to his place."

"Any chance you can tap his phone?"

Lily hesitated. "Look, boss… you know I respect you. And if you want me to try and plant some kind of ears-on hardware on him, I'll do my best. But—"

"But what?"

He could almost hear her shrug. "But he feels clean to me. I've been tailing him for over a week, he works, he goes home, he goes shopping, he goes to the club to see his friend. If he's not to be trusted, he's hiding it really well."

Dominic sighed. "Okay. Drop the caution to yellow, be prepared to shadow him again if I need you to, but otherwise you can back off."

Lily hung up, and Dominic dropped his forehead into the couch cushion. Farid was queer. He was into BDSM, and, apparently, threesomes. Dominic groaned. *He is so out of my league.*

4

DOMINIC WAS on the verge of a panic attack. He knew the signs—the shortened breath, the tightness in his chest, the prickling along his skin that heralded the moment when he lost control and the fear took over—but he couldn't seem to stop himself.

Cory's last day was today. He couldn't function without Cory, and she was *leaving*. Dominic gripped the desk, his knuckles turning white, and labored for air. Sparkles danced across his vision, and panic buffeted his mind, filling his ears with white noise.

He couldn't, he *couldn't*—

Someone was speaking to him, gripping his shoulders and calling his name.

"*Dominic!*" The speaker shook him, and Dominic's head snapped back. He bit down and tasted blood as he focused on Farid, bending over him with worry in his dark eyes. "Breathe," Farid said. "Focus on me. Breathe with me. In through your nose—" He demonstrated and Dominic struggled to follow suit. "Out through your mouth. Keep going. You're doing great."

Dominic watched Farid's face, thick lashes framing liquid eyes, aquiline nose and perfect mouth, and wondered vaguely what it would be like to kiss him.

Farid's hands were steady on Dominic's shoulders, their faces only inches apart. All he had to do was lean forward—

"Oh my God, Dom!" Cory rushed into the room and Farid pulled away, stepping back so Cory could cup Dominic's face in her cool hands. "You idiot," she scolded. Dominic closed his eyes and leaned into her touch. "I'm not going away forever. Farid's going to take good care of you. Aren't you, Farid?"

"Of course I am." He was on the other side of the room, it sounded like, and Dominic wanted him back, wanted his hands on him again, but Cory was speaking, and Dominic forced himself to listen.

"I'm only ever a phone call or text away," she was telling him. "If for some reason Farid can't help, you can always call me."

Dominic swallowed the blood in his mouth. "Cor—" He was a mess. A red-hot pile of neuroses and insecurities, who said the wrong thing to reporters more often than not and had no patience for niceties. How was he supposed to get through the next six months without his best friend since college, who knew him better than anyone else and always knew what to do when he fell apart?

Cory's eyes softened. "I know. But you can do this, I promise." She squeezed his hand and straightened, muffling a groan.

Guilt surged through Dominic. "You should have left weeks ago," he said. "I kept you here because I'm selfish and scared—I'm so sorry—"

"You really think you could have kept me here if

I'd wanted to leave?" Cory said tartly. "Believe me, Dom, I stayed because I wanted to. Now get off the guilt train and help me downstairs."

Dominic waved goodbye to Cory and Melissa as Farid stood beside him, tilting his face up to the sunlight and closing his eyes like a cat. Dominic swallowed the by-now familiar fizz of desire at the sight of Farid's long, elegant throat and instead turned to go back inside the building.

They rode the elevator up in silence, Farid leaning against the mirrored wall and watching Dominic contemplatively.

"You have a one o'clock with *PC Magazine*," he said as the car stopped and the doors slid open. "The journalist has been warned not to ask you any questions about your love life."

Dominic whipped his head around, but Farid stepped out of the elevator and strode down the hall, leaving Dominic no choice but to follow.

He waited until they were in the office before confronting him. "You told the journalist not to ask me about my love life?"

Farid nodded, sitting down at Cory's desk. Dominic shoved down the irrational fury at seeing him in her place.

"You might as well have put a sign on my forehead advertising that I'm single and desperate," he hissed. "Every news outlet from here to New York will run that as their top story and I'll be flooded with offers from lonely guys in their mothers' basements, hoping for a free ride. Thanks a fucking lot, but I don't need your *help.*"

Farid's mouth fell open, but Dominic stormed past him and into the inner office, slamming the door and just barely stopping himself from punching it for good measure.

Stupid, stupid—how could you think this would work? Cory's the only one who can do this job.

He sat down but he couldn't concentrate on the code he'd been writing. Cory was gone. He'd been left with an incompetent idiot who probably couldn't find his own ass with both hands and a map. *Six months* of having to deal with Farid not knowing the first thing about him—

Farid opened the door, bumping it wide with his hip. He was carrying a basket, which he set on the only clear spot on Dominic's desk.

"Lunch," Farid said calmly.

"Fuck off, I'm not hungry," Dominic snapped.

Farid arched an eyebrow. "Is that so?" He lifted the lid of the basket, and Dominic's traitorous stomach growled as the smell of roast beef and sourdough floated out.

To his credit, Farid didn't smile. He just lifted the sandwich out and set it on the desk before placing a pomegranate soda beside it.

"You don't know me," Dominic snarled. "Don't think you do just because you got my lunch order right."

"I would never be so presumptuous," Farid said. The door was silent when he closed it behind him, leaving Dominic staring at the food on the desk.

After a minute, he sighed and picked up the sandwich. No sense going hungry.

He was too distracted to savor the tender roast beef.

———

Farid did his best to focus on work, on keeping Dominic's empire running smoothly, but the man himself kept intruding on his thoughts.

Dominic was volatile, neurotic, and an undeniable genius. He was also devastatingly attractive and wildly irritating, with his mood swings and unpredictable behavior. Farid couldn't get a handle on him yet. It was a given that Dominic had trust issues, considering the tail he'd put on Farid for the first week. He hadn't seen the pretty Indian girl in a while, though, so maybe Dominic had decided Farid was to be trusted, at least marginally.

Which was good, because—

As if on cue, his phone rang. Salma's name flashed on the display. Farid glanced toward Dominic's office, then answered.

"What's wrong?"

"Dad's upset," Salma said, her voice tight with tears. "He's yelling."

"Because of you?"

"Partly," Salma said. "Partly at Nasim, who's playing video games and won't take out the trash. I'm sorry to call you at work, I'm just—"

"Come here," Farid said abruptly.

"What?"

"Bring your laptop," Farid said. "Dominic won't care if you stay downstairs in the bakery all day if necessary. There's free Wi-Fi, and you can use my employee card to get any food you want."

"Are you *sure* Dominic won't care?"

"He won't even know you're here," Farid said.

"Okay," Salma said, the relief in her voice palpable. "I'll be there in fifteen minutes."

She texted him when she was outside, and Farid glanced at the clock and rose to put his head into Dominic's office.

"I'm taking my break," he said. "Do you want anything from the bakery?"

"You take breaks?" Dominic asked, raising his head and blinking. He looked exhausted, and Farid pushed down the urge to smooth away the worry lines on his forehead.

"Occasionally, I like to pretend I'm a functioning human being and not an automaton," Farid said lightly. "I'll bring you back an almond croissant, how's that?"

Dominic mumbled something, and Farid headed for the elevator. As he stepped inside, a young man came panting up, his round cheeks flushed and blond hair falling in a tousled flop over his forehead, brown eyes bright with enthusiasm.

"Harvey," he said, thrusting a hand at Farid. "I work in R&D. I don't think we've met."

Farid accepted his hand. "I'm Farid. Dominic's new assistant."

Harvey's eyes went comically wide. "You're his new assistant?"

"Why is that hard to believe?"

"It's not!" Harvey said, waving a hand frantically as if to erase the assumption. "I meant—you get to work with Dominic. You're so *lucky.* What's it like to be so close to him all the time?"

Someone's got a crush, Farid thought, hiding his amusement. "It's… never boring."

"I'll bet not," Harvey breathed. "He's such a genius. His procedural algorithms are just incredible. Isn't it awesome to see how his mind works? Not that I get to very often, just when he comes down to R&D, but it's always so great when he shows me stuff he's come up with. And he listens to my ideas too!"

Farid nodded gravely. "He's a good man."

Harvey beamed at him as the elevator dinged and the doors slid open. "It was great to meet you, Farid."

Farid rode the rest of the way down and stepped out in the lobby to find his sister staring around her, eyes big with wonder at the steel and marble that soared over their heads. She caught sight of him and hurried across the floor, clutching her laptop to her chest.

"This place is amazing," she hissed.

"The croissants are pretty good, too," Farid agreed, grinning. "Come on, I'll buy you something and get you set up."

Salma followed him to the bakery, glancing around as Farid led her past the security guards' station and into the cozy bakery tucked off the side of the elevators.

Melissa wasn't behind the counter, of course. She was at home with Cory, waiting out the last month of the pregnancy. In her absence, her sous chef, Rod, had taken over. A big man, flour covering his rotund frame and cheeks pink with the heat from the ovens, he beamed at Farid as they entered.

"Who's this?" he said. "She could be your twin!"

Farid couldn't help the laugh. "Maybe because she

is. Rod, this is Salma, my twin sister." He drew Salma forward, and Rod blushed even redder.

"Beg your pardon, ma'am."

Salma smiled at him. Farid never got tired of her smile. He'd seen it so rarely of late, and all he wanted was to put it back on her face.

"Can we get a couple of almond croissants and whatever Salma wants to drink? Anything she wants, just put it on my account."

A small, round young woman popped up out of the back, balancing a tray of scones on strong arms. Her hair was so pale it was almost white, trapped under a hairnet.

"Hot as balls in there," she said over her shoulder.

"*Senna*," Rod hissed. "*Customers.*"

Senna nearly dropped the tray as she spun, a look of almost comical dismay on her face. She had a snub nose dusted with flour and big, blue eyes, and her fair skin blushed dark pink in her mortification.

"I'm so sorry," she said in a rush. "I didn't see you, I'm so sorry, please don't report me to the boss—"

"It's okay," Farid said, holding up a hand. Senna was older than he'd thought, closer to his age of twenty-seven than the teenager he'd initially expected. He gave her a smile, bringing his dimples into play. "It happens to all of us. I'd hate to work back there, I don't know how you do it."

Senna set the tray down and wiped her hands on her apron, still crimson, and Farid turned to Salma.

"I have to get back to work. Rod, can I get those croissants?"

Rod handed them over, and Farid dropped Salma a wink.

"Stay as long as you like, they won't care."

He rode the elevator back up, the croissants warm in his hands, and found Dominic asleep with his cheek on the desk. Farid left the bag by his head and tiptoed back out.

———

BACK AT HIS DESK, he went to work streamlining the schedule Cory had left him. After a little while, he heard shifting, and then paper rustling. Farid smiled to himself. Dominic had needed the rest, and he was glad he'd gotten it.

His cellphone rang, and Farid answered absently, eyes on the monitor.

"Farid Qadir."

"Mr. Qadir, my name is Peggy. I represent a company that would very much like to speak to you about your particular skillset."

"Sorry," Farid said, glancing toward Dominic's office. "I'm off the market right now."

"So we understand," Peggy said. Her voice was smooth and cool, no emotion in it, and Farid narrowed his eyes.

"How do you even have this number?"

"That doesn't matter," Peggy said. "What matters is you have something we want. And we have something you want. We would like to propose a trade."

"You have *nothing* I want," Farid growled.

"Not even transitioning for your sister?"

Farid froze, halfway to his feet, all the oxygen gone from his lungs. "How—" he croaked, and stopped to clear his throat.

"We have ways," Peggy said, sounding smug. "Meet me tonight at Aperture. Seven o'clock."

AFTER, Farid wasn't sure how he got through the day. He couldn't think. All he could see were Salma's sad eyes. He avoided Dominic's office, operating on autopilot, and was out the door at 5:00 p.m. instead of waiting for Dominic.

Salma was still downstairs, tucked up in one of the overstuffed chairs and typing on her laptop, brow furrowed in concentration. She looked up and saw him, a smile spreading across her lovely face, and Farid's heart seized. He needed her to be happy like a physical ache in his chest, needed her at peace in her own body.

He crossed the bakery toward her, thinking hard. Of course they wanted him to spy on Dominic. It wasn't his first time being approached by a rival company. He'd made himself quietly indispensable in whatever role he chose to fill, and others wanted him, both for his skills and for what he learned in his positions.

It was the first time he'd been tempted to say yes, though.

He dropped into the chair beside Salma.

"You look tired," she observed.

"Long day," Farid said. He leaned his head back against the chair and rolled it to look at Salma's profile as she continued to type. "What are you working on?"

"Paper for school," she said. "Due Friday."

"Aren't you tired of college?" Farid teased gently.

Salma rolled her eyes. "More than you know."

"Master's in Information Technology, PhD in Computer Science—girl, you're going to have the world at your feet." Farid nudged her arm with his forehead, and Salma sighed.

"If I ever get there. If Baba will ever leave me alone."

Farid looked up at her, head still sideways on the chair. Salma's mouth drooped, and she closed the laptop gently and folded her hands on top of it.

"What did he say?" Farid asked.

"The usual," Salma said. She rubbed a thumb across the vinyl cover on her laptop. "When am I going to get a job, when am I going to help support the family like you do, Nasim might be a useless lazy lump but at least he's not wearing dresses and flouting God's will."

Farid clenched his fists, sick fury rolling through him. "I have got to get you out of there," he growled.

"Mama needs me," Salma reminded him. "She needs you too. And Nasim needs someone who can show him how to be a real man and not like Baba."

"Nasim is eighteen years old. *He* needs to get off his ass and find a job. He could help Mama as much as you do. More, since he's not in school."

Salma rested her cheek against Farid's head. "An apartment for the two of us," she murmured. This was a game they'd played since they were little. "A full-time nurse for Mama. Nasim to get a job. Baba to accept me."

"Transitioning for you, while we're dreaming," Farid said sourly, and sat up. Senna was cleaning the tables on the other side of the bakery, and she glanced up, caught Farid's eyes, and ducked her head again, a blush racing up her throat. "I think she's scared of me," Farid said out of the corner of his mouth.

"She's nice," Salma said. She uncurled her legs. "Ready to go home?"

Farid cleared his throat. "I actually have some other stuff to do. I'll meet you back there, okay?"

"Thanks for letting me stay," Salma said, touching his arm. "Do you think I can come back tomorrow, after class?"

"Anytime you want." Farid slung his arm around her and pressed a kiss to her soft hair. "I'll see you at home."

HE WASN'T GOING to say yes. He told himself that, over and over, on the taxi ride to the coffee shop. He would go in, tell her he wasn't interested, and leave. That was all.

Peggy was a tall, slender woman, with blonde hair artfully streaked with white pulled back from a high forehead and glasses that glinted with the light.

Farid didn't shake her hand when she extended it, and she arched a brow but gestured him to take a seat.

"I'm not a spy," he said as he sat down.

"And yet, you're here," Peggy observed over her espresso cup.

Farid clutched the fabric of his pants. "I won't spy for you."

"Perhaps I can put forward some facts, and then you can consider them," Peggy said. "Fact number one: your sister is transgender and unable to transition at the moment. Fact number two: your mother has leukemia. Fact number three: all your money is currently going toward treatment for her as well as supporting your family, since your father is not employed."

Farid worked to swallow.

"You provide well, but not enough to pay for your mother's treatments *and* for your sister to transition safely, especially since you're paying for her college education."

"That doesn't mean I'm going to betray my employer," Farid spat.

"We can offer you a position in our company with a significant raise, once the data is delivered."

"No." Farid shook his head. "I won't. I can't. I *won't*."

"Twenty-four-hour home health nurse for your mother," Peggy said. "Around the clock attendance for a year, and end-of-life services, should it come to that before the year is up. Full medical costs of transitioning covered, from doctors' visits to hospital stays and everything in between. Hormones, physical therapy after surgery. All of it."

Farid shook his head again, but it was a helpless movement.

As if sensing him weakening, Peggy leaned in. "Your sister deserves a life, don't you think? Not this stasis she's currently trapped in, caring for your mother, going to class, rinse, repeat. All while you struggle to provide for a family of five with almost insurmountable health costs."

Farid worked moisture into his mouth. "You can't ask this of me," he whispered.

"Two-year scholarship for your brother to the university of *your* choice, not his, here in Seattle," Peggy said. "That's the best I can do."

Farid stood. "No," he spat. He spun on his heel and left without looking back.

<hr>

BUT WHEN HE GOT HOME, it was to Salma huddled on the front steps of their house, knees drawn to her chest and hand over the rapidly darkening bruise on her cheek.

Farid bent over her, cupping her chin in one gentle hand even as rage made his vision sparkle and breath come short.

"Where is he," he said through his teeth.

"Den," Salma said. "'Rid, don't—"

Farid caught her reaching hand and gently put it back in her lap. "He has to be told," he said. "You stay here. Is Mama okay? Where's Nasim?"

"Of course," Salma said, and sniffled. "She's asleep, and Nasim is out with friends."

"Do you want me to call the cops?" Farid asked. He didn't want to, didn't want the publicity and talk it would bring, but Salma's safety was the most important thing.

She shook her head, though. "God, no. I just want him to stay away from me."

Farid touched her silky black hair. "Stay here," he repeated, and stalked into the house.

It was dark and quiet, a light shining from under the door in the den at the end of the hall. There was a dim glow from the kitchen, and Farid put his head in there first. He set his jaw at the sight of the refrigerator standing open and milk spreading in a creamy white puddle across the floor.

The door to the den opened, and Farid turned. His

father stood with his back to the light, slim and lean-framed just like Farid, with three days' growth on his jaw and shadows under his eyes.

"Guess he went crying to you," Adil said.

"She," Farid said through a throat so tight with anger he was afraid he'd choke on it. "*She*, Baba, she is not a man, stop referring to her that way!"

Adil flung up a hand and turned to go back in the den, but Farid caught his arm.

"Let go of me," Adil growled, voice dangerously low.

"You listen to me," Farid said. "Mama still loves you, which is the only reason I allow you to stay. *I* provide for this family. *I* pay the bills, buy the food, arrange taking Mama to her appointments. You've done nothing since you were laid off except sit in the house and sulk and make jabs at Salma *and* Nasim about getting jobs when you don't even have one *yourself*."

Adil tore his arm free, snarling. Farid let him go and used the momentum to push him over the doorstep into the den. Caught off-balance, Adil staggered backward. The light from the fireplace glinted on his dark eyes and the sudden fear in them.

"Touch her again and I'll put you out on the street with the clothes on your back," Farid said. "Do you hear me?"

Adil glared at him, mouth working bitterly. "He's an affront—"

Farid slapped him open-palmed, the sound cracking like a whip. The shockwave traveled down his arm, and he took a step back as Adil clutched his face, clearly stunned.

"*She* is your child, whether or not you approve of

her choices. She deserves your respect, and if you can't give that, then at least your silence."

Adil opened his mouth, but the front door slammed and running footsteps pounded down the hall.

Farid spun and caught Nasim before he could hurl himself at their father, pushing him back over the threshold and into the hall. The door to the den shut hard but Farid didn't look, too busy keeping Nasim where he was.

"He hit her, he—let me go, 'Rid, let me—"

Farid wrapped an arm around Nasim's skinny waist and pulled him back, down the hall. "I took care of it, 'Sim, stop *fighting* me, goddammit, *listen* to me—"

Salma slipped through the front door and caught Nasim's arm. "*Stop*," she ordered.

Nasim stopped struggling and slumped against Farid's frame, hiccupping raggedly. Farid held him, tucking Nasim's face into his shoulder as Salma rubbed his back.

After a moment, Nasim pushed away. "Don't comfort me," he said, swiping at his cheeks. "Salma's the one he hurt."

"I'm fine," Salma said and cupped Nasim's face in both hands. Farid watched them in the light from the window, two of the people he loved best in the world, and his heart twisted. Salma whispered something to Nasim, who nodded and pressed his forehead to hers.

"Let's go in the kitchen so I can clean up the mess," Farid said.

They followed him, and Farid brought out the mop as Salma and Nasim settled at the table.

"Do you want to tell us what happened?" Farid asked as he mopped.

Salma shrugged. "The usual. He was angry and spoiling for a fight."

"Did Mama hear?"

"I'd already given her a sleeping pill," Salma said. She propped her unbruised cheek on her hand with a sigh.

"I won't leave you alone with him anymore," Nasim said. He looked younger than usual, tears still on his cheeks, and his chin wobbled, but he set his jaw, and Salma took his hand.

"He won't touch you again," Farid said. "I made sure of that." He rinsed the mop in the sink and set it back in its corner, then touched Salma's hair. "I have to go do some stuff. Call me if you need me, okay?"

In his room, he pulled his phone from his pocket and stared at it, sitting on the end of his bed. Finally, though, he firmed his mouth and pulled up the call log.

The phone rang once.

"I'll do it," Farid said before they could speak. "One other thing."

"What?"

"You have to make sure they don't know it was me." Peggy inhaled but Farid kept talking. "You're asking me to put my career, my *life*, on the line here. If word gets out I'm the one behind this, you know I'll never work in big business again. You'll ruin me. You have to promise me that I'm kept out of it."

Peggy was silent for longer this time. "I promise," she finally said. "You will be in the clear. No one will suspect you."

"I'll be in touch." Farid hung up.

5

———————

Farid was late the next day, a fact Dominic only realized when he surfaced from the code and reached for coffee that wasn't there.

He put his head into Cory's office, but it was dark and empty. Dominic reached for his phone but the outer door opened and Farid burst through, panting.

"I'm sorry," he gasped. "I overslept, I—"

Dominic cut him off. "Are you all right?"

Farid didn't look all right. His normally sleek hair was rumpled and on end, dark circles under his eyes and the skin around them drawn and taut.

"I'm fine," he said, running his hand through his hair in a futile attempt to tame it. "Just… insomnia. Didn't get much sleep and then didn't hear my alarm."

"How's your mother?"

Farid stiffened. "What?"

"Background checks are required for employment," Dominic said carefully. "You knew that when Cory hired you. I'm sorry if I overstepped—"

Farid turned away, tugging sharply at his cuffs. "It's fine," he said over his shoulder. "I'm getting coffee. Have you had breakfast?"

"Um… no," Dominic said. He opened his mouth to defend himself, point out the code was more important, but Farid just nodded and left.

When he came back, he was much more his usual, contained self. He'd found a comb somewhere and subdued his hair, although it still curled enticingly behind his ears in a way that Dominic tried not to notice, and he set coffee and an almond croissant on Dominic's desk with something like his normal manner.

"Eat," he said.

Dominic tore the edge off the croissant and nibbled at it as Farid moved around the room, neatening as he went.

He drew the curtains back, and Dominic blinked in the bright sun that flooded the room. Farid stood in front of the windows, haloed in the light, and looked out over the city. His shoulders drooped, and Dominic frowned.

"Are you sure you're okay?"

Farid turned. "I'm fine," he said quietly, but his smile didn't quite reach his eyes. "I'll let you get back to work. You have a meeting with Sales at eleven, and Legal at one."

"Oh God, murder me now," Dominic moaned, slumping back in his chair. "The only thing worse than Sales is Legal. Both in one day? *Why?*"

Farid frowned. "I'm sorry, I didn't realize they were both so stressful or I wouldn't have allowed them both to schedule appointments in the same day."

Dominic straightened. "No, it's fine, I just—I don't care about sales, you know? I don't want anything to do with that side of things, and I usually end up getting roped into something I don't want to do. And Legal—" He shuddered. "The less said about them, the better."

"Maybe it won't be too bad this time," Farid suggested.

Dominic ran a finger through the crumbs of the croissant as a pattern formed in his head. Dimly, Farid spoke again, but Dominic barely heard him. After a minute, the door closed, but Dominic was already deep in code again.

At eleven, Farid came back. Dominic growled at being interrupted, but truthfully, he was ready for a break. He stood and stretched with a satisfied sigh.

"Did you figure out the problem?" Farid asked.

"One of them," Dominic said. He shook his hair off his forehead. "I was looking at it the wrong way. Came at it from a different angle, and bam. Pieces fell into place."

"Well, good," Farid said. "The conference room is ready for you."

Dominic settled in at the table as Farid took a seat in a chair behind him, against the wall. Across from him were his two least favorite people. Maggie Stone gave him a smile that was all teeth and pinched eyes, her dark red hair scraped back off her forehead. Derek James folded his hands and arched an eyebrow, his smile supercilious and dark blue eyes wary.

"Thank you for agreeing to meet with us, Mr. Spector," he said. "We have some things we think are very exciting, and all we need is your approval to move forward with them."

Maggie stood and turned to the whiteboard on the wall. "First," she said, her voice harsh and dissonant, "we have to go over some numbers."

Dominic fought the urge to sag in his chair and instead nodded, fixing a politely interested look on his face.

The next hour dragged as Maggie droned on about sales and stock shares and company market value. Dominic rubbed at the tension headache forming in his temples and struggled to pay attention.

"As you can see," Derek said, "clearly it's the best option."

Dominic nodded. "Sure." Anything to get him to stop talking.

"Great! So if you'll just initial here, here, and here, and then sign these forms, we'll get out of your hair." Derek pushed the papers across the table and Dominic reached for the pen, but Farid was suddenly there, whisking the entire sheaf of paper away.

Dominic blinked as Derek protested.

"You're not signing that," Farid said.

"He agreed!" Derek said.

Farid flicked through the pages. "Pretty sure Dominic would rather put his head in a hornets' nest than agree to host the public unveiling of the new app, let alone attend a party with a hundred of the shareholders in one week."

"What?" Dominic yelped.

Derek shrugged irritably. "You said you would."

"He said nothing of the kind," Farid said flatly.

"Take this shit away and retool it, removing Dominic from the spotlight and rescheduling the shareholder meeting for in the daytime, here in the building, at least a month from now."

Derek's mouth opened and closed, and Maggie snatched the papers from Farid's hand as he held them out.

The door shut behind them, and Dominic turned to look at Farid, who looked unruffled.

"Good thing one of us is paying attention," he finally said, and Farid smiled. It looked real for the first time that day.

"Time for lunch. The usual?"

WHEN HE BROUGHT the roast beef sandwich in, Dominic had already gotten sucked back into the code.

"Legal rescheduled," Farid said, putting the food on the desk and setting the pomegranate soda beside it. "Apparently they weren't as prepared as they thought."

Dominic narrowed his eyes. "Did you—"

Farid just smiled again and left the room.

AS HE WAS GETTING ready to leave, his cellphone buzzed. It was Lila Rathbone. Dominic frowned as he answered.

"Lila? Everything okay?"

"Hello, Dominic, it's nice to hear your voice too." Lila sounded amused, and Dominic could almost see her, with her silver hair and perfectly tailored suits, those sea-glass green eyes that always seemed to hold a secret. Dominic didn't fully trust her, not when she was his closest competition, but he couldn't help liking her.

"I'm fine, by the way," she continued. "I just wanted to give you a head's up on something. We recently discovered—and fired—a spy working for Cubits."

"*What?*"

"I've sent you the relevant information," Lila continued. "I just felt you'd want to know. Can't have Cubits giving away all our secrets, after all."

Dominic sank back to his chair. "Thanks, Lila," he said. "Were they working alone?"

"As far as I know. Investigation is ongoing. How's business for you?"

"Same as ever," Dominic said, amused in spite of himself. "I'm not giving you any company secrets."

"Can't blame a girl for trying," Lila sighed. "Stay sharp, Dominic. I'll be seeing you."

THE HOUSE WAS quiet when Farid let himself in that night. Everyone seemed to have gone to bed or at least retired to their rooms for the evening. Farid drew a breath of relief and stepped out of his shoes by the front door, then padded to the kitchen.

"Mama!" he said, and his mother straightened from looking in the fridge and put a finger over her lips. "What are you—where's Trevor?"

Ebrah tucked her hair behind her ears and swayed,

and Farid rushed to her side. He slipped an arm around her waist and guided her to a chair.

"He's asleep," Ebrah said in her husky voice. "I just woke up, and I wanted a snack, and I didn't want to bother him or anyone else, so I thought I'd sneak down. I'm fine, love, don't fuss."

Farid knelt in front of her. She smiled down at him, huge dark eyes luminous in the moonlight from the window, her cheeks hollowed with shadows. She'd lost more weight, he realized with a pang.

"What do you want?" he asked. "I'll make it for you."

"Cocoa," Ebrah said immediately. "Enough for both of us, and then you'll sit here and you'll tell me more about this job of yours that's got you so tied up in knots."

Farid sighed and rose to obey. As the milk heated, he leaned a hip against the counter and told her about Dominic.

"He's so smart, Mama, he's—his mind is constantly going, I'll be talking to him and a few minutes in realize he's completely stopped hearing me because he's coding in his head." He huffed a laugh and stirred the milk. "The other day, someone mentioned offhandedly that some kind of shopping app to help keep track of budgets and lists would be great, and he wrote the entire skeleton code in about three hours. Handed it off to R&D and told them to 'pretty it up,' but it was basically already done."

Ebrah leaned her cheek on her fist. "Sounds like you like him a lot."

"I admire his mind," Farid corrected. "He's also a gigantic pain in my ass."

Ebrah snorted quietly. "How so?"

"Oh… he's constantly working himself up into anxiety attacks over various things, some strange notion that he's not good enough, won't be able to deliver what he's promised, and then he lashes out, and *then* he's like a kicked puppy, all big apologetic eyes for losing his temper."

"Is he dangerous with his anger?"

"No," Farid said immediately. "No, not at all. He doesn't even show it except around me or Cory and then it's just shouting and the occasional slammed door because he's 'a failure and the whole world's about to know it.'" He shook his head. "He has no idea how brilliant he is."

"You definitely like him," Ebrah said.

Farid sighed and reached for the cocoa powder. "Definitely don't."

"Liar," Ebrah said, her voice amused.

Farid set the cocoa in front of her and kissed her temple before sitting down beside her. "You're just desperate to pair me off with someone."

"Someone good enough for you," Ebrah corrected. "Is Dominic good enough for you?"

Farid hunched his shoulders, betrayal and guilt gnawing under his breastbone. "He's *too* good for me," he said in a low voice. "Besides, I'll only be there until Cory gets back from maternity leave."

Ebrah touched his hand, her fingers like roughened silk, dry and wrinkled. "We know not what is in the wind," she murmured.

"Would you like to go somewhere this weekend?" Farid asked. "The museum or the park or… anywhere you want."

Ebrah smiled at him. "I just want to spend time with you and the others."

"We can do that," Farid said. "I'm sorry I'm so busy."

"It's for us," Ebrah said, patting his hand. "You're a good man, Farid. A good man and a good son."

Farid ducked his head, unable to meet her eyes, and took a sip of cocoa.

6

———

"Team-building day," Farid said a week later, and Dominic dropped his forehead to the desk and groaned.

"I'm busy," he told the maplewood.

"It'll do you good to take a day off," Farid said. He set a cup of coffee on the desk beside Dominic's head, and Dominic took an appreciative sniff without moving. "Give your brain time to recharge, all that good stuff."

Dominic sat up and ran his hands through his hair. "I'm on a schedule. I can't take a day to go run around a theme park, the release for Wraith is getting closer every day and I'm still not quite there, it's not gelling, I've made promises I can't keep, and you want me to just ignore those obligations? While you're at it, go ahead and take out a front-page banner ad for me while you're at it that reads Dominic Spector Fails to Deliver!"

Farid appeared unmoved, folding his arms. "Dramatic and a little over the top, I'd say. Seven out of ten for delivery, but the Russian judge thinks you need to lighten up."

Dominic gaped at him. "You have a sense of humor," he finally said blankly.

"When it suits me," Farid said. "Bus leaves in thirty, I have a casual outfit hanging in the closet for you. How's Cory?"

Dominic couldn't help his smile. "She's good. Due any minute and can't wait to give birth. Melissa is waiting on her hand and foot, which she's milking."

"Good for her," Farid said. "Go change."

Dominic scowled but didn't argue. When he emerged, wearing a dark green shirt and a pair of slacks, Farid was waiting. His shirt was pale pink, and his faded jeans clung to muscular thighs in a thoroughly disconcerting way.

"I don't know how I feel about you in civvies," Dominic said, and Farid's lips twitched.

"Like a turtle without its shell, I know. Ready?"

"Under protest."

Farid led the way to the elevator, politely holding the door as Olivia and Ryan from R&D panted up. Olivia beamed at Dominic as Ryan punched the button.

"I'm so excited. Aren't you excited, Dominic? This is going to be so much fun. I've been looking forward to this for six months, oh my God, this is so exciting!" Olivia was small and round, her pale face glowing with her delight.

Ryan, tall and lanky, punched the button for the first floor. Dark eyes and darker hair, he smiled at Olivia, who was bouncing up and down on her toes.

"I'm going on every ride at least twice," Olivia told him.

Ryan nodded. "You said."

"And I'm going to eat cotton candy and corn dogs and drink horribly sugary drinks until I feel sick."

Ryan nodded again. "You said that too."

"And we're going to take pictures in front of every single ride."

"I remember." Ryan's tone was endlessly patient.

Farid slanted an amused look at Dominic, who fought his smile. Olivia's excitement was adorable, but he still wanted to get back to his office and work on the code, and he was losing an entire day. He was so *close*, if he could just—

"So, Farid," Olivia said, "how do you like working for Dominic?"

"He's a very good boss," Farid said, smiling at her.

"You do realize you're going to have to address the troops and keep everything organized, right?" Dominic interjected. "I'm not—I don't do that stuff."

"Of course." Farid seemed unfazed. "Cory briefed me thoroughly." His lips quirked. "Everything is well in hand. All you have to do is look pretty and wave."

"He's good at that," Olivia said.

Ryan snickered, and Dominic felt a blush firing the tips of his ears. He hunched his shoulders and shoved his hands deep into his pockets as the doors opened on the ground floor. Some fifty employees were milling around the marble-floored lobby, everyone turning to look as Dominic and Farid stepped out, Olivia and Ryan on their heels. An excited babble erupted, and Dominic just barely kept the flinch internal, pasting a smile on his face and waving.

Farid stepped in front of him and raised both hands, asking for quiet he instantly received. Dominic stayed silent as Farid looked over the faces in front of them.

"For those who haven't met me, I'm Farid Qadir," he said, his voice somehow pitched to fill the big room without shouting. "I'm filling in for Cory while she's on leave, so if you need to speak to Dominic, you go through me. Now, I know we're all looking forward to this, but please remember to move in an orderly fashion onto the buses." Farid pointed over their heads and as one, the crowd swiveled to see. Farid continued before anyone could move for the doors. "Your entry is paid for, as are all the rides. There is an all-day buffet at the King's Ransom, in the middle of the park. For anything else, you're on your own. Let's go!"

Outside, Dominic stopped and craned his neck to get a glimpse past the buses. "Where's Amber?"

"She's on the second bus," Farid said. "We're on the first."

"I don't even get to have my car?" Dominic dug in his heels.

Farid just cocked his head. "Cory was very clear on this point. You ride on the first bus, right up front where everyone can see you, and you smile and you're sociable to anyone who approaches you."

"You're fired," Dominic snapped, and pushed past him toward the bus.

"Sure thing," Farid said equably, right behind him. "Soon as Cory gets back."

The bus was huge, spacious, and smelled like lemon Lysol. The driver smiled cheerfully, her blue eyes bright as she clutched a wheel bigger than she was.

"Hello!" she chirped. "I'm Jess. I'm your driver today."

Dominic eyed her. "Do you even have a license?"

"Of course she has a license," Farid said. "Don't needle the poor girl. Here's our seat."

Dominic slumped into it and crossed his arms, slouching against the upholstery as people filed past them to find their seats. Farid leaned in.

"Cory said when you sulk, to remember that you're the face of this company, and that if you don't smile and actually be as charming as we both know you can be, she'll—well, she said to remember what happened senior year of college."

Dominic gulped and straightened. Farid's brows rose.

"What on earth happened senior year of college?" He lifted a hand to forestall Dominic's reply. "Not my place, forget I asked."

"Hi Dominic, hi Farid!" Olivia said, bouncing past with Ryan on her heels. "This is gonna be so fun!"

Dominic dredged up a smile that quickly turned genuine when he recognized Senna, her dandelion hair semi-tamed by a flowered headband and a streak of flour on her cheek. She was clutching a small child's hand, the same puffball hair betraying their relation.

"Hi," Senna said, ducking her head and pulling the child closer. "This is my sister, Bug."

Mouth open to greet them both, Dominic paused and blinked. "Bug?"

The little girl grinned, displaying several missing teeth. "Bug," she said firmly.

Senna shrugged, a movement clearly performed countless times. "Her name is Abigail, but she refuses to be called that."

Farid leaned forward, eyes warm. "Hello, Bug. I'm Farid. This is Dominic. May I ask why you named yourself that?"

Bug considered him for a minute. She was a carbon copy of her sister, with a spray of freckles across her sunburned nose and pale hair in wild disarray framing her round face.

"I'm gonna be an ento—ent—entomologist," she announced, and pointed to the large plastic insect in improbable pink pinned to her overalls.

Dominic leaned around Farid. "When you get bigger, will you become Beetle instead of Bug?"

Bug's giggle was high and delighted, pealing out across the bus as Senna blushed with mortification.

"C'mon," she said, pulling on Bug's hand. "Our seats are down this way."

Bug waved goodbye as Senna towed her past and Dominic and Farid waved back before facing front again.

"I love kids," Farid said. "Don't you?"

"Not little ones," Dominic said. "That age where they're mobile and… and… sticky, and into everything…." He shivered.

"Germophobe?" Farid inquired.

"Have you *seen* what maple syrup does to a circuit board?" Dominic snapped. "Talk to me when you have."

The bus doors closed, the gears groaned, and the wheels began to move. They were on their way.

The trip to the theme park wasn't too long, thankfully. Dominic was all too aware of Farid's warm weight against his shoulder. He smelled like cinnamon and coffee and rich aftershave, comforting and solid. *Steady*, Dominic thought. No matter how much he raged and stormed, Farid was there, a rock for Dominic to batter himself against until he was finally calm. And somehow he never lost his temper, never snapped back or allowed Dominic's frustrations to bleed over into dangerous territory.

Dominic took a deep breath and stared at the fractal pattern on the back of the driver's seat. It was not dissimilar to the code he was working on, he thought absently, fingers twitching. If he could just tweak things by a decimal of a point, it would fall into place, he knew it would.

He ignored his surroundings as the bus rolled through Seattle, and was rudely startled back to awareness by Farid gently shaking his shoulder.

Dominic held the growl in with effort. "What?"

"We're here," Farid said. "And you're done working."

"I am *not*," Dominic snapped. "You may be able to drag me out here but you can't force me to enjoy myself."

"We'll see about that," Farid said, and stood as the last of the bus's passengers filed past.

Dominic followed reluctantly, blinking in the bright sunshine. People were hurrying toward the entrance, a pair of huge plaster swans guarding the gates, elegant heads bent and beaks touching.

"Driver's been tipped," Farid said from his elbow. "Let's go. I want a funnel cake."

They walked toward the gates, shoulder to shoulder.

"I'll make you a deal," Farid said.

Dominic squinted suspiciously at him.

Farid just smiled, hands in his pockets. "If I can make you admit that this is fun, then I win. And if you're still sulking and bored by the end of the day, then you win."

"What are the stakes?" Dominic asked, diverted.

Farid shrugged. "If you win, I'll let you hole up in your office until you get this code hammered out, meetings and interviews be damned."

Dominic raised his eyebrows. "And if I lose?"

"You do what I say, when I say it, without arguing, for a full week."

Dominic stopped dead, and Farid paused, looking over his shoulder.

"Think you can't handle it?"

Something fizzed in Dominic's chest. Farid ordering him around. He wasn't sure how he felt about that, but he wanted—

He cleared his throat. "I have a deadline—"

"And I'll do my best to help you meet it," Farid said. "But the rest of the time… you're mine."

The words jolted through Dominic, and he swallowed hard. *Mine.* He hadn't meant it that way, he told himself. Farid wasn't the innuendo type.

"Do we have a deal?"

Dominic shifted his weight. Farid didn't look away, eyes sharp and almost predatory.

"I—yeah," Dominic blurted.

The tension bled from the air immediately, and a smile transformed Farid's solemn face.

"What are you waiting for? Let's go have some fun."

FARID'S first stop inside the gates was a cotton candy vendor. Dominic watched the pink concoction form dubiously, and nearly dropped it when Farid shoved it into his hands.

"I don't want cotton candy," he protested.

"It's not for you," Farid informed him, digging out his wallet. "You're just holding it for me." He handed the money to the vendor and thanked her with a smile.

"Keep track of how much you spend," Dominic said, following him as Farid headed down the smooth flagged path. "Payroll will reimburse you."

Farid pulled a piece of cotton candy off with nimble fingers and popped it into his mouth, eyes bright. Dominic watched as he licked his fingers and shook his head.

"No way," he said when he'd swallowed. "Hey look, that roller coaster looks fun, let's ride it first."

"What am I supposed to do with the cotton candy?" Dominic objected.

"Shit, you're right." Farid pulled another piece off but didn't eat it. "Open up."

Before Dominic could think better of it, he opened his mouth and Farid pushed the sugary treat inside. It melted on Dominic's tongue, but he didn't even taste it as Farid smiled at him and sucked his sticky fingers clean.

"Let's take a look at the other rides, then, or—I have a better idea. Senna!"

Dominic blinked and shook himself as Senna and Bug hurried toward them. Farid whispered something in Senna's ear, and she nodded, looking resigned.

"Special occasion, right?"

Farid whisked the cotton candy out of Dominic's hand and presented it to Bug, who squealed with glee and shoved a huge swath in her mouth.

"Can I leave her with you when the sugar high hits?" Senna asked Farid, who laughed.

"I love kids, you can totally dump her on us." He grinned at Bug, still eating spun sugar. "My little sister used to love cotton candy too. Now that she's grown up she thinks she shouldn't eat it. Isn't that dumb?"

Bug nodded, her mouth full.

Dominic shifted his weight, feeling like a fifth wheel and wondering when he'd be allowed to go back to the office. Farid glanced at him and tossed a wave at Senna and Bug.

"We're off to ride the worst roller coasters here," he said, and caught Dominic's wrist loosely. "Bye, girls!"

They waved as Farid towed Dominic toward the original ride, an alarmingly huge structure painted lurid yellow and green. The sign out front proclaimed it The Terminator, and Dominic dug in his heels again.

"I don't want to," he said when Farid stopped and turned to face him. "Can't we do a...." He hunched his shoulders. "A smaller one first?"

Farid cocked his head. "Are you afraid of heights?"

"Have you seen the view outside my office?" Dominic retorted. "I just don't want to do this at all, okay? And I haven't been on a roller coaster since I was a teenager."

"No time like the present to get back on the bicycle," Farid said easily, but he steered Dominic away from the Terminator down the path. "I feel like doing one of the water rides, I think."

Dominic let him take the lead, watching the way his shoulders moved under his shirt, the way the faded denim clung to Farid's legs as they walked. He closed his eyes briefly, pushing back against the now-familiar hot surge in his chest. He couldn't feel this way about an employee. It was impossible.

"This one looks fun," Farid said, and Dominic glanced up, called back to his surroundings.

The entry was connected to a bridge that spanned

a wide, shallow, manmade current. As Dominic and Farid watched, a coaster car topped the crest of the track and plunged down toward the river as screams of delight shattered the air. At the bottom, the car hit the water and plumes of spray billowed up, soaking the bridge and darkening the wood.

"You're kidding me," Dominic said.

Farid's smile was almost ear-to-ear. "Come on, you promised."

Dominic sighed and followed him onto the wet planks, setting his feet down gingerly until they were safely across and in the tunnel that led to the cars lined up patiently waiting for occupants.

Olivia and Ryan were there, and Senna and Bug joined them, cotton candy nowhere in sight, as they got in line.

Farid stepped into the car and sat down, beckoning to Dominic, who stepped hesitantly into the tiny metal box and sat beside him.

"I'm too tall," he said, relief filling him. "Look, the bar won't—"

Farid put a hand on his knee, cutting him off. "Cross your feet."

Dominic obeyed, watching Farid's fingers so close to his inner thigh, and Farid pushed down with one hand and pulled the metal bar over Dominic's lap with the other.

"There," he said, sounding satisfied, and lifted his hand away. "Uncross your feet."

Dominic did, wishing his warmth back, and realized the bar was settled in the locked position across his thighs with perfect ease.

Farid's eyes were bright. "See?"

Dominic scowled and put his hands in his lap as

the attendant, lanky, spotted, and perpetually bored, drifted along the line of cars, checking that each bar was locked.

Finally, they were deemed ready to go, and the car clanked and jostled its way out of the tunnel and into the bright sunlight, making them blink and shield their eyes.

Bug was talking at top speed to Senna, behind them. In front, Olivia was saying something to Ryan, who was nodding amiably.

The car inched up the first long hill and Dominic looked around, taking in the amusement park spread out below them. Several people waved, and Dominic waved back, fighting the smile that suddenly wanted to appear.

At the top of the hill, there was a pause that felt interminable, and Dominic held his breath, leaning forward as if he could urge the car forward by sheer force of will.

It plunged down the slope, flinging Dominic back against the seat, and he whooped despite himself, wind whipping his hair as they careened around corners, slinging them sideways into each other. Every time Dominic righted himself, they hit another corner and he ended up half on top of Farid again, breathless with laughter. They rocketed along a long stretch, and then the big hill was in front of them, the last stretch of the ride.

The car slowed and crept up the slope, and Dominic glanced at Farid. He was smiling, hands resting on the safety bar and eyes intent on the hill ahead of them, and Dominic squeezed his eyes shut against the sudden wild urge to kiss him.

When he opened his eyes, they were at the top of

the hill, teetering on the apex. Farid turned toward him, mouth opening to say something, but the car careened down the track and whipped the words from his mouth. Dominic clutched the bar, and they hit the water at the bottom with a mighty splash that soaked everyone, leaving Dominic gasping with the cold as his wet shirt clung to his frame.

The coaster rolled sedately back into the tunnel and the bars unlocked. Dominic levered himself out as Farid stepped onto the platform and turned to face him.

"It's *cold*," Dominic said, plucking his shirt away from his stomach.

Farid's hair was plastered to his scalp, and he laughed and shook his head, flinging water droplets everywhere, then ran his hands through his hair. It stood up in tiny black spikes, giving him a rumpled, disheveled air.

Dominic followed suit, shaking his head like a wet dog, and laughed when Farid yelped as drops hit him.

"Come on," he said, and left the tunnel, Farid on his heels.

They emerged into sunlight, and Dominic turned to face him, walking backward. Drops of water glistened in Farid's hair, iridescent in the sun's rays.

"What were you going to say," Dominic asked, "at the top of that last hill?"

Farid's smile widened. "I was going to say 'I win,'" he said, and lunged forward to catch Dominic's arm just before he backed into a hot dog cart.

Dominic stumbled and straightened, turning to apologize to the alarmed vendor. "Ooh, hot dog. Want one?"

Farid shook his head. "Halal," he said.

"Right." Dominic paid the vendor for his own hot dog, feeling stupid.

"I'll take a pretzel, though," Farid told the girl, who blushed and nearly dropped the soft pretzel before fumbling it into a paper bag and handing it over.

"On me," Dominic said, mouth already full of processed meat and bread, and handed his card back to the vendor.

They meandered down the path, taking in the sights around them, and Dominic rolled his shoulders with a sigh.

"Fine," he said abruptly. "You're right, you win. This is fun."

Farid didn't gloat, though. He just smiled down at his pretzel and took another bite.

"What's next?" Dominic asked.

"Anything you want," Farid said.

Dominic snorted. "Dangerous words."

"I mean it, though," Farid said, and caught his eyes. "What do you want?"

You. Dominic opened his mouth and closed it again. He couldn't say that. *Wouldn't* say that. It was crossing too many lines.

"To do," Farid added. "What do you want to do?"

Same answer. Dominic shrugged. "I don't care. It's been twenty years since I went to an amusement park, so I don't even know what the protocol is these days."

"So we'll wander for a while, see what grabs our fancy." Farid took a bite of pretzel and set off down the lane, Dominic close behind.

THEY DIDN'T LEAVE the park until the sun was

setting, a burnished-orange glow throwing the roller coasters into stark relief. Dominic's nose felt sunburned, and he prodded it with one finger as he and Farid crossed the parking lot to reboard the bus.

"It'll peel," Farid said, slanting a smiling look at him. "I should have made you wear sunblock—I wasn't thinking."

"You're definitely fired," Dominic said, and bumped him with his shoulder. Farid's smile widened.

"So. A full week. Think you can handle it?"

"A deal's a deal," Dominic said. "You're not going to make me do anything too embarrassing, are you?"

"I'll go one better," Farid said, standing aside so Dominic could step up into the bus's cool interior. He smiled at the driver and sat down beside Dominic, crossing his legs and folding his hands in his lap. "The only time I'll expect you to do my bidding is when we're alone. No witnesses, I promise."

Relief filled Dominic's chest, and he leaned back against the seat, struggling to hide it. "What are you going to make me do, anyway?" he asked. Senna and Bug bounced past, smiling at them, and Dominic waved at Bug.

"Don't worry," Farid said. A smile played around the corners of his mouth. "Nothing too onerous. You might even enjoy it."

7

———

Farid gazed up at the stars, flat on his back on the roof of the house. The night air was crisp and cool, bringing with it a promise of rain in the morning, but for now it was dry, the breeze sweet when it touched him. *What was he doing?*

There were moments when he could breathe through the guilt choking him. When his mother smiled at him or Salma laughed. When Trevor took Ebrah to a routine appointment that Farid didn't have time for. When Salma got back from her first consultation with the doctor who would be overseeing her transition, she was glowing, and Farid had hugged her, fighting tears.

But then he got to the office, and it would all come rushing back, and suddenly he was drowning again.

He'd been unable to do much yet. Take a few pictures of Dominic's monitor when Dominic was in one meeting or another. Most of his time was spent in Dominic's proximity, so finding time alone, especially alone in Dominic's inner sanctum—was almost impossible.

You're doing this for family, he told himself for the thousandth time. *Dominic will be fine. He's a genius— he'll have a new app or software program out in a month.*

The window opened, and Farid rolled his head to see Nasim climbing through to join him, Salma on his heels.

"Thought you'd like some company." Nasim dropped cross-legged beside him, all gangly teenage limbs, and held something out. "Salma fried pies."

Farid accepted the crescent-shaped pastry, still warm, and bit into the sweet, apple-filled center with a hum of approval as Salma settled on his other side.

"How are you doing?" she asked.

"Fine," Farid said around his mouthful. "Swell, even." He poked Nasim's bony knee. "Who's the latest in your love-life?"

"Emily," Nasim said, lighting up. "She's so pretty, 'Rid. And she writes poetry. She says she'll let me read some someday."

Farid glanced at Salma, whose lips were twitching.

"Who was it last week?" she asked.

"*Two* weeks ago," Nasim corrected, scowling. "Brenda. But she turned out to be a bitch."

Farid straightened. "Sorry, what?"

"She was transphobic," Nasim said. "Called Salma some gross stuff. I dumped her ass."

Farid settled back. "Okay, then." He touched Nasim's knee again. "Thank you for watching out for her."

Nasim shrugged. "'S no big deal. What about you?"

"Still a nope," Farid said.

Salma leaned back, arms under her head, and gazed up into the night sky as Nasim wriggled with wordless frustration.

"But… ever? You have sex, right? How can you *not* fall in love?"

"I'm not discussing my sex life with you, first of all," Farid said. "Second, I don't know, it just doesn't happen. Hasn't happened. I'm not a poetry and roses kind of guy. I don't do romance. It's… confusing. I don't understand it."

"Maybe you will someday," Salma said. She turned her head to look at him, and her smile was soft, meant only for him. "But it doesn't matter if you don't. There are many different ways to love a person."

Farid took another bite of flaky pastry and apple filling, and Nasim stretched out beside him. They stared at the stars as Farid ate his pie and thought about love, the endless variations of it, and what he would do for those he *did* love.

HE WENT to work the next morning still thinking about it.

The door to Dominic's office opened, and Farid jumped as Dominic put his head through.

"You have an intercom," he said, more sharply than he'd intended.

Dominic's eyebrows rose. "I needed to stretch my legs. Something wrong?"

"Of course not," Farid said. "What can I do for you?"

Dominic shrugged and stepped into the office,

shoving his hands in his pockets. "Hit a wall. Thought I'd take a couple laps in the gym, clear my head."

"You have a gym? Of course you have a gym." Farid half-laughed at himself and swiveled back to his computer. "Have fun."

"Wanna come?"

Farid blinked, turning back. "I—thank you, but I have plenty to do here."

Dominic nodded and retreated, presumably to change.

Farid waited until he was gone, making sure he got on the elevator and the doors were closed, before he made his move.

He slipped into Dominic's office with his breath held, heart picking up. His feet were silent as he approached the desk. The screen was unlocked, the code glowing rainbow-hued on black, a jumble of letters and numbers and symbols that made absolutely no sense.

Farid pulled out his phone and took a picture. Making note of where the cursor was on the screen, he scrolled up and took several more pictures, then down and did the same. The sweat was forming on his forehead, nerves jumping at every noise, imagined or real. Where had he stopped? Did he need to page back twice or three times?

Holding his breath, he backed up three pages and then, nerves stretched to breaking, hurried for his office.

He'd managed to get his breathing under control by the time Dominic reappeared, dressed in comfortable clothes and hair damp with sweat. He looked relaxed and happy for once, and Farid couldn't help making a mental note of that. *Tire him out so he doesn't fret himself to death.*

Dominic wiped his forehead and smiled. "I had an idea on the track."

Farid made an encouraging noise.

"It means scrapping everything I did today," Dominic continued, oblivious to the way Farid stiffened, "but it'll be better in the long run." He disappeared into his office as Farid stared after him.

Alone, he dropped his forehead to the desk and moaned softly. He wasn't cut out for this. Still, he couldn't deny the relief that trickled through him at the realization that he wouldn't have to betray Dominic. Not yet, anyway.

DOMINIC WORKED LATE THAT DAY. Halfway through the night, he stretched out on the couch and fell asleep, still working through code as he drifted off.

Farid woke him the next morning by pulling the shades, and Dominic groaned and rolled over to press his face against the couch cushions.

"Go 'way."

"Breakfast," Farid said. "And you're getting up to eat right now."

Dominic grunted and didn't move.

"*Now*," Farid said, the whip-crack of command in his voice, and Dominic jolted upright in shock. Farid didn't look angry, standing calm and relaxed in the middle of the office, perfectly turned out as usual, but Dominic regarded him warily.

"Remember our agreement?" Farid asked.

Still half-befuddled from sleep, Dominic struggled to marshal his thoughts. "The—oh."

"Exactly. Everything I say when we're alone together. So get up, go take a shower, and then come back and eat some breakfast."

Dominic stared at him but Farid just arched an eyebrow.

Finally, Dominic sighed and stood.

He didn't want to admit that the shower helped clear his head, coming out damp and rumpled to find a full breakfast on his desk. Eggs, several rashers of bacon, and waffles, as well as coffee that smelled enticing—Dominic sighed happily and sat down to dig in.

Farid came back before he was done. He moved around the room, picking up and neatening the space, and Dominic watched him while he ate.

"Have *you* eaten?" he asked between bites.

"I'm not the one who regularly forgets what food is," Farid said. "When you're done with breakfast, you have two hours to code."

"That's *it?*" Dominic yelped.

"For now," Farid said serenely, and left the office.

Two hours later on the dot, he was back. Dominic growled, but Farid didn't seem to notice.

"Up, let's go."

"I don't want to," Dominic protested.

Farid gave him a look. "And yet you promised. Up."

Dominic groaned and obeyed. He followed Farid out of the office and down the hall, still sulking, and it took him awhile to realize where they were. He perked up as Farid stopped at the door to R&D and gestured.

"Badge us in, then."

Dominic swiped his card, and the door opened with a soft click. Inside, Harvey was alone, working busily away in his corner. He looked up, and his eyes got wide.

"M-Mr. Spector!" Harvey scrambled to his feet, brushing at his shirt.

"I've told you to call me Dominic," Dominic said. "Have you met Farid?"

Harvey bobbed something between a curtsy and a bow in nervous acknowledgment, and Farid smiled at him.

"How's it going, Harvey? Made any breakthroughs?"

"I'm close," Harvey said breathlessly. "Do you want to see, Mr.—uh, Dominic?"

Farid tried to step back and let them geek out together, but Dominic gestured to him.

"Come look," he said.

Farid followed him to Harvey's desk, and Harvey handed Dominic a small, square device.

"This is Phantom," Dominic said to Farid. "It's a smart-driving app." He turned it on, and a tiny ghost floated into view and waved. Dominic flicked through options. "Here, this automatically gauges mileage and alerts the driver when an oil change or tire rotation is due."

Farid made appropriately admiring noises as Dominic switched to another screen.

"This one calls for roadside assistance in the event of a wreck. It automatically dials emergency services if a collision is detected and the driver is unable to respond."

Harvey was nearly bouncing on his toes, all pent-up energy. "I had an idea, M—Dominic, could I maybe run it by you?"

"Sure," Dominic said.

"Well, what about an alert sent via text or email to the owner of the vehicle if the vehicle is taken beyond a set parameter, like say, twenty square miles or something? It would help parents keep better track of—"

"*No.*"

Harvey blinked, opening and closing his mouth. Farid felt much the same, watching the tension bunch and slide in Dominic's shoulders.

"No," Dominic repeated, and set down the device. "I won't have any watchdog functions on any of my creations, are we clear?"

Harvey's head drooped. "Yes sir." His voice was small. "I—I'm sorry, sir, I thought—"

Dominic gripped Harvey's shoulder. "Hey, I didn't mean to sound so abrupt. It's a good idea, okay? It's just not for me."

Harvey nodded.

"Come on, show me what else you've been working on," Dominic said.

Farid took a step back, and this time Dominic let him go as Harvey began speaking, slowly but with growing confidence as Dominic nodded encouragingly.

There were no security cameras in here. That would make it easier, when it came time. Because it was going to have to be Phantom. He was going to have to find a way to get into the lab. Random pictures of code weren't going to be enough. He needed the real deal.

Farid put aside the now-familiar guilt and waited until Dominic looked up and around for him. Then he stepped forward, giving Harvey an apologetic smile.

"Thanks for having us," he said.

Harvey bobbed his head again and Dominic gave him a smile and followed Farid from the office.

"More field trips?" he asked.

Farid shook his head. "Back to code with you."

Dominic brightened, and Farid had to lengthen his step to keep pace, hiding his smile.

———

HE MADE sure Dominic was absorbed in his computers again before he placed a call to Cory.

"Oh thank God," she said when she answered the phone. "I'm going out of my mind with boredom. Give me something to do. How's Dom?"

"He's fine," Farid said, smiling. "He misses you."

"I miss him too. I miss working. I miss seeing my *feet*."

"Anything I can do?" Farid said, trying to hide his amusement.

"Bring Dom to visit me," Cory said immediately. "He probably needs a break anyway. How many meltdowns has he had?"

"Not too many," Farid said. "I've learned to spot them, and I can usually head them off."

Cory made a thoughtful noise. "Is that so? Can I talk to him?"

"How about I send him over this afternoon instead?" Farid countered. He glanced toward

Dominic's office, his head just visible behind the monitors. "He says he's getting close to a breakthrough on this piece of code." *And that will give me some time alone in the office.*

"I have a feeling I'm going to have a very interesting conversation with him," Cory said, and hung up.

8

———

Cory and Melissa lived in a bungalow on the north side of Seattle, the streets wide and welcoming and shaded with foliage from the huge oak trees that lined the pavement. Dominic's driver nosed the car into the space in front of the sprawling wood and brick house and parked.

"I'll text you when I'm ready," Dominic told her.

"Take your time," Amber said cheerfully. "I'll explore the neighborhood."

Dominic knocked on the door and waited.

"It's open!" Cory called.

Dominic turned the handle and stepped inside. The hall was huge and airy, a stained glass panel above the door reflecting rainbow light onto the gleaming mahogany wood. Pictures of Cory and Melissa—and more than a few of Dominic—lined the walls leading to the living room where Cory was struggling to her feet.

"Stay there!" Dominic exclaimed, rushing to her. She was somehow, impossibly, even bigger, her belly taut and rounded, but her skin was glowing and her eyes were bright.

"Get over here," she said, and pulled him into a tight hug. "God, I've missed you. Do you want something to drink? Are you hungry?"

Dominic released her, smiling. "A drink would be great, but I can get it. Same place in the fridge?"

"I might have rearranged some," Cory said, lowering herself gingerly back into her recliner. "But just poke around until you find something."

Dominic took his shoes off and headed for the kitchen—his favorite room, with its cream-colored walls and large skylights. "Where's Melissa?" he called as he bent to rummage in the refrigerator.

"Shopping," Cory said, and muffled a grunt. "She had some last-minute things to pick up before the baby gets here."

Dominic came up triumphant with a bottle of lemon fizz and some Perrier for Cory. "And you? How are you feeling?" He went back into the living room and handed the water to her before sitting down on the overstuffed couch opposite her.

"Like I'm about to pop," Cory said, rubbing her stomach. "Pregnancy does horrible things to a body. The nosebleeds are driving me *crazy*."

"Nosebleeds?"

Cory scowled and took a sip. "My gums bleed too. It sucks. Also I pee when I sneeze. Whose idea was this? Did you know the smell of french fries makes me throw up? I thought pregnant women got cravings, not aversions, this is bullshit."

Dominic hid his smile and drank hastily. When he lowered the bottle, Cory was regarding him with narrowed eyes.

"What?" Dominic brushed at his face. "What is it?"

"How's Farid working out?"

Dominic stiffened. "He's, um. Fine."

"Fine," Cory echoed. "Yeah, *and* he's a good assistant." She snickered at Dominic's expression. "You have to admit he's gorgeous."

"I don't have to admit anything," Dominic muttered.

"How was the team-building day?"

"He made me ride roller coasters."

Cory snorted a laugh. "Poor baby. Was it awful?"

"No. It was actually kind of… fun." Dominic resisted the urge to squirm as Cory's eyes sharpened.

"You like him." It wasn't a question.

"I don't *hate* him," Dominic parried weakly. "He's not you, but—"

"No, you *like* him," Cory said. "As in, you think he's hot, and you'd probably like to date him."

Dominic drained the bottle in several long gulps without answering.

"I knew it!" Cory crowed. "Even I can see it, and I'm as gay as they get. Have you thought about asking him out?"

"He is my *employee*," Dominic said flatly. "It's inappropriate, and… taking advantage, and… I don't even know if he's interested."

"He's interested," Cory said, and sipped her water.

"What? How do you know?"

"I saw the way he looked at you when you weren't looking. Trust me, Dom, he's totally into—" She cut off and pressed a hand to her stomach with a grimace.

"Are you okay?" Dominic was on his feet in a

heartbeat, taking Cory's water from her and then hovering, not sure what to do. "What's happening?"

"The baby's doing the salsa on my bladder is what's happening," Cory said. She caught Dominic's hand and pulled it to her stomach. "Feel."

A protest formed in Dominic's throat but it died as something fluttered under his hand, a series of rolling taps there and gone again so quickly he would have thought he was imagining it except for the delighted smile on Cory's face.

"She likes you," Cory declared.

"Don't be silly," Dominic said. He rubbed Cory's stomach, though, his smile matching hers. "Have you decided on a name yet?"

"Still batting a few around. God, why is this week taking so long? Why can't it be Thursday already? I want my *body* back."

Dominic retreated to the sofa and curled his legs under him. "Sales tried to trap me again."

Cory stiffened. "What happened? I'm going to kick their asses, I swear to God—"

"Farid stopped them. Sent them packing with their tails between their legs." Dominic smiled at the memory.

Cory sighed. "Ask him out, Dom."

"Even if I weren't his employer, what would I say? 'Hi, I'm a hopeless virgin but I can't stop thinking about kissing you and maybe doing more than that?'"

Cory stared at him. "More than that? Dom, do you want to have sex with him?"

"*No*," Dominic protested. "Maybe. I don't know, Cor, I've never felt like this before, I don't know what I'm feeling. It doesn't matter, though, because I'm his boss, and it isn't happening."

"You won't be his boss forever," Cory said. She raised an eyebrow at Dominic's expression. "Well, you won't. And if you're interested in him…. Dom, you never feel this way about anyone. Don't you owe it to yourself to find out where it goes?"

Dominic squirmed. "I—"

"Give it time," Cory said gently. "Once I come back and he's not your employee anymore, why don't you ask him out?"

"I don't even know if he feels the same way," Dominic muttered.

"Oh, he feels the same way," Cory said. Her tone was unshakable in its conviction. "If he has eyes, he feels the same way. I'd—" She broke off with a grunt and pressed a hand to her abdomen. "Ow."

"You okay?"

Cory looked up, opened her mouth, and folded forward over her stomach. "Oh fuck, oh *fuck*, Dom, call Melissa *right now.*"

Dominic scrambled for his phone. "Why?" he asked, dreading the answer.

Cory made a peculiar noise and arched back against the chair cushions. "Because my fucking *water just broke*, wait, shit, don't call my wife yet, *call an ambulance*!" Her fingers were claws, clutching at the chair arms, a tendon standing out in her neck.

Dominic dialed 911 with shaking hands, flinching as Cory dragged in air and then screamed. "My friend is having her baby," he shouted into the phone when the line went live. "Get an ambulance here now! Please! 725 Broken Wing Road, *hurry.*"

"Sir, the nearest ambulance is on its way to you." The dispatcher's voice was brisk and reassuring.

"What do I do?" Dominic begged her. "She's… is this normal?"

"I can't tell you from here," the dispatcher said. "Is she bleeding?

"Cory, are you bleeding?"

"How the fuck should I know?" Cory snarled. She pulled herself upright with a moan, and Dominic caught her questing hand. "Up," Cory said, yanking on his arm. "Get me up, I have to stand, help me, dammit—"

Dominic helped her to her feet, phone caught between his ear and shoulder. "I don't think she's bleeding," he told the dispatcher. "But she's… dripping. It's clear fluid." It puddled around Cory's bare feet as she bent almost double, fingers digging into Dominic's arm.

"Her water's broken. Tell her not to push, or you're going to be delivering that baby on your own."

"Oh *God*. Don't push," Dominic told Cory. "Fuck, right, I have to call Melissa."

"My phone," Cory said through her teeth.

<hr>

MELISSA ARRIVED LESS than a minute before the ambulance, bounding up the walk and taking control of the situation. Dominic surrendered Cory to her gratefully, hovering just out of range as Melissa rubbed Cory's back and murmured gentle words to her.

"Are you sure she's okay?" Dominic asked.

Cory groaned again, hunching over, as the paramedics knocked and charged inside.

Rendered completely superfluous, Dominic took

two big steps to the outside of the room and waited, hating the helplessness.

The paramedics were quick and competent, unfolding the gurney and helping Cory maneuver herself onto it with gentle hands. Melissa was right beside her as they headed out the door, leaving Dominic alone in their living room wondering what to do.

Farid would know. Before he thought better of it, Dominic dialed his number.

"How's Cory?" Farid asked. Just the sound of his voice, calm and competent, soothed Dominic's nerves.

"Giving birth," he blurted.

"Which hospital?" Farid asked, sharply focused suddenly.

"Um—" Dominic rubbed his forehead. "Mercy West, I think? I don't—"

"Are you okay?"

"I don't know what to do," Dominic said. He turned in a circle. "They're gone, I'm still at the house, I don't—"

"Lock up," Farid interrupted. "Lock the house, and call Amber. Tell her to take you to the hospital. I'll meet you there." He hung up before Dominic could protest.

Dominic obeyed Farid's instructions on autopilot, locking the house with his own key. Amber pulled up to the curb, and Dominic went to meet her.

"Mercy West," he said as he slid into the back. "Cory's having her baby. Step on it, please?"

Amber obeyed, sliding out into traffic and navigating with breathless speed through the streets of Seattle as Dominic clung to the door handle and fought to calm his overactive brain.

Farid was already there when Amber stopped in front of the emergency room entrance, as unruffled as ever. Dominic nearly fell out, and Farid caught his arm.

"I talked to a nurse," he said, his grip warm and reassuring. "She's upstairs in Labor and Delivery. Cory put instructions on file last month to disclose information to you and your assistant as necessary."

Dominic shook this off impatiently. "Is she okay?"

"She's fine," Farid said. He led him through the sliding doors and toward the bank of elevators. "Well, she's—"

Terror drove jagged teeth through Dominic's spine. "*Tell me.*"

"The baby's breech," Farid said reluctantly. "But that's not uncommon. She's going to be fine, I promise."

"You don't know," Dominic said, following him blindly into the car. "She's almost thirty, complications go up then, anything could go wrong, *what if she dies,* Farid?"

The doors whooshed shut, and Farid caught Dominic's face in both hands, forcing him to meet his eyes.

"Breathe," he ordered.

Dominic tried to shake his head. His vision was tunneling, sparks dancing behind his eyes as he labored for air. His best friend was in danger. He was going to lose her. He couldn't make it without her and she was dying—

Farid said something but Dominic couldn't make sense of the words. He tried again to pull away but Farid tightened his grip and dragged Dominic's head down until their lips met in a forceful, demanding kiss.

Farid's mouth was rough, almost bruising against Dominic's, insisting he pay attention to the matter at hand. He didn't ask for entry so much as insisted on it as Dominic opened to him, his knees suddenly like water.

Then Farid gentled the kiss, hands loosening their grip and one sliding up into Dominic's hair, the other cradling his jaw.

Dominic still couldn't breathe, but for an entirely different reason. Farid was an even better kisser than Dominic had ever dreamed, lips and tongue skilled and gentle as he coaxed Dominic back from the edge of the panic attack and onto solid ground.

Farid let go with one hand, and Dominic made a protesting noise but couldn't open his eyes to see what he was doing until the elevator shuddered to a stop.

Then that warm hand was back on Dominic's face, maneuvering him into position, and Farid's mouth was wet and sweet on his again.

When Farid finally broke the kiss, it was a minute before Dominic could open his eyes, and it was to the sight of Farid smiling at him from a few inches away.

"You—" Dominic stopped to clear his throat. Farid was so beautiful, hair mussed and falling over his forehead, eyes heavy-lidded and lips wet and red with kisses—*I did that*, Dominic thought, and it shook him to his core. *I made him look like he's about to have the best fuck of his life.*

"I brought your laptop," Farid said before Dominic could say anything else. "You can work while we wait." He reached back and pressed the elevator button, and the car rose swiftly and smoothly to the third floor as Dominic tried to figure out what had just happened.

HE FOLLOWED Farid out onto the maternity ward floor, still dazed. The hall was decorated with bright pastel murals of baby animals and balloons, but it smelled like antiseptic, and Dominic could hear someone moaning in pain a few doors down. The panic crept back, and his breath shortened.

Farid found a nurse, spoke to her briefly, and then turned to Dominic.

"We're in here," he said. When Dominic didn't move, Farid wrapped long fingers around his wrist. "Come on," he said gently, and tugged.

Dominic managed to get his feet moving and stumbled after him into a small, cheerfully decorated waiting room.

His laptop was already set up on the table in the corner. Farid herded him to the chair, and Dominic sank into it, head still spinning.

"Can you work?" Farid asked.

Dominic hesitated and then shook his head. "I can't—what if—"

"She's fine," Farid said, taking a step closer.

Dominic tilted his head to look up at him. Farid smiled.

"You trust me, right?"

Dominic nodded without hesitation. Something flickered through Farid's eyes, there and gone, and then the smile was back in place.

"Then you can believe me when I tell you that Cory is in the best hands possible. She's in good health, and so is the baby. The doctors here are the best in the state. They're both going to be fine. So what you have to do is trust me and wait for news and work on your code."

"I can't," Dominic whispered. "I'm—I can't focus. I can't think, how can I *work* right now?"

Farid took a step back, and worry flashed through Dominic. Had he upset him? But Farid just bent to pick up a briefcase Dominic hadn't noticed.

"New plan," he said. He opened the case and lifted something out. "Solve this," he said, and handed Dominic a spherical object.

Dominic turned it over in his hands. It was made of polished wood, smooth and dark. Dominic ran a thumb over the satiny outside and looked at Farid, who sat down beside him and adjusted his cuffs.

"What is it?"

"What do you think it is?" Farid countered. "It's a puzzle. Solve it."

"*How?*"

"I guess you need to figure that out, don't you?"

Even smug was a good look on him, Dominic noted absently, but most of his attention was on the wooden ball in his hands. He turned it over. It was perfectly round, appearing like nothing more than a carved toy at first glance. Only closer inspection revealed the joins, almost invisible strips against the grain of the wood, so neatly did they fit together.

Solve it. How? Dominic rubbed the wood again, turning it in his fingers and exploring every inch of it. It was perfectly made, no imperfections or blemishes marring the surface, no clues to show him how it should be solved, or even how it was a puzzle.

Dominic glanced up at Farid, who'd pulled out his

phone and was seemingly absorbed in it. He turned back to the ball. If it was a puzzle, that meant it had to open somewhere. He scraped the wood gently with a fingernail. The seams were so tight he barely even felt them, even knowing they were there.

He held it to his ear and tapped it. It sounded solid. He turned it and tapped again. There—it sounded slightly more hollow there. Dominic kept tapping, making note of where the hollower places were. There seemed to be four of them, evenly spaced. Dominic pressed on one of them. Nothing happened. He pressed a little harder.

"Don't break it," Farid said without looking up. "It's not about how strong you are."

Dominic scowled but eased his grip. If it wasn't about strength, then it had to be about pressure, applied in the right spot. He put a thumb on one of the hollow-sounding spots, and his index finger on the opposite one and squeezed.

Nothing happened. Dominic huffed out a breath and changed his fingers' positions.

Still nothing.

He almost dropped the puzzle when the door opened and a nurse stepped inside. She was Hispanic, short, and curvy in scrubs with tiny ducks printed all over them, and she smiled at Dominic, who scrambled to his feet as Farid followed suit.

"Is she okay?" Dominic asked.

"She's fine," the nurse said soothingly. Her name tag said Justina on it. "The labor's coming along fine. The baby hasn't turned yet, though, so we may have to do a C-section."

Dominic stiffened. "She doesn't want surgery."

Justina grimaced. "She may not get a choice. If the

baby doesn't turn soon, the labor will progress too far, and we'll have to perform the surgery to save them both."

Dominic's head spun, and Farid gripped his arm.

"Breathe," he ordered. "She's in good hands. Right, nurse?"

"Right," Justina said. "I just wanted to let you know where we stand. Her and the baby's vitals are both very strong. They're going to be fine."

The door shut behind her, and Farid squeezed Dominic's arm, guiding him back to his seat. Dominic sat obediently and bent forward, elbows on knees, puzzle ball almost forgotten in one hand. Farid sat beside him, palm warm and reassuring on Dominic's back.

"I'm such an asshole," Dominic whispered.

"What?" Farid sounded startled.

Dominic squeezed his eyes shut so he wouldn't have to see the condemnation on Farid's face. "This whole time," he managed, words sour in his mouth, "all I've been thinking about is what I would do if I lost her. What would happen to *me* if I didn't have her." The puzzle made a dull *thunk* as it hit the floor, and Dominic covered his face. "I should be worried about *her*. About the baby, about Melissa. I'm a selfish *prick*."

There was silence for a moment, and then Farid lifted his hand from between Dominic's shoulder blades. Dominic only had a brief second of panic that he was leaving before he'd knelt in front of him, taking Dominic's wrists and pulling his hands away from his face.

"Listen to me," he said, tone gentle but firm. "You *are* worried about her. Her *and* the baby *and* Melissa.

Of course you're thinking about what her loss would do to you personally—you're human. That doesn't make you an asshole. It makes you a normal person."

Dominic shook his head wordlessly, unable to argue as disgust with himself welled.

"You're a good man, Dominic," Farid said, squeezing his wrists. He was so close, kneeling almost between Dominic's feet, face turned up and eyes dark, and Dominic leaned forward and pressed their mouths together before he thought better of it.

Farid caught his breath, but his fingers tightened on Dominic's wrists and he kissed back, lips parting and tongue warm and wet as he leaned in and deepened the contact.

"I'm sorry," Dominic whispered between kisses.

Farid shook his head a fraction and mouthed along Dominic's jaw, one hand sliding up into his hair. "Don't be," he murmured, breath warm on Dominic's skin.

"You're always having to—"

Farid caught his mouth again, and Dominic forgot what he was saying in the giddy rush of Farid's taste and smell, intoxicating on his tongue.

When they separated, Farid sat back on his heels and took a shaky breath. "God, what you do to me."

Dominic touched his own mouth with one finger. His lips tingled, and he was lightheaded. "What are we doing?" he managed.

Farid's face lit with his smile. "Fuck if I know."

Dominic couldn't help his laugh. "I think that's the first time you've ever sworn in front of me."

"Is it?" Farid's smile widened. "Not very professional of me, but then, neither is making out with my boss." He stood up in a fluid motion and smoothed his pants. He bent and scooped up the puzzle, setting it back in Dominic's palm. "Back to it."

Dominic rubbed a thumb over the wood, watching Farid as he settled in the chair beside him again. God knew he shouldn't have kissed him, should have put a stop to it the *first* time, let alone done it a second, but he couldn't stop thinking about the way Farid tasted, the soft noises he made, and the intoxicating smell and feel of him.

He wanted to do it again, lay Farid down and cover his body with his own and see just what kind of noises he'd make when pushed to the edge—his cock stirred and he crossed his legs hastily, angling away from Farid.

This was new territory for him. Recognizing that in theory he would be interested in having sex with Farid and having an erection at the thought were two very different things, and Dominic wasn't sure what to do. He couldn't have sex with a subordinate. He *couldn't*. It was all kinds of wrong. And just because Farid had kissed him didn't mean *he* wanted sex. Dominic knew better than most that kissing didn't necessarily indicate interest in further activities.

Farid tapped the ball in his hand, making Dominic jump.

"Stop overthinking whatever's going on in your head and solve the problem in front of you," he said.

Dominic scowled, repositioned his fingers, and pressed again.

The puzzle fell apart in his hands, and he gasped. A small piece of paper was nestled among the fragments, and he lifted it out with finger and thumb.

One day with no interruptions. He looked up at Farid questioningly.

Farid smiled. "All day to yourself, coding or doing whatever you want to your heart's content. Sound good?"

"Like heaven," Dominic said fervently.

"Good," Farid said. "Now put the puzzle back together."

Dominic groaned and went to work.

It should have been easy. It *looked* easy, innocuous strips of wood lying in his palm. Surely they would go back together the same way. But every time he got one curved piece in place, the next would refuse to fit beside it.

It took him more than an hour, swearing steadily under his breath as Farid read peacefully beside him, before he had it back together.

"Now what?" he said, dropping the puzzle into Farid's hand.

Farid turned the ball one way and then the other, a smile playing on his lips, and Dominic throttled the urge to kiss him. Before Farid could speak, though, the door opened, and Melissa burst inside, startling them both to their feet.

There were dark circles under Melissa's eyes and blood—*blood*—on her hands, but a smile stretched her generous mouth from ear-to-ear.

"Would you like to meet your goddaughter?" she asked.

Dominic's mouth fell open, and he looked at Farid, who grinned and made a shooing motion.

"Go. I'll be here."

9

———

FARID SANK BACK onto the chair after the door closed behind Dominic and Melissa. *What the fuck am I doing?* Kissing Dominic hadn't been on his to-do list, no matter how enticingly rumpled he was or the way his eyes got big and he waved his hands when he was excited.

But he'd been so *panicked* in the elevator, and it was either hit him or kiss him to snap him out of it. Farid had chosen the more attractive option. What he hadn't counted on was the way Dominic had kissed back, or how he'd gone to putty in Farid's hands. Farid had had the distinct feeling he could have put Dominic on his knees right there in the elevator and Dominic would have gone willingly.

And wasn't *that* a mental image—Dominic kneeling, hair mussed and lips wet and parted, gazing up at Farid beseechingly.

Farid slapped himself, the sharp sting steadying his thoughts. *Focus.* Maybe this wasn't a bad thing. It could be a way to earn Dominic's trust faster. An idea swam into soft focus, and he ignored the worm of self-hatred that writhed through his gut.

He could use this. And if he hated himself by the time it was over, well…. Salma and their mother were taken care of, and that was all that really mattered.

WHEN DOMINIC CAME BACK, his eyes were wet, and his mouth wobbled when he smiled. "She's beautiful," he managed, and swiped at his face.

"Red and squashed and wrinkly?" Farid asked. He pulled a handkerchief from his pocket and held it out.

Dominic's laugh was soggy as he accepted it. "*So* wrinkly. And pissed off—she's got better lungs than my father with a—" He stopped and cut a glance at Farid, who pretended not to have noticed the slip.

"What's her name?"

"Um. Dominique?" Dominic's voice sounded like he was still having trouble wrapping his brain around the fact that a baby had been named after him. "They're calling her Nicki."

Farid smiled at him. "I can't wait to meet her. When do they get to go home?"

"Cory's running a fever, so they want to keep her until that goes down. Probably tomorrow."

"Do you feel you need to stay too?" Farid asked.

Dominic eyed him. "You'd stay too, if I said yes, wouldn't you?"

"It's my job," Farid said, lifting a shoulder.

"You're really good at it," Dominic said. "But no, they said she's fine. I think we can go, and—" His stomach growled and he winced.

"And get something to eat," Farid said. "On it."

At the restaurant, a small, private club with enclosed booths, Dominic devoured his burger with vigor as Farid watched, amused.

"Sorry," Dominic said halfway through. "I don't know why I'm so hungry."

"Never apologize for your appetites," Farid said, and Dominic stilled.

His eyes were uncertain when they lifted to Farid's, but there was hunger in them, hunger and need and something that looked almost like hope.

Farid toyed with his straw, not breaking his gaze. "Cards on the table?" he suggested.

Dominic swallowed hard and nodded.

"I want you," Farid said baldly. Dominic's eyes widened but he said nothing. The silence wrapped around them was almost hypnotic, a cocoon they hung suspended in. Farid leaned forward. "I think you want me too. Am I right?"

Dominic's throat bobbed but he nodded again, jerky and unsure this time.

"So…." Farid drew the word out, tracing the shape of Dominic's mouth with his eyes. "Would you be open to an… arrangement?"

"What—" Dominic's voice broke and he squeezed his eyes shut briefly. "What kind of… arrangement?"

"Purely sexual," Farid said. "Put bluntly—I want to dominate you."

Dominic's mouth fell open and he tried several times to speak.

Farid waited.

"What would… that mean?" Dominic finally managed.

"It would mean I'd want not just your body, but also your mind," Farid said. Dominic's eyes were huge, fascination and fear warring in their depths. "I want to control you, to tell you to get on your knees and have you obey instantly, to push your limits, tie you up and—"

"*Stop.*" Dominic's voice was strangled and he hunched forward, breathing harshly through his nose. His knuckles were white where he clutched the table.

Farid waited, triumph welling within him. He'd been right. He'd known—but it had still been a gamble.

Finally Dominic lifted his head. "How… would it work?"

"After-hours only," Farid said, and Dominic's bearing eased. "In the office, you'd still be the boss, no question. But after…." He let the words trail off and smiled. "You'd be mine to do with whatever I want."

Dominic shuddered all over. "You—but—what if I don't—"

Farid took a chance and reached across the table to touch the back of his hand. "This would only be entered into with full, willing, and continuous consent. I would never do anything to you that you didn't *want* me to do. And we could and can stop any time, for any reason."

Dominic was unmoving under his touch and Farid went a little further, caressing the pad of his thumb and sliding his finger over Dominic's pulse. It was fast and thready, and Farid hid his smile.

"Are you in?"

Dominic hesitated. "And we'd be… discreet?"

"Completely," Farid assured him. "This would be between the two of us and no one else. I'll even sign something to that effect, if it would make you feel better."

Dominic swallowed a few times, and guilt pricked Farid's skin. He would never forgive himself if he didn't at least *say*—

He leaned forward, catching and holding Dominic's eyes.

"Let me be clear," he said in a low voice. "This is highly unethical. If we're discovered, it could be used against you even though it was my idea, because you're my superior. There could be blowback. Are you willing to risk that?"

"What kind of blowback?"

Farid lifted a shoulder. "I'd probably be fired, which since I'm leaving soon anyway, wouldn't be much of a problem. But it could affect your reputation."

Dominic looked serious, generous mouth drawn down at the corners. "I'm out, I don't care about that. What about you?"

"Push comes to shove, Lockheed Martin will take me back," Farid said. He rubbed Dominic's pulse again, making him twitch.

Dominic took an unsteady breath. "In that case… yeah. Yeah, I'm—" He shivered again. "I'm in."

Farid tilted his head and smiled at him. "Your place?"

AT HIS APARTMENT BUILDING, Dominic was a bundle of nerves as they rode the elevator up, his hands clasped and his eyes on the control panel, bouncing on his toes and seemingly unaware of it.

Farid kept still, hands in his pockets. One wrong move could set Dominic off, he could feel it, and he couldn't mess this up.

Dominic lived in the penthouse, a huge, open space drenched in sunlight from the floor-to-ceiling windows on all sides. Farid stood in the center of the living room and tilted his face up, letting the late afternoon sun's rays soak into his skin and sighing in appreciation.

"Why do you do that?" Dominic was standing in front of him, holding out a glass with what looked like scotch in it.

Farid accepted the glass and took a sip. It *was* scotch, and an excellent one at that. "Do what?"

"Every time you're in the sun," Dominic said. "You tilt your face up, like you're drinking it through your pores. Like you're… praying."

"My mother calls me a sun-worshipper," Farid said. "If I don't get enough sunlight, I get irritable and cranky."

Dominic looked fascinated. "But you work in an office."

Farid shrugged. "It pays the bills." He turned to take in his surroundings, the plush carpet, overstuffed furniture, and rich wall hangings. "This is nice."

"Why did you kiss me?" Dominic said.

Farid turned back, and Dominic ducked his head, embarrassment flickering across his face.

"Forget it," he mumbled. "I—it was a stupid question."

"Was it?" Farid set the tumbler down and closed the space between them. He drew a line down Dominic's jaw with one finger. "Do you really not know why I'm attracted to you, Dom?"

Dominic's eyes fluttered shut. "Is—is it only that?"

"Only what?" Farid said softly. "Only that you're beautiful?"

Dominic swallowed hard and said nothing.

"No," Farid breathed. "It is much, much more than that. It's your spirit, your fire, and this… desperate need of yours to be dominated."

Dominic drew away, his eyes widening. "What? But I'm—"

"You spend all day, every day, in control," Farid said, stepping nearer still. "You run a multimillion dollar company. You're a boss. *The* boss. And you *crave* subjugation, with all your heart. You long to be taken out of your head, to be forced to give up control."

Dominic stared at him, breath rapid and short. "I —I don't—you don't know me. You can't—"

"I knew the minute I kissed you in the elevator," Farid interrupted. "But I suspected five minutes after I met you."

Dominic was trembling, frozen in place as if unable to move.

"You can trust me," Farid said gently. "Will you allow me to give you this?"

He waited as Dominic fought an internal battle and finally nodded jerkily.

"Sit down," Farid said. "At the table."

Dominic obeyed, looking unsure, and Farid seated himself opposite, out of reach.

"Now we're going to talk."

Disappointment flickered across Dominic's face. "I thought—"

"I don't know your limits," Farid interrupted. "*You* probably don't know your limits. So we're going to discuss a few, see what you think you might like and dislike. First off, do you want to be hurt?"

"No," Dominic said instantly, but there was shame in his eyes. "I'm—does that mean—"

Farid wanted to kiss him but he didn't move. "There are so many things I can do to you that don't involve pain. I'm glad you trusted me enough to tell me that."

Dominic's expression eased subtly, and he took a careful breath.

"So no pain," Farid mused, tracing a pattern on the table with one finger. "How about kneeling?"

Dominic blinked. "Just… kneeling? What's the point?"

"Kneeling in a dominance and submission context can be a beautiful thing," Farid said. "The person on their knees is giving over control of everything to their Dom. They're saying 'do what you want with me, I have no say in the matter.' It's total trust, and some subs can hit subspace just by kneeling, without a finger laid on them."

"Subspace?"

"Some people describe it as flying," Farid said. Dominic looked confused but fascinated, no warning signs in his body language. "It's a mental escape, like freefall, but knowing you're safe and your Dom won't let anything hurt you. It's an incredible feeling. People have been known to get addicted to it."

Dominic's throat worked. "You think I—" He gnawed on his lip.

"I very much want to try and help you find subspace," Farid admitted. "A sub who goes down like that is the most beautiful thing in the world to me. Helping you get there does it for me, in a big way."

Dominic digested that, eyes thoughtful. "What else?" he finally asked.

"You said no pain, so that rules out cutting, burning, blood-play, hitting, and whipping," Farid said.

Dominic's eyes went wider with every word. He swallowed hard but said nothing.

"Bondage?" Farid said. "Tying you up in such a way that you're not in pain but you're immobile?"

"Oh God," Dominic said faintly. "I—yeah."

"Good," Farid said, smiling at him. "Breath-play?"

"I don't—" Dominic swallowed. "I don't know?"

"How about humiliation?"

Dominic's brow creased. "Like what?"

"Degrading things said during a scene," Farid offered. "Calling you a slut, or filthy, dirty, bad… that kind of thing."

Something flashed across Dominic's face. "No," he said, and it was clearly difficult for him. "I can't—I don't w-want…."

Farid switched tacks immediately. "Blindfolds?"

It took Dominic a minute to follow, but then he nodded. "I mean… I think so. I don't know."

"Gagged," Farid suggested. "You'd still have a way to safeword, even with your mouth closed."

Dominic considered but finally lifted a shoulder. "I don't know." His mouth drooped. "I'm sorry, I d-don't—"

"You're doing well," Farid said, and Dominic lifted his eyes, clearly surprised. Farid smiled at him. "So well. You're telling me what you think you'll like, what you know you won't. This is good. It's *really* good."

"I'm saying no so much, though," Dominic whispered. A curl had fallen forward over his forehead, and Farid resisted the urge to smooth it back.

"There's no limit on how many times you can say no," he said instead.

"But—it won't be fun for you," Dominic said. "I keep telling you what you *can't* do to me."

"You've given me plenty to work with," Farid said, keeping his tone soothing. "Now, just to be completely clear—you want this to be sexual as well as mental, right?"

Dominic nodded immediately. "If… that's okay."

"More than okay," Farid said. "What do you like, as far as that?"

Dominic shrugged again. "The, um. Usual."

Farid narrowed his eyes. "Blowjobs, handjobs, penetration, being held down during sex, or tied up?"

Dominic squirmed, flushing bright red. "Yes," he managed.

"I think that's enough for now," Farid said abruptly, and he didn't miss the relief that flashed across Dominic's face. "On your knees."

Dominic slid out of the chair and sank to his knees, watching Farid with hunger in his eyes.

"Hands behind your back, lace your fingers together," Farid directed.

When Dominic obeyed, Farid crowded in close, pushing him back on his heels and wrapping one hand around his throat. He didn't squeeze, just held him steady as Dominic swallowed hard and relaxed into it, going pliant in Farid's grip.

"Good," Farid said approvingly. "Now. Choose a safeword."

Dominic blinked. "A what?"

"It's your guarantee of safety," Farid said. He stroked Dominic's long throat, tracing up and along the line of his jaw as Dominic shivered. "If at any point what we're doing is too much, you can use it, no questions asked. There will be no judgments, no condemnations. Choose a word you wouldn't use in casual conversation."

Dominic's mouth worked, and Farid thumbed his lower lip again, smiling.

"P-pomegranate," Dominic managed.

"Very good," Farid said.

Dominic's posture eased, and he settled back on his heels.

Farid moved away so he could appreciate the picture Dominic made, kneeling abjectly before him.

He backed up and sat down on the couch as Dominic watched him, confusion in his eyes.

"What are you—"

Farid held up a finger. "Be quiet."

DOMINIC SHIFTED HIS WEIGHT, baffled. Farid had pulled out his phone and was seemingly absorbed in it, completely ignoring Dominic. He crossed his legs and flicked through pages, fingers quick and deft on the screen.

Frustration welled inside Dominic's chest. He'd thought they were going to—he opened his mouth and closed it again, remembering what Farid had said. *Be quiet.* This was a test. He could be quiet. He could be good, show Farid how obedient he was.

He settled his weight, relaxing into a comfortable position, and closed his eyes. Silence fell over the room, and Dominic's mind wandered.

He wanted to put his mouth all over Farid's body, to explore every detail of him, taste the soft skin on his inner elbows, suck livid marks into his thighs, feel Farid gasping, sinking his hands into Dominic's hair to hold his head still. He wanted Farid to explore *him*, to take him over body and soul, crowding out every sound and thought and sensation until all that remained was the dark-eyed man currently sitting on the sofa.

He swallowed again, tightening his grip on his own hands. *Be quiet.* Farid still hadn't even looked at him.

Dominic took a deep breath and let go. He released the anxiety that rode his shoulders like a watchful gremlin, the fear that was never far from his mind, and floated, free and serene, safe from the panic that buffeted him constantly.

He was only vaguely aware when Farid got up and left the room, returning a few minutes later and cupping Dominic's jaw.

"Doing so well," he murmured, and Dominic leaned into his touch, luxuriating in the simple contact. "Would you like to come?" Farid asked.

Arousal was the furthest thing from his mind, but an orgasm sounded nice. Dominic nodded dreamily, and Farid huffed a quiet laugh.

"Get up," he said.

He helped Dominic to his feet and to the couch. Dominic sank down into its cushions, coming back to himself enough to realize that Farid was on the floor in front of him between Dominic's spread knees.

He caught his breath, and Farid looked up. "Be quiet," he said again, and unzipped Dominic's slacks.

Dominic couldn't have spoken if he'd wanted to. He was paralyzed, watching Farid pull his pants down and free Dominic's soft cock, and Dominic swallowed shame. Farid wouldn't want him now, would think he wasn't good enough—but Farid had leaned forward and was blowing gently on the head of his cock.

"Did you know that it's possible to train you to come at the sound of my voice?" he asked, looking up.

Dominic shook his head, and Farid smiled at him.

"Maybe we'll do that someday," he murmured. "Tie you down, maybe slip a vibrator inside you, and see just how hard I can make you come just from my voice."

Dominic's breath hitched, and his cock jerked, stiffening. Farid made a low, triumphant noise.

"There you are." He pulled a condom from his pocket and rolled it into place. He followed with his mouth, hot and wet and filthy, and Dominic stuffed his knuckles between his teeth to keep himself quiet as Farid worked him over with lips and tongue.

He'd never had a blowjob before, and there was distress somewhere deep inside him that he couldn't enjoy it properly, couldn't truly appreciate the magic Farid was working with his mouth. But he was still half out of his body and only partially aware of what was happening physically, and finally he gave up and let go completely, floating free.

It didn't take long before the feeling of impending orgasm made his muscles twitch, tendrils of ecstasy spreading outward from the base of his spine. Farid pressed on the skin just below his balls, and Dominic seized and curled forward, emptying into the condom soundlessly in helpless jerks. Farid eased him through it, humming around his mouthful, and finally pulled off and wiped his mouth.

Dominic went limp, boneless with exhausted bliss, and Farid laughed quietly.

"You did it," he said. He crawled onto Dominic's

lap, straddling his thighs. "You didn't make a single noise." He bent and kissed him, and Dominic opened for him, tasting scotch and latex. "I'm going to jerk off on your very expensive shirt," Farid informed him when he pulled away. "And you're going to watch."

He freed his erection from his pants, and Dominic bit back a moan of appreciation. Farid's cock was as beautiful as the rest of him, long and slim, and Farid's hand wrapped around it only made it better.

Dominic opened his mouth and closed it again. He hadn't been given permission.

"You may, ah—speak," Farid said.

"Can I suck you off sometime?" Dominic whispered.

"Of course you can," Farid said as he stroked. "God, that'll feel good, your mouth on me… I've been thinking about it nonstop ever since I kissed you that first time—" He caught his breath, hand quickening, and his thighs tensed as he came, bending forward so their foreheads were pressed together as wetness splattered Dominic's french linen shirt. Farid shuddered, half-laughing. "*Jesus.* Ah, God, I needed that."

Dominic was content to lay quietly, Farid a solid weight on top of him, and enjoy the afterglow, but all too soon Farid stood and pulled him protesting to his feet.

"Cleanup and then dinner," Farid said, pushing him toward the bathroom.

"Dinner? It's barely four!" Dominic said, but as he spoke he realized the sun was setting.

"You were in subspace for over an hour," Farid said, laughter in his voice, and chivvied him into the shower stall, where he helped him tug his clothes off and start the water.

WHEN DOMINIC GOT out of the shower, he found Farid making himself at home in the kitchen, poking through Dominic's cupboards.

"You have no food," Farid said. "None. How do you *live*? Wait, no, I found some crackers. Do you have any cheese?"

"I have a delivery service," Dominic said, running his hands through his damp hair. "They should be here… any minute, actually."

Farid shook his head. "Must be nice."

"It is," Dominic said. "And you can share it with me if you want, they usually bring enough for leftovers."

"Sure, why not?" Farid said, smiling at him.

THEY ATE lobster carbonara sitting on the couch, legs tucked beneath them as the sun sank below the horizon and the lights came on in the city at their feet.

It was a comfortable silence, easy and companionable, but finally Dominic cleared his throat.

"How is this going to work?" he asked.

Farid swallowed his mouthful. "I'm assuming you mean us having sex."

Dominic hunched his shoulders and nodded.

"In the office, you're the boss," Farid said. He nudged Dominic's knee, eyes creasing with amusement. "You can tell me what to do all day long if it makes you happy."

Dominic huffed a reluctant laugh.

"Outside the office—" Farid lifted a shoulder. "It's

up to you. Personally, I'm not interested in a total power exchange. Too much responsibility on me, and you're a grownup, you've been making your own decisions for years."

"Total power exchange," Dominic echoed. "Does that mean what I think it means?"

"Master and slave type deal, yeah," Farid agreed. "Not my thing."

"Mine either," Dominic said hastily. "I like making my own choices."

Farid nodded. "Good. But when we're scening, I'm in charge. If you disobey, you'll be punished. Sometimes you'll enjoy the punishments, sometimes… you won't."

Dominic shivered. "I don't… know what—"

"You're new to this, I know," Farid said. "You don't know what you like yet. We'll take it slow, talk it out beforehand if you want. In any case, if I ever do anything you don't like, you can always safeword."

Dominic set his plate on the coffee table and drew his knees to his chest. "What got you into this?"

"I figured out early on that I liked bossing people around," Farid said. His eyes were amused. "Had a girlfriend who introduced me to BDSM, and I've gone from there. I have to say, for your first time scening, you did really well. You took my orders perfectly."

"First time with everything," Dominic mumbled. "I had no idea what I was doing."

Farid dropped his plate on the table with a clatter. "Say what now?"

Dominic looked up, startled. "What?"

"First time—" Farid clutched his hair. "Please, dear God, please tell me I didn't just take your virginity."

"It's not a big deal," Dominic said, and Farid nearly fell off the couch in his scramble to stand.

"Oh my God," he said, covering his mouth with one shaking hand. "Oh my *God* you were a *virgin*? And I—that was—why didn't you *say* something?"

Dominic stood too, still baffled. "Because it doesn't matter! I wanted this, Farid, I could have said no at any time!"

"But—" Farid turned away, rubbing his face, and then turned back. "If I'd known, I would have—"

"Treated me differently, yeah," Dominic snapped, anger suddenly flooding him. "Which is what I didn't *want*."

"Okay," Farid said. He took a deep breath and sat back down on the couch. "Okay, Dom, I'm sorry. Sit, please?" He patted the cushion, and Dominic sank down beside him. Farid blew out a breath. "I'm sorry. It's just—I assumed… you've had boyfriends, and you've got money, and *looks*, and I—*how* were you still a virgin?"

Dominic lifted a shoulder. He was defensive, on edge, and angry with it. "I've never… wanted it before," he finally said.

Farid waited while Dominic searched for words.

"I thought—I thought I was broken, I guess," he whispered. "I didn't want anyone. But I knew I liked boys, and the thought of kissing boys, so I figured I was gay. I just didn't want *sex*. So I didn't have it. Ever. I mean, there were a couple of near-misses that didn't… work out. So I figured it was better to just… not do it."

Farid looked horrified, and Dominic rushed to clarify.

"Until you. I can't stop thinking about… sex with

you. Which—it's never happened before, so I didn't know what to do, and then you offered and I—I'm *sorry*, I should have told you but I didn't want—"

Farid leaned in and covered Dominic's mouth, stopping the flow of words.

"You're not broken," Farid said. "You're *not*. It does sound like you're on the asexual spectrum, though."

Dominic blinked. "But I *do* want—"

"Spectrum," Farid repeated. "There's a whole gamut of different asexuality colors you could be, and I suspect you're somewhere in the demi or gray-asexual shade. Meaning you don't want sex until you've formed a bond with someone, or you only want it rarely, or any other of a dozen things."

"But I do," Dominic said. It was important that Farid understood. "I *want* it. With you. All the time, honestly."

Farid laughed quietly and leaned forward to press their mouths together. "That's good," he said against Dominic's lips. "I want it with you too. But we're going to take it slow. And if you ever *don't* want it, you tell me, okay?"

Dominic nodded. "How do you know so much about it?"

"My little brother dated an ace girl briefly in high school," Farid said, sitting back. "Salma and I did our reading up on it."

"And you're… okay with… it? Me?"

"Of course," Farid said. "After all, I'm aromantic. I'd be a hypocrite if I had a problem with someone who identifies as ace."

"You're… you don't fall in love?" Dominic hazarded.

"Got it in one," Farid said easily. "Which is why this will be strictly sex. No messy feelings."

"Right," Dominic said. "That makes it… less complicated."

Farid gathered the dishes and took them to the kitchen and then came back to the living room. "I'll get out of your hair and let you enjoy your evening," he said.

"Oh." Dominic chewed on his lip. "No more sex today? I can—I mean…."

Farid laughed and straddled Dominic's lap, bending to kiss him, his weight grounding Dominic and calming his mind. "Not a good idea to have too many intense scenes back to back, especially when you're so new to it." He kissed him again, threading his hands through Dominic's hair. "Don't worry," he breathed. "We will."

"Okay," Dominic managed.

Farid stood and straightened his clothes. "Watch for a subdrop," he said as Dominic followed him to the door. "If you get upset, anxious or irritable, call me immediately. Make sure you hydrate too."

He went up on tiptoe and pulled Dominic down into one more kiss.

"God, you're delicious," he sighed. "I can't wait to take you apart."

Dominic shivered, and Farid grinned at him and slipped out the door.

10

Farid's phone rang in the elevator, and his smile faded as he looked at it.

"Yeah."

"Progress report," Peggy said.

Farid scowled at himself in the mirrored wall. "It's only been a few weeks. Even I can't work that fast."

"But you've already kissed him," Peggy said.

Farid stiffened. "How—"

"Please," Peggy snapped. "Give us some credit. You think you're *not* being watched?"

"You don't trust me." The doors slid open, but Farid didn't move.

"We don't trust anyone," Peggy pointed out. "You're not special. Have you gotten anywhere yet?"

Farid tugged on his jacket and stepped out of the elevator. "Not yet. But I will. He's on his way to trusting me."

"Work fast. We don't have a lot of time."

Farid hung up and strode across the lobby, clenching his fists.

Dominic was already in the office when Farid arrived the next morning. Farid found him reading his notes for the press conference, lips moving as he scanned the cards. By now, Farid could parse the lines on Dominic's forehead—stress and anxiety and fear that he'd flub the entire thing, probably.

He waited, but Dominic didn't seem to notice him. Farid cleared his throat, and Dominic jumped, dropping his cards.

"*Fuck*. How long have you been there?"

"Long enough to see you're working yourself up to a panic attack if you're not careful," Farid said. He stepped into the room as Dominic went to his knees to pick up the cards. "How's Cory?"

Dominic glanced up, a smile replacing the anxiety. "She's fine. Baby too." He scrambled to his feet. "How do I look?"

"Would it be inappropriate to say hot as fuck?" Farid quipped.

Dominic passed a hand over his face, trying and failing to hide the smile.

"Your hair's a mess, though," Farid said. He moved close. "Hold still."

Dominic gulped, eyes widening, but he stayed motionless as Farid reached up and gently disentangled a knot over his ear, running his fingers through the strands as they curled and clung to his hands.

When he was satisfied, he lowered his arms. Dominic's gaze was hungry, but he didn't move.

"The look in your eyes," Farid murmured. "I want to bend you over that desk and fuck you until you *beg*."

Dominic squeezed his eyes shut, the by-now familiar sign that he was struggling for control. Farid waited.

"Can I see you tonight?" Dominic finally whispered.

Farid tilted his head. "There's a distinct possibility," he allowed. "Nail this press conference and the rest of your appointments today and maybe you'll get a reward this evening."

Dominic shot his cuffs, a determined look on his face. "On it."

Farid couldn't help his laugh as he followed him out of the office and down the hall to the pressroom.

FARID STAYED IN THE BACKGROUND, watching Dominic work the room. Despite his earlier nerves, he was doing well. His shoulders were tight and hands fidgeting on the podium out of sight of the room as he fielded questions, but his voice was calm, and he didn't hesitate over his answers.

The reporters gathered sent Farid a few inquisitive glances but seemed content to accept him as Cory's replacement, focusing their attention on Dominic. That was fine by Farid. He worked best behind the scenes, and this way he could make sure Dominic was handling the questions easily.

A reporter raised her hand, and Dominic pointed to her.

"We've been hearing news that you broke up with Lance because he was just after your wealth, is that accurate?"

Dominic tensed. "We're not here to discuss my love life."

"But—"

"We're done," Farid said, stepping forward. "Thank you all for coming."

He touched Dominic's elbow and turned him toward the door, giving the assembled group an impersonal smile as they left.

Back in his office, Dominic yanked his tie off with a muttered curse. "I fucking *hate* it when they do that. And they *always* do it. Why can't they stop pestering me?" He ran his hands through his hair, leaving it standing on end. "It's none of their fucking business!"

Farid shut the door behind them. "Like it or not, you're a public figure. Which means that every aspect of your life is laid bare to scrutiny. It sucks, but there's not really a way around it."

"I don't *want* to be a public figure!" Dominic snapped. "I just want to write my code and be left alone." He blew out a breath and Farid smiled in sympathy.

"R&D wants to see you now."

"Fine," Dominic said. He rubbed his face and reached for the door, pausing when Farid followed him through. "You don't need to come with me for this one."

"Oh." Farid stopped. "Sorry."

Dominic shot him a smile. "I'll be back soon."

He disappeared, and Farid sat down at his own desk. He'd have to find another way to get back inside the Research and Development lab for a more thorough recon.

When Dominic came back, he was buzzing with excitement, his shirtsleeves rolled up and collar unbuttoned. His hair was disheveled, like he'd been running his hands through it again, and Farid suppressed a smile.

"Go well?"

"Hm?" Dominic's eyes were distant, fingers tapping an invisible code in midair. "Oh, yeah. It did. They've got some great ideas. Harvey came up with this particular sequence of code that's going to revolutionize what we're doing."

"Oh yes? How?"

Dominic glanced at him, clearly still deep in his thoughts. "Oh. It's—I don't think I can explain it. I have to—do you mind—"

"Go on," Farid said, waving him away. "Leave the dunce out of it."

Dominic flashed a smile and vanished into his office.

When the sun went down and Dominic still hadn't emerged, Farid went in search.

The lights were off again, the only illumination in the room the monitors Dominic was hunched in front of as he typed rapidly.

Farid flicked the light on, and Dominic yelped and shielded his eyes.

"Warn me," he complained.

"Sorry," Farid said, lips twitching. "It's late, and you haven't eaten."

"Are you my nanny now too?" Dominic said. He

stood and stretched, arms over his head and moaned with relief when his back popped.

"Do you want me to be?" Farid countered. He leaned against the wall and made no effort to conceal the fact that he was admiring the view as Dominic dropped his arms.

"Nah." Dominic rounded the desk and loomed over Farid, bracing an elbow on the wall above his shoulder. "So. I think I did pretty well at the press conference. I seem to recall someone mentioning a reward."

Farid lifted an eyebrow. He could feel the heat radiating off Dominic's body but he made no move to close the space between them. "Is that so?" This close, he could smell Dominic's aftershave, spicy and sweet, and his mouth watered.

"I mean, if you've changed your mind…." Dominic drew away, and Farid went after him in a rush, fisting both hands in Dominic's shirt and yanking him down into a bruising kiss.

Dominic huffed a laugh against Farid's mouth and pulled him in, arms around Farid's waist as their lips and tongues slid together wet and hungry.

It was several minutes before Farid managed to break away, panting. "Careful," he said, licking his lips. "Or I'll put you on your knees right here."

Dominic's eyes widened, and he glanced at the door, firmly closed.

"Like the thought of that, do you?" Farid husked. He reached between them and cupped Dominic's erection, running a thumb over the taut fabric. "Maybe you've got a bit of an exhibitionist streak. Do you want to be put on display? Stripped down and—"

Dominic shivered and twisted away. "Don't—"

"Don't what?" Farid asked, suddenly worried. Had he gone too far? Pushed too hard?

There was shame in Dominic's eyes when he glanced up. "I'm gonna come in my pants if you don't stop," he whispered.

Oh. Farid drew a deep breath and forced himself to take a step back. "To be continued," he said, and opened the door, gesturing for Dominic to precede him through.

He waited until they were in the car, the window closed between them and the driver, to speak again. "I want to be clear on something."

Dominic lifted his eyes, apprehension on his face.

Farid took his hand, thumbing the skin over Dominic's knuckles. "Nothing you do is wrong," he said quietly. "Even if you weren't a—"

"Virgin," Dominic offered. "You can say it."

Farid smiled. "Yes. But even if you weren't a virgin, you're in a new situation and it's okay for you to not know what you're doing. I won't punish you for coming because I've worked you up to that point, okay?"

"Unless I want to be, right?" There was sudden mischief in Dominic's eyes, and Farid laughed.

"If it's deliberate, pet, then yes. You *will* be punished."

Dominic shivered.

"Pet," Farid said carefully, tasting the word, and Dominic closed his eyes, dark lashes sweeping down.

"Again?" he whispered.

Farid unbuckled and slid across the seat to cup Dominic's face. "Are you my pet?" he murmured, and kissed the line of his jaw.

Dominic's throat worked silently, his eyes still closed.

Farid nipped Dominic's chin, making him jerk. "My pretty pet. I'm going to take you apart, beautiful boy. Break you down, make you come screaming, make you *beg*—"

Dominic grabbed the door and covered his mouth, hips bucking as Farid watched, amazed and delighted.

"I'm sorry," Dominic gasped after a minute, trembling.

"What did I just say?" Farid said. "Nothing you do is wrong." He rubbed the wet spot on Dominic's crotch, and Dominic twitched as Farid grinned suddenly. "I told you it was possible to come with just the sound of my voice."

"I don't—I didn't want—"

"Oh, we're nowhere near done for the evening," Farid promised.

Dominic sagged back against the seat, chest heaving. "I am not going to survive this."

WHEN THEY GOT to Dominic's building, Farid refused to sneak in the side entrance.

Dominic stared at him, clearly horrified, and Farid smiled.

"We're walking right through the lobby," he said.

"But—"

"But what?" Farid interrupted. "But anyone could see? Anyone who looks at you will know you just came? I guess you'd better walk fast, then."

Dominic's mouth firmed, and he unbuckled and

took a deep breath. Then he pushed the car door open and stepped out.

Instead of angling away and scuttling by the doorman, a balding, kind-eyed man with the name-tag Jerry on his chest, Dominic lifted a hand in greeting, although he didn't slow his pace across the lobby.

"Jerry, how are the girls?" he called.

"Laura's set to graduate college," Jerry said, and the elevator dinged as he pressed the button for it. "And Melly is taking a gap year and going to Ecuador this summer."

Dominic glanced at Farid. "Send Laura a graduation gift," he said out of the corner of his mouth. Lifting his voice, almost to the elevator, he said, "Jerry, this is Farid, my new assistant. He's to be allowed up whenever he wants, all right?"

"You got it, Mr. Spector," Jerry said.

The elevator doors slid open, and Dominic and Farid stepped inside.

Farid waited until they closed before crowding into Dominic's space. "Definitely got a bit of an exhibition kink, do you?"

Dominic's throat bobbed. "I'm—I've never done anything like that."

"Did you enjoy it?" Farid asked, trailing a finger along Dominic's jaw.

Dominic nodded jerkily.

"Interesting." Farid thumbed Dominic's lower lip. "You've given me a few ideas."

Dominic's eyes were wide, and there was already a telltale bulge at his crotch again. He swallowed hard several times, mouth working. "Like what?" he asked hoarsely.

"Oh, you'll see," Farid said.

The elevator dinged and the doors slid open. Dominic turned and stepped out, Farid right on his heels, crowding up against his back as Dominic unlocked his door.

Farid pushed him over the threshold, and the door swung shut as Dominic stumbled and went to one knee and Farid pounced. He caught a fistful of hair and cranked Dominic's head back, crowding in close.

Dominic's eyes closed, and his Adam's apple bobbed, but he said nothing, loose and pliant in Farid's hand.

"Safeword," Farid said, bending to nose along Dominic's jaw.

"P-pomegranate," Dominic managed. "Farid—"

"You can stop me at any time," Farid said.

Dominic nodded, and Farid stepped back, adjusting his cuffs.

No matter how much Dominic said he wanted what they were doing, the truth was that he had no idea what he was in for, and it was going to be Farid's job to keep him safe as they learned his boundaries. That meant carefully monitoring his emotional state, even if Dominic didn't safeword.

Dominic didn't look scared, though. He was utterly still, watching Farid's face, so Farid put a foot on Dominic's chest and pushed until Dominic went over and landed flat on his back with a grunt.

Farid turned away. "Take your clothes off," he said over his shoulder and headed for the bedroom. He'd found condoms behind the bathroom mirror, a brand-new unopened box, that first time they'd scened. After, he'd imagined Dominic buying them, jittery and keyed up, maybe for his most recent boyfriend. Hoping he was different, perhaps? Farid didn't know, but it made him extra aware of how careful he had to be.

There were no noises from the living room, and Farid sat down on the bed and pulled out his phone.

This was another test, of course. He wanted to see what Dominic would do with scant instructions. Would he come looking for Farid? Get bored and give up? Farid couldn't wait to find out.

He gave it fifteen minutes and went back out.

Dominic was on his knees, right where Farid had left him, naked with his hands clasped behind his back and his eyes fixed on the door. He drew a visible breath of relief when Farid appeared, but didn't move.

Farid couldn't help his smile, and some of the tension left Dominic's shoulders. Farid crossed the room to him and bent to run a thumb over Dominic's cheekbone as Dominic leaned into it.

"What a good pet," Farid whispered.

Dominic closed his eyes, and Farid kissed him. Dominic tasted tart and sweet, like the pomegranate soda he liked so much, and Farid pressed in, taking command and holding Dominic's jaw to keep his head steady as he swept his tongue inside Dominic's mouth.

When he drew back, Dominic swayed after him. Farid trailed a hand over Dominic's broad chest, through the softly curling hair, as Dominic sucked in a breath. Farid put his shoe on his thigh and pressed, watching as Dominic's cock thickened, and then slid it farther up, until his toe nudged the tip of his shaft. Then he lifted his foot away, not missing the disappointment that flickered across Dominic's face.

"You're a natural, pet," he said. "Get up."

Dominic scrambled to his feet, and Farid tilted his head back and smiled up at him. He stepped close and ran one finger down Dominic's erection, flushed a dark red.

Then he stepped close and wrapped his hand around Dominic's cock. Dominic groaned and folded forward, and Farid caught and steadied him, his free arm around Dominic's neck as he stroked him, their cheeks pressed together.

"When's the last time you masturbated?" he asked.

Dominic swallowed audibly, hips jerking. "Y-yesterday."

"Did you think about me?" Farid asked.

Dominic whimpered.

"Did you?"

"*Yes*," Dominic blurted. "I thought about—Farid, *please*—"

Farid slowed his strokes. "What did you think about?"

Dominic's groan sounded ripped from him. "*You*."

Farid smiled against Dominic's curls. "Mm, yes, but what in particular? Did you think about sucking me off? Me fucking you? You fucking *me*?"

Dominic twisted violently away, and Farid let go as Dominic stumbled backward, shoulders hunched, every muscle tensed.

It was several minutes before his breathing eased and he lifted his head to meet Farid's eyes.

"God, I love how sensitive you are," Farid said. He took a step forward. "I can use that."

Dominic shuddered but didn't move.

"The 'no pain' thing puts an interesting spin on it," Farid mused, running a finger along Dominic's pectoral. "It means I have to think outside the box. Usually by now I'd have whipped you or used nipple clamps or any number of other things, but—"

Uncertainty flickered across Dominic's face, followed by resolution. "Do you—you can… hurt me, I guess."

"Oh no," Farid said. He took Dominic's jaw in one hand, a firm grip just this side of pain. "You said no pain. Now is as good as time as any to say this." He pulled Dominic's head down so their faces were level. "Hear this, Dominic. I will never hurt you in any way I can avoid. I will take care of you. You are safe with me. This I promise. Do you understand?"

Dominic nodded fractionally, chin still imprisoned in Farid's grip, but something around his eyes eased.

"You can always safeword," Farid continued. "No matter what we're doing, if it's too much for you, I *want* you to safeword. Okay?"

Dominic's lashes swept down, and he took a slow, careful breath. "Okay," he whispered.

"Beautiful, beautiful boy," Farid murmured. "Do you know what you do to me?" He wrapped a hand around Dominic's cock and stroked again, relishing the minute vibrations that rippled through Dominic's body with every movement of Farid's hand.

Dominic's breathing was harsh and ragged in the quiet room, his hands still behind his back and hips bucking into Farid's grip.

"Not—yet," he begged after a minute. "Please, Farid, I—"

Farid eased off, and Dominic sucked in air and straightened. Farid put a hand on his chest, appreciating the firmness of the muscles that flexed under Dominic's skin, and impulsively bent to drop a kiss on the mole just over Dominic's collarbone.

Dominic's breath stuttered.

"Like that, do you?" Farid did it again, kissing his

way along Dominic's left collarbone and then over to the right. He set his teeth against the jut of bone, and Dominic jerked.

"P-please—"

Farid glanced up. "Please what, pet?"

Dominic's mouth worked. "Wanna—will you —bed?"

Farid laughed and pulled him down into a kiss. "You want me to take you to bed?" he murmured against Dominic's mouth, and Dominic nodded fractionally.

"Please?"

"Lead the way, pet," Farid said.

Dominic immediately spun for the bedroom, and Farid followed, admiring Dominic's firm ass and those endless legs. He leaned against the doorjamb as Dominic crawled onto the bed and turned to face him on his knees.

Uncertainty crossed his face, and Farid smiled at him. "Just enjoying the view." He pushed away from the doorway and took his shoes off while Dominic watched him. Farid undressed slowly, unbuttoning his shirt and taking it off in calm, controlled movements. Next were his pants and underwear, and finally his socks until he stood naked in front of Dominic, whose eyes were wide.

"On your back," Farid instructed. "Do you have lube?"

Dominic froze halfway into position and nodded. "B-bedside drawer." He lowered himself to the bed as Farid rummaged in the drawer and came up with the bottle of lube.

He crawled onto the bed and leaned down to look into Dominic's eyes. They were still blown with lust but there was wariness in them now too, fear of whatever Farid had in mind.

"We can stop at any time," Farid reminded him.

Dominic firmed his mouth and nodded, and Farid kissed him, quick and gentle, and then slid between his open legs. Dominic's shaft was flushed where it lay against his stomach, and Farid glanced up.

"Have you ever played with yourself down here?"

Dominic propped himself on his elbows and shook his head. "I—no. I've just always...." He made the jerking off motion and shrugged, and Farid laughed quietly and popped the cap on the lube.

"We're going to see what you like," he said, and coated a finger.

Dominic flinched when Farid touched the flexing knot of muscle but stayed still, holding his breath. Farid explored the area thoroughly but didn't push inside, waiting for Dominic to relax.

Finally Dominic took a deep breath, and some of the tension in his frame bled away. "That... I think I like that."

"Yeah?" Farid slid his finger inside up to the first knuckle, and Dominic jerked, a sharp noise falling from his mouth. "Still okay?"

Dominic's eyes were closed, a frown wrinkling his forehead. "I—don't know."

"Breathe slow and deep," Farid instructed. "It can take a little while for it to start feeling good. Bear down against me when I push in more."

He pulled out and added more lube and then pressed in again, up to the second knuckle. Dominic's breathing was rapid and unsteady, a flush pinking his chest and his eyes still closed.

Farid began to work his finger in and out in slow,

steady movements, watching Dominic closely as uneasiness formed a spiky ball in his chest. He didn't like the way Dominic was frowning or the way he'd gathered handfuls of the bedspread as he fought to relax.

But Dominic didn't say anything, so Farid kept going, sliding in and out of that silken heat until Dominic's body was accepting the intrusion. Farid pushed deep and rubbed—there—and Dominic jerked and cried out.

"What—*ah*—"

"That's your prostate," Farid said, smiling up at him. "Does it feel good?"

Dominic shook his head and then nodded. "No—yes… it's… *intense.*"

"Keep breathing for me," Farid said. He pulled out and added more lube again. But this time, when he breached the ring of muscle with two fingers, Dominic made a noise that was definitely pain.

"S-stop."

Farid froze, two knuckles in. Dominic's chest heaved, his mouth set, and Farid grimaced and pulled back.

"No—I'm okay," Dominic managed.

Farid hesitated.

"Please?" Dominic whispered. "I want to do this—for you. *With* you."

Farid dropped a kiss on Dominic's knee and began to move again, even slower. Dominic relaxed into it, but he was still tight around Farid' fingers—*too* tight.

Farid took a deep breath and added a third finger, and Dominic flinched and stifled the noise with a fist against his mouth.

"Nope, we're done," Farid said, pulling out.

Dominic sagged with relief even as he opened his mouth to protest.

"No," Farid said. "It's hurting you. Look, you're not even hard anymore."

Dominic glanced down at his soft cock, and shame filled his eyes. "I can handle it," he insisted. "Please, Farid—I want to—"

Farid leaned over and stopped him with a kiss. Dominic arched up into it, his eyes closed, and Farid caressed his cheekbone with his clean hand.

"I have to take care of you," he said when he pulled away. "You were nowhere near subspace and you weren't truly enjoying what we were doing, and that means I'm not going to continue. Even if you *were* into pain, there's a difference between pain you're into and pain you want to stop. That was pain you wanted to stop, wasn't it?"

Dominic bit his lip but finally he nodded. "I'm sorry," he whispered. "I wanted—"

"Trust your body," Farid said. "*Listen* to it. And don't ever force yourself to accept what I'm doing if you're in genuine pain, do you hear me? The only time I'm going to get angry is if you endure what I'm doing rather than enjoy it."

He sat back on his heels and pulled Dominic to a sitting position. Dominic didn't meet his eyes, and Farid caught his chin in an iron grip.

"Stop blaming yourself," he said flatly.

"I ruined—"

Farid gave Dominic's chin a rough shake. "You didn't ruin a *thing*. Don't you realize how many different ways there are to have sex? Penetration is not the ultimate endgame, Dom. Besides." He grinned. "This means *you* get to fuck *me*."

Dominic sucked in a startled breath. "What?"

"You heard me," Farid said. "Now come on, we're showering, and I'm going to give you a blowjob while you wash my hair. But you can't come until my hair is completely clean, and if you do, you'll be punished."

Dominic's throat bobbed, and he followed Farid off the bed and into the bathroom wordlessly.

IN THE BATHROOM, Farid turned on the water and pulled Dominic into the shower stall with him. Steam billowed forth as the water poured out, and Farid leaned in and pressed a quick kiss to the corner of Dominic's mouth.

"Remember what I said?"

Dominic nodded wordlessly as water beaded on Farid's lean torso and slid in rivulets down his brown skin.

"You have to wash *and* condition my hair," Farid said and went to his knees. "And you're not allowed to come until it's done."

Dominic fumbled for the shampoo and knocked it off the shelf. He swore under his breath, and Farid laughed, slanted eyes gleaming, and handed it to him.

"That's the last help you're getting from me," he said, and leaned forward to nuzzle Dominic's groin. His breath was hot and wet against Dominic's abdomen, and he licked a path down as Dominic struggled to remember how to open the shampoo bottle.

Hair, he thought desperately, his hands feeling oversized and clumsy. *His hair needs to be wet first.*

Farid had reached Dominic's shaft, which was

thickening rapidly, and Dominic took a step back before Farid could take him into his mouth.

Farid looked up, irritation flickering across his face, and Dominic swallowed fear.

"Your—" His voice shook. "I have to—get your hair wet."

"Oh." Farid moved sideways until the water cascaded over his shoulders, tilting his head back and closing his eyes as he let the stream pour down his face.

He was beautiful in the way a panther was beautiful, sleek and deadly, preening under Dominic's hungry gaze. Dominic forgot how to breathe as he watched, until Farid opened his eyes and arched an eyebrow.

"Wet enough for you?"

Dominic cursed his awkward tongue. Why wasn't he smooth and polished like Farid? Why did he have to stand where he was, rooted to the floor and gawping like a hick seeing the big city for the first time?

Farid's eyes softened, and he beckoned. Dominic managed to get his feet moving. Farid curled his fingers around Dominic's palm, the press of his skin wet and soft and reassuring.

"You can't fuck this up," he said as he held Dominic's eyes.

"But—" Dominic struggled to find the words. "If I—"

"If you lose this game?" Farid prompted.

Dominic nodded wordlessly.

Farid stood in one easy movement, and Dominic made an inarticulate noise of protest.

"Relax, pet, we're not done," Farid said. He squeezed Dominic's hand. "But we will be if you don't talk to me."

He waited as the steam billowed around them, filling the stall, and Dominic tried to figure out how to explain.

"I don't want—" He trailed off. *I don't want to be punished, I don't want to be beaten or whipped, I don't want to remember what it was like—*

Farid seemed to take pity on him after a minute. "You don't want pain. We established that. But there's something else going on here."

"I—yes," Dominic said. "But I—" He ducked his head and steeled himself. "It's more than just not wanting pain," he said in a rush. "It's—physical punishment reminds me of—" *Don't talk about that don't talk about that don't—*"I don't want to be locked in a dark room or screamed at or—"

He waited for Farid to pull away, to tell him how disappointed he was, and he hunched his shoulders and stared at the floor, braced to be rejected.

Farid laughed instead, low and delighted, and Dominic jerked his eyes up. Farid laced both hands behind Dominic's neck and pulled him down into a damp kiss.

"I'm so proud of you, pet," he breathed against Dominic's mouth.

"But—" Dominic's head spun. He couldn't figure out what he'd done right.

Farid nipped his chin lightly, still smiling. "You communicated. Instead of letting me hurt you because you thought it was what I wanted, you stood up and told me what *you* wanted."

He took a step back, and hope stirred in Dominic's chest. Maybe he hadn't completely ruined things after all.

"So my punishments need to be creative," Farid

mused. He pulled Dominic around until he was under the spray, and Dominic spared half a thought to be grateful for his bottomless water heaters as the almost-scalding water hit his skin and turned his muscles to taffy.

Farid handled him effortlessly, seeming to know exactly how to hold him still, one hand tilting Dominic's chin back as the other worked through his wet hair, massaging his scalp.

He drew away and retrieved the shampoo bottle and then tapped Dominic's shoulder. "Knees. Hands behind your back."

Dominic folded obediently to the floor and gripped his left wrist with his right hand. The water beat down on his shoulders relentlessly as Farid gripped his jaw, pulling his head up.

"Same game, slightly different rules," he said. "You're going to suck me off while I wash your hair. Your goal is to make me come before I'm done, and if you do, then you'll be rewarded. If you don't… you won't be allowed to come at all." He squeezed shampoo onto Dominic's scalp and with his free hand, pressed a thumb into his mouth. "Open."

Dominic obeyed, and Farid pushed his cock inside. The taste of his precome registered first on Dominic's tongue, salty and bitter, and then the heavy, silken feel of Farid's skin, satin over steel.

Dominic floundered briefly as Farid slid deeper, his hand tight in Dominic's wet hair. He didn't know how to give a proper blowjob, what was he doing? There was no way he was going to win this game.

Farid groaned above him. "*Fuck*, that feels good. Tap my thigh if you need to stop, okay?"

Dominic's mouth was too full to answer so he

made a slight noise of assent and cautiously slid his tongue along the underside of Farid's shaft. What was he supposed to do?

Farid wasn't moving, hands still buried in Dominic's hair as he waited for Dominic to relax.

Break down the problem, a tiny voice said in the back of Dominic's mind. *Remember what Farid did to you? And you know what feels good when you touch yourself. Apply logic to the situation.*

Dominic tightened his grip on his wrist and began to suck. Rhythm and steady pressure were the key. Farid hissed through his teeth as Dominic swallowed him deeper, bobbing his head as he ran his tongue along Farid's frenulum.

After a minute, Farid began to work the shampoo into Dominic's hair, his hands unsteady, but Dominic took little notice. He was too focused on the issue at hand, cataloging every noise Farid made, every fractionally tightened muscle, the way his thighs trembled when Dominic hit an especially good rhythm.

There—Farid hunched forward, sucking in air as he fought off his climax, and Dominic almost smiled, but his mouth was full.

Instead, he took Farid deep, relaxing his throat and sliding down until his nose was brushing the wet curls at Farid's groin. Tears sprang to Dominic's eyes and he fought his gag reflex, swallowing hard around the intrusion. He was so intent on what he was doing that he was only dimly aware of Farid swearing in a thick voice and curling over, hands suddenly, brutally tight in Dominic's hair. He pulled back and hot, bitter liquid flooded Dominic's mouth.

Dominic swallowed it all, filing away the taste and

texture and deciding it wasn't pleasant but more than worthwhile.

Finally Farid eased back, and Dominic sucked in air. His wrist hurt, he realized vaguely—he'd been clutching it so hard he'd bruised himself. He ached with the need to come, his skin tight and tingling in desperation, but Farid hadn't said he could touch himself, so he stayed where he was, mouth clamped shut to keep from begging.

Farid bent and kissed him, one soapy hand cradling Dominic's jaw. "You did so well, pet," he breathed when he drew away. Dominic watched him hungrily, and Farid smiled. "You've earned your reward, but first, let's get the shampoo out of your hair. Turn—there you go—now, tip your head back and close your eyes."

His hands were deft and gentle as he rinsed the soap from Dominic's hair, and Dominic sighed, peace settling over him soft like silken feathers. He'd done well. Farid was pleased with him. He didn't have to worry about making mistakes anymore.

"Up," Farid said. He helped Dominic to his feet, and Dominic swayed, leaning into Farid's slim frame. Farid laughed under his breath. "You've hit subspace, haven't you?"

Dominic nodded dreamily. He still needed to come, but it felt so good to let go, to trust Farid to take care of him. His mind drifted, free of its moorings, as Farid pulled him down against him with an arm around his neck and took hold of Dominic's shaft with his other hand.

Nerves fired under his touch, and Dominic jerked, twisting, but Farid held him still, his rhythm steady.

Dominic's knees were butter, liquefying more with every smooth stroke, and he fought to stay on his feet.

"Hold on to me, arms around my neck," Farid said against his cheek.

Dominic obeyed, and Farid pressed a kiss to the skin under his ear. Fire was building in Dominic's groin, spreading in rippling waves, and still Farid stroked him, his touch confident and practiced.

"Need—" Dominic's tongue was thick in his mouth, words slow to form. "P-please," he begged.

"You need to come?" Farid murmured.

Dominic nodded desperately, bucking into Farid's fist with frantic need, and Farid made a quietly triumphant noise.

"Come for me, pet," he ordered.

Dominic choked on a sob as his orgasm rolled over him in an unstoppable wave, as inexorable as a freight train, and his knees buckled. He went down in a help-less heap, taking Farid with him, and they sprawled on the hard floor of the shower, Farid half-across Dominic's chest.

It took a minute for Dominic to realize Farid's shoulders were shaking, and shame and horror flooded him.

"I'm s-sorry," he stuttered, trying to sit up, but Farid pushed him back to the floor. He stretched to reach the faucets and turned the water off, and silence assaulted Dominic, his heartbeat pounding like a hammer in his ears as he waited for Farid to tell him how badly he'd fucked up.

But Farid was smiling, he saw, amusement dancing in his eyes as he pushed damp curls out of Dominic's face. He'd been *laughing*.

"You okay?"

Dominic nodded dumbly and Farid's smile widened. He slid off Dominic's chest and stood. Dominic watched, still expecting him somehow to say the whole thing was over, that he'd failed, but Farid just held out a hand.

Dominic hesitated, and Farid arched a brow.

"Just going to stay down there on the hard tiles?"

Dominic accepted his hand, allowing Farid to pull him to his feet. He felt oversized and awkward next to Farid's neat, contained figure, and he couldn't figure out what to do with his hands.

Farid didn't seem to notice. He just opened the shower door and grabbed a towel off the warming rack.

"*Heated*," he said in clear delight, and wrapped the warm, fluffy fabric around Dominic's shoulders.

Dominic dried himself off with automatic motions as he watched Farid out of the corner of his eye.

For his part, Farid didn't even seem to notice. He hummed to himself as he dried off and draped the damp towel over the rack. Then he turned and held out a hand for Dominic's towel.

He was utterly unselfconscious in his nudity, muscles sliding under sleek skin, the curve of his spine and ass a perfect sine wave, and Dominic was struck dumb by his beauty yet again.

Farid beckoned, and Dominic followed him out of the bathroom into the bedroom.

"Get dressed," Farid said. He sat down on the end of the bed, leaning back on the heels of his hands. "If you have anything that might fit me, that'd be great."

Dominic was still tongue-tied, not entirely sure he hadn't fucked everything up, and he rummaged silently in the drawers. He found soft sweatpants and a faded

Star Wars T-shirt for himself, and then dug deeper. Lance had been about Farid's size, and he'd left clothes at Dominic's apartment occasionally, a subtle hint that Dominic hadn't acknowledged.

He came up with a pair of bright yellow flannel pajama bottoms, and his lips twitched as he handed them and a T-shirt over.

Farid stared blankly at the pants. "You're shitting me."

Dominic shrugged as he pulled the shirt over his head. "It's that or go naked—you'll drown in anything of mine."

"Going naked has more appeal," Farid muttered, but he stood long enough to tug them on and then sat down again. He crossed his legs and waited as Dominic finished pulling his own pants on, then pointed at the floor in front of him. "Knees."

Dominic blinked. Were they still scening? Hesitantly he sank to his knees and clasped his hands behind his back, gazing at the carpet.

Farid leaned over and tipped Dominic's chin up with one finger. There was something like affection in his dark eyes, and Dominic was trapped in his gaze, a butterfly pinned to a board.

"What did you do right?"

Dominic fought to focus as the tension drained from his muscles. Maybe someday he'd stop and parse out exactly why Farid taking control gave him such a sense of security, but right now he couldn't make his brain work anyway.

Farid tapped Dominic's jaw. "Answer the question."

Dominic opened and closed his mouth. "I—" Fog

was creeping in around the edges of his mind, and he swayed. "'Rid, what's… happening to me?"

Farid bent and looked into his eyes. "You're hitting subspace again," he said gently. He sounded very far away. "You're safe, Dom. Tell me what you did right."

Dominic settled on his heels with a sigh and closed his eyes. "I… told you… what I didn't want. Don't… wanna be beat… again."

"Who beat you?" Farid asked.

"M' dad," Dominic slurred. He was so tired suddenly. All he wanted to do was sleep. He swayed, and rustling noises came from the bed as Farid stood.

"Get up," Farid said. His voice was brisk, but his hands were gentle as he helped Dominic to his feet and led him out to the living room with slow, easy steps.

There, he sat down on the couch and spread his legs, pointing to the floor between his feet. "On your knees again, put your head on my thigh."

Dominic obeyed willingly, sinking to the floor and resting his cheek against Farid's inner thigh. He sighed, warm and safe, and Farid combed his still-damp hair off his face as Dominic squirmed until he was comfortable, one arm under Farid's leg.

"Sorry… I fell on you," he slurred.

Farid's body vibrated with his silent laugh. "Rest, pet."

DOMINIC WOKE in the same position, cheek still pressed to Farid's thigh and Farid's hand combing through his hair, fingers deft and gentle against Dominic's scalp.

He lifted his head, blinking, and Farid smiled at him as he muted the television.

"Have a nice nap?"

Dominic sat back on his heels and rubbed his face, muffling a yawn. "How long was I out?"

"Not long," Farid said. He crossed his legs, and Dominic couldn't help his smile at the ridiculous yellow pants. Farid arched an eyebrow. "Don't mock me, pet, or I'll have to punish you."

Dominic couldn't quite stop the snicker. "I just— have a sudden burning need to find you some clown shoes."

Farid laughed outright and patted the cushions. "Get up here, asshole. We need to talk about a few things."

Dominic scrambled to his feet and sat on the couch beside Farid, who still looked amused.

"So we need to address a couple of issues," Farid began.

Dominic tensed and drew his knees to his chest.

"It's nothing bad," Farid said, touching Dominic's shin. "But do you remember... what you said during and after our scene?"

"I—about being beaten?" Dominic said, clutching his knees.

"Yes," Farid said. His eyes were warm and encouraging, and Dominic relaxed a fraction. "You were abused?"

Dominic shook his head. "I wasn't... no. I just don't like—I don't want to be whipped or beaten."

"Your father beat you, yes?"

Dominic nodded. "But only when I was bad."

Farid flinched. "Dom... that's abuse."

"Not if I deserved it," Dominic protested. "It's just

—it's not like he left bruises. I mean… not usually. And it was only when I disobeyed, but I don't like being reminded of it, I—"

Farid leaned forward and cupped Dominic's hand in one warm hand. "So you don't want to feel you're being punished physically, is that right?"

"Yeah," Dominic whispered.

"Okay," Farid said. "So punishment should be incorporeal?"

Dominic nodded. "Is that okay?"

"Of course it is." Farid looked sad, and Dominic wondered briefly what he'd done to upset him. But then Farid lifted his eyes and smiled, and the shadows fled. "The other thing is, this was your first intense scene. You're probably going to drop. I'd like to stay the night, make sure you're okay."

Dominic recoiled, shaking his head. "No. *No*, 'Rid, you can't—no one can know about this, about… us." Panic prickled the back of his throat at the thought of the tabloid headlines and he rubbed his arms, the tiny hairs rising, as he curled in on himself.

"Easy," Farid said. He sounded alarmed. "That's fine, Dom, you know I won't tell, but I also don't want you to ride out a drop alone."

"I'll be fine," Dominic managed, lifting his head. "I—it's not a big deal."

"You don't know what a drop can be like," Farid pointed out.

Dominic wrapped his arms around his legs again and rested his cheek on his knee. "I'll be fine," he repeated.

Farid said nothing, beside him, and the silence felt crystalline, poised to shatter.

Dominic closed his eyes. "You should go."

Farid didn't move for a long minute, but finally he sighed and stood up. Dominic listened as the sound of his footsteps faded in the direction of the bedroom, but when he came back, Farid didn't go straight to him. Instead he headed for the kitchen and opened the refrigerator.

Dominic looked up as Farid pulled something out and came back to the living room, back in his workday suit.

"Drink this," he said, holding out a bottle.

Dominic sat up and accepted the Evian, turning it in his hands. "I'm not really thirsty."

"If you're not going to let me help you through this," Farid said, sounding angry for the first time and making Dominic's eyes snap up, "then you're damn well going to do what I tell you to make sure you weather this as easily as possible. Drink the fucking water, Dominic."

Dominic stared at him for a minute, and Farid made an impatient motion toward the bottle. Dominic fumbled with the cap and finally managed to twist it off.

The water tasted wonderful as it slid down his throat, cold and sweet, and Dominic closed his eyes and drained the bottle as Farid watched.

When he set the empty container down, Farid smiled, although there were still lines of frustration around his eyes.

"Better. Now, your food service will be here soon, right?"

Dominic nodded silently.

"Good. I want you to eat and relax. Try to watch some TV or read a book."

"What if I get an idea?" Dominic protested. "I

have to write it down, you can't ask me to just stop thinking—"

"Actually, the entire idea is to keep thinking," Farid said. He stepped between Dominic's knees and ran a finger down his jaw, making Dominic shiver. "The drop will tell you lies, make you irritable or grouchy, or tell you you're not worthwhile or a good person. It's your body's way of compensating for the high you get during a scene. So keep your mind occupied however works best for you, but—" He bent and nipped Dominic's lower lip gently. "Just take care of yourself."

His breath was warm, and a frisson rippled through Dominic.

"I could—can I text you if I need you?" he asked. Farid's mouth was so close, and Dominic wanted desperately to lean up and taste it, but instead he held his breath and waited for Farid's answer.

"That's an excellent idea," Farid said approvingly and lowered his head until their mouths were touching.

Dominic wanted to melt into the couch, he wanted to draw Farid down with him and memorize every little thing about him, explore his lean body with lips and tongue, but—he sighed regretfully and drew away.

Farid straightened and pulled his cuffs down. "Text me any time tonight, even if it's late."

11

—————

Farid avoided his reflection in the mirror as he rode the elevator to the ground floor.

Jerry was still on duty, and Farid nodded at him but didn't stop for small talk. Instead he strode outside and hailed a cab, waiting until he was in the warm, tobacco-scented interior, the partition up and the driver blasting music, before pulling out his phone.

"Report."

"I don't have much," Farid said. "He's working on something big that's going to drop soon, but I don't have details yet."

"Well, you'd better get them," Peggy said. There was a faint clicking, like she was tapping her nails on something. "You were hired because you were the best at your job, Mr. Qadir. If you don't deliver—"

"Save it," Farid interrupted, irritation making his voice tight. "I don't need to be threatened. I'm well aware what's at stake here."

"Fine. Then *get it done.*"

Farid's phone beeped, signaling the call had been

terminated, and he growled and shoved it back in his pocket.

He needed something to take his mind off Dominic's anxious eyes, the way he tried so hard to be good and was so afraid of failure.

He couldn't leave town, not with Dominic in imminent danger of dropping. Even if Dominic wouldn't let him come over, he wanted to stay close. He pulled his phone back out and called Sanyam.

It was Fox who answered, though, voice cool and sardonic above the background noise of the club. "What do *you* want?"

Farid couldn't help his smile. "Hello, Fox. How's the art?"

He could almost see the toss of Fox's head. "It's fine. I have another show next month, biggest one I've done so far; are you coming?"

Farid had known Fox long enough to read between the lines. *Please come, I'm scared out of my mind and need all the support I can get.*

"Of course I'm coming," Farid said. "Send me the details, and I'll be there."

Fox blew out a breath. "I guess you want to talk to San?"

"If he's available."

Rustling and voices in the background, and then Sanyam's deep, warm voice greeted him. "I hear you're coming to Fox's show."

"Wouldn't miss it," Farid said. "Is he going out of his mind with nerves?"

"Naturally," Sanyam said, sounding amused. "I do my best to keep him... distracted."

Fox's voice was suddenly close to the mouthpiece again. "If you come up, you can help distract me too."

Farid laughed, even as electricity jolted through him at the memory of the night they'd shared. "I wish, but I can't leave town right now."

"Pity," Fox commented, voice fading.

"You sure?" Sanyam said. "What's keeping you down there?"

"New job," Farid said. He leaned his head back against the tattered upholstery as the taxi went around a corner. "And… new sub."

"Oh?"

"He's actually my boss *at* the new job," Farid admitted.

"And that's a good idea?"

"Probably not, but…." Farid rubbed his eyes. "He needed it. *Needs* it. He's brilliant and gifted and neurotic and I wasn't thinking the first time I kissed him, it just sort of happened, but God, San, the way he submits. It's… poetry."

"Are you falling for him?"

Farid dropped his hand. "No. No! I'm *not*. You know I don't do that."

"I know you never have," Sanyam said. "I also know you might be surprised by what's inside you."

"What does that even mean?" Farid demanded, suddenly testy.

"It means don't rule anything out," Sanyam said. "And be careful."

"Yeah." Farid signaled the driver to stop, paid him, and stepped out. It was a beautiful night, the sky indigo painted with spangles above him. "I think I'll walk awhile, try to clear my head."

"Keep in touch," Sanyam said.

"And don't forget my show!" Fox yelled from the background.

Farid smiled as he disconnected. Cars rolled by, the city's sounds distant in his ears. He put his hands in his pockets, thinking. He'd never been one for romance. Roses and teddy bears and heart-eyes didn't make sense to him. He'd lost more than one relationship because his partners hadn't felt "cherished," as one girlfriend had put it.

It wasn't that he was callous. He'd *tried*. But inevitably he'd forget an anniversary or other meaningful event, or not bring home flowers "just because," and the frowns and the sighs would start.

Farid kicked a pebble out of his path as his phone buzzed.

Dominic: *U said I shld work but I can't think*

Farid hit the call button.

"You didn't have to—I didn't mean to interrupt anything," Dominic began.

"What do you mean, you can't think?"

Dominic sighed. "I—it's like my brain is too loud, signals are jamming, I can't—I can't make anything make *sense*."

Farid hailed a taxi and it pulled to a stop in front of him. "Will you let me come over?"

"*No*," Dominic said sharply. "No, 'Rid, it's too late, the doorman will know, I like him but he's a gossip, I know he's sold stories about me to the tabloids before. Please, I can't—"

"Okay," Farid said, sliding into the taxi. "I won't come over. Hold on." He gave his home address to the driver and sat back. "Still there?"

"Yeah," Dominic whispered.

"Where are you right now?"

"Living room. I'm… I was pacing. Now I'm— sitting up against the glass, looking down at traffic."

"Have you eaten?"

"I tried," Dominic said miserably. "I couldn't...."

"You need to eat," Farid said, putting a note of command in his voice. "Is the food still out?"

"Yeah."

"Pick up the fork and take a bite."

He heard shuffling noises as Dominic shifted himself over to—presumably—the coffee table, and then clinking as he picked up a utensil.

Farid waited until he heard chewing. "Good, pet," he said. "So good for me. Take another bite now, go on."

Dominic made a muffled noise of protest but kept eating. Finally, he sighed and the fork clinked again.

"I'm done," he said.

"So good," Farid repeated. "Do you have a drink?"

"Pomegranate juice."

"Drain the glass."

The glass rang against the table as Dominic set it back down, and Farid smiled.

"Well done, pet. Now, gather up your dishes and take them to the sink. Come back and tell me when you're finished."

He waited, head against the cool window of the taxi, as Dominic obeyed.

The taxi had pulled up to Farid's house and he'd paid and was halfway up his steps before Dominic came back.

"I did it," he said. He sounded tired, and Farid hesitated in the middle of pulling his keys from his pocket.

"Give me a minute to get inside," he said. "You brush your teeth and get in bed while I'm doing that."

"Okay."

Farid let himself into the house, moving silently to keep from waking the other occupants, and ghosted down the hallway to the kitchen. There, he turned on the stove light and began assembling ingredients.

"I'm in bed," Dominic said.

"Good," Farid said. "How are you feeling?"

"A bit better, I guess—kinda hating myself."

"For calling me?"

"For needing help, for bothering you, take your pick." Dominic sighed, and Farid heard rustling as he rolled over.

"First of all, I told you to text me for any reason. Second, you're not bothering me. I was out for a walk by myself, so you didn't interrupt anything. And third, that's the subdrop talking, making you doubt yourself." Farid tucked the phone between his ear and shoulder and pulled the milk from the refrigerator.

"What are you doing?" Dominic asked. He sounded sleepy. *Good.*

"Making myself cocoa," Farid said.

Dominic huffed a quiet laugh. "You didn't strike me as a cocoa kind of guy."

"Appearances can be deceiving, pet," Farid said, smiling as he turned on the burner. "I'll make you some next time I come over."

"I'm not a fan of chocolate," Dominic admitted.

Farid dropped the phone. It hit the floor and bounced, and Farid swore and scrambled to pick it up.

"—hello? Farid?"

"Sorry, dropped the phone," Farid said. "How can you not be a fan of chocolate? I thought everyone liked chocolate."

"I don't know, I just—" Dominic broke off to yawn. "Sorry."

"Think you can sleep now?"

"Yeah," Dominic said. "See you in the morning?"

"Of course. Goodnight, Dom."

Farid hung up and poured the milk into the pan, thinking about his evening, the lost, scared look in Dominic's eyes and the startling protectiveness it had triggered in himself.

It's just sex, he reminded himself. *It's a way of getting him to trust me so he'll let some secrets slip. Nothing more.*

He was so engrossed in his thoughts that he didn't hear the approaching footsteps until his sister spoke.

"You usually talk to your boss at this hour?"

Farid spun, and milk flew from the whisk in fat, white drops.

Salma lifted a dark eyebrow. Her hair was tousled, like she'd just gotten out of bed, and there were shadows under her black eyes.

"I woke you," Farid said. "I'm sorry, I dropped the phone, I was trying to be quiet—"

"I wasn't sleeping much anyway," Salma said. She pulled her silk robe tighter. "Is there enough there for me?"

"Yeah, of course," Farid said. He added more milk and rested a hip against the counter, watching his sister out of the corner of his eye as she slid onto a bar stool and propped her pointed chin on her hand. "Everything okay?"

Salma shrugged. "Dad. On my case again."

"I'm sorry," Farid said. "I'll talk to him, try and get him to back off."

"It won't help." Salma traced the swirling outline of the marble on the counter in front of her with one slim finger. "He keeps using my deadname. He won't stop, says it's the name he gave me when I was born and it's the name he'll go to his grave with."

Farid winced as he added the cocoa and sugar and stirred them in. "You're an adult, you legally changed your name, he has no right to do that." He poured the cocoa into two mugs and set one in front of Salma before sitting down beside her.

"He's offended that I wanted to change it, I think." Salma took a sip and sighed. "When can we move out and get our own place, just the two of us?"

"As soon as this job is done," Farid said. He covered her free hand with his. "It'll pay for the rest of your transition, plus at least six months of hormone treatments."

Salma rested her head on his shoulder. "I hate that you had to move home for me."

"Hey, you cook for me too, it's a win/win," Farid said into her hair.

"I feel guilty all the time," Salma mumbled.

"Don't," Farid said. "This was *my* choice, understand? I'd do it again in a heartbeat. You didn't force me into anything—I *wanted* to do this."

"So, Dom."

Farid stiffened. "What about him?"

"It's kind of late, is all." Salma studied him.

"I talk to my employer any time he wants to talk to *me*," Farid said. "That's why I get paid so much money."

Salma's lips curved, and she took another sip.

"I have to be up early," Farid said. He bumped shoulders with her, gently so as not to spill her cocoa. "Night, sis."

"'Night," Salma said.

Farid slid off the stool and carried his cocoa down

the basement steps. Safely in the lower level of the house, he flicked on the lights and took off his shoes before padding through to his bedroom.

He dug comfortable clothes out of his dresser and took them into the bathroom to change and get ready for bed.

Teeth brushed, he crawled in between the covers. It was nowhere near as nice as Dominic's bed, but it was home, warm and comforting and peaceful.

Farid closed his eyes and relaxed. Tomorrow, he had to make some progress in getting hold of some of Dominic's code, but for now, it was time to sleep.

DOMINIC ARRIVED to find Farid already at his desk, cool and composed as if they hadn't shared scorching sex the day before.

"Morning," Dominic muttered, and hurried past, clutching his cream cheese bagel and coffee to his chest.

Safe in his office, he flicked on the lights and rolled his shoulders, shaking off the tension. He set the bagel and coffee on his desk as the door opened behind him and Farid slipped into the room.

"What?" Dominic said, knowing he sounded sharp.

Farid leaned back against the door, looking him up and down. "Just trying to get a feel for how you are."

"I'm fine," Dominic said. "Don't you have a job to do?"

Farid arched one elegant brow. "As I recall, you *are* my job." He stayed where he was, but his voice dropped to a throaty purr. "Does that mean you want me to do *you*?"

Dominic swallowed a groan and twisted away. "I'm fine," he repeated over his shoulder. "Did you want something?" He closed his eyes in mortification but it was too late, and Farid was laughing quietly behind him.

"Walked right into that one, didn't you?"

Dominic fought his own smile and managed to compose himself before he turned to face him. "I really am fine."

"Good," Farid said, putting his hands in his pockets. "Subdrops aren't something to mess around with. I'm glad you texted me when you did."

Dominic hunched his shoulders and crossed to sit at his desk. "It was stupid."

"It was *smart*," Farid corrected. "And you were doing what I told you to do, so it was also obedient. Which means—" He put his hands on the desk and leaned forward, for all the world looking from the outside like he was simply having a conversation with his boss. "It means a reward, pet," Farid breathed, and Dominic clutched the armrests, unable to move.

But instead Farid smiled and straightened, dropping him a wink. "Right now, however, I have actual work to do, so I think I'll go do that."

Dominic watched him leave the room as desire surged in his blood, and he gritted his teeth, struggling to throttle it back.

After a minute, he leaned forward and pressed his forehead to the cool maplewood of his desk. He had a feeling he'd gotten himself in way over his head, but he wasn't sure he cared.

His computer dinged at him and Dominic lifted his head to read the message. It was from Farid.

R&D meeting this morning at 10:30. Interview with PC Magazine at 1. Call Cory. I sent her flowers from you, btw, so if she thanks you, that's why.

Dominic winced and tapped out a quick acknowledgment before digging out his phone and dialing Cory's number.

"Dom, honey, I'm so glad you called!" She sounded tired but happy, and Dominic was suddenly overcome with missing her.

"Hey," he managed, his throat tight. "How—" He stopped to swallow. "How's the baby? And you?"

"We're both fine," Cory said. "Melissa's got her right now, she had some colic, and Mel said they'd go for a walk, get some morning air. How are *you*?"

"I'm fine, really. When can I come see you guys?"

"Next week," Cory said. "We're having a week alone to get to know baby Nicki, and then next week we're having visitors. You're the first—after our parents, of course."

"I can't wait," Dominic said. "Did you like the flowers?"

"Yes, tell Farid he has excellent taste." Cory laughed when Dominic said nothing. "Dom, you really think I wouldn't know he sent them? You'd forget your own head, let alone sending flowers. But I loved them, and I know they were from you in spirit."

Dominic smiled. "Promise you'll come by to visit soon too? It's not the same without you here."

"Of course," Cory said. "Email or call me any time, okay?"

He sat for a while after they hung up, thinking hard. He needed to work, to get back to the software rollout they were planning for fall, but Farid's dark, amused eyes were all he could focus on.

From where Dominic was sitting, he could just see the outline of Farid's sleek head through the fogged glass window beside the door. Farid seemed to be on the phone, talking quietly so as not to disturb Dominic.

Dominic scowled and turned back to his computer. The subdrop had scared him more than he wanted to admit. Enough that he didn't want to scene again?

He shook his head. *No.* Even the buzzing of his brain after wasn't enough to deter him from wanting more, wanting to see how far Farid would push him, what he'd meant by taking him apart.

Dominic shifted in his seat. He was the boss, he could take the day off, go home with Farid, and have all the scorching sex he wanted, and no one would say a word to stop him.

His computer monitor glowed softly in the dim light of his office, and Dominic rubbed his face. He had to get back to work. His team was counting on him.

He sighed. Being an adult *sucked*.

12

———————

When ten thirty rolled around, Dominic was deep in code, engrossed in unpicking a knot that had been fighting him for a month. He was so close, about to solve the puzzle and turn the tangle into an elegant flow that would streamline the entire application, and when the overhead lights flicked on, he jerked his head up with a snarl.

Farid didn't seem impressed. "R&D, remember?"

"Busy," Dominic said, turning back to his bank of monitors. "Reschedule."

"Sorry, boss, but I can't. This particular meeting is about Phantom's unveiling in six weeks, and it can't be pushed."

Dominic growled and shoved his hands through his hair. He swore when he hit a tangle, scalp smarting with the pain.

"Do you even own a hairbrush?" Farid asked, amusement threading through his tone.

Dominic glared at him and stood, not bothering to dignify that with a reply.

"Well, hold still so I can fix it for you," Farid said, and stepped in close.

RESEARCH AND DEVELOPMENT was one of his favorite places, Dominic had to admit. Everyone there was as excited about his toys as he was, if not more so, and it was delightful to be surrounded by minds that thought in ones and zeros like his own.

Harvey pounced the minute Dominic walked in the door, nearly vibrating with excitement.

"Mr. Spector, sir, do you have a minute?"

"I need to talk to Selene first," Dominic said, smiling at him. "Soon as I'm done, though, I'm all yours."

Harvey blushed, but his lips tugged up as he stepped back. "I'll be at my desk."

"Over here, Dominic," Selene called, and Dominic smiled at Harvey and headed toward her.

Selene was tall and elegant in a suit that had probably cost more than some cars, but it made the most of her curves. Her auburn hair was swept up into a sleek chignon, and she unbent enough to smile as Dominic joined her.

"How are we doing?" he asked. "Are we going to make both rollouts?"

"So far so good," Selene said. "My team is the best. I have every faith that we'll be ready in time." Selene led him toward the back wall, where the demo products were laid out. Dominic picked up a phone and tapped on the icon of the ghost sitting behind a wheel. The ghost flickered in and out as the app loaded.

"So how's Phantom?" he asked absently as he watched the screen.

"There are still some wrinkles in the code," Selene said. "I've got Harvey working on them, and he's definitely one of my best coders, but I think it needs your touch, to be honest. Harvey doesn't have the experience yet."

The ghost solidified and then dissolved into a puff of smoke that read *Welcome to Phantom!* Dominic touched the menu and scrolled through the options before glancing up at Selene.

"He showed me what he was working on last week. I've got to get Wraith closer to ready for rollout first, but then I can take a look at Phantom's code, see if I can tweak it. Say in a week? Will that work?"

Selene nodded. "I wanted to give you a run-through on Wraith, show you those bugs I mentioned," she said. "And then I think Harvey wants to talk to you." She pulled up the Wraith operating system and began to point out her issues.

Dominic was halfway back to his office when his phone rang. He didn't recognize the number but answered it absently, still working through code in his head.

"Hello, darling," Lance purred, and Dominic jerked to a stop.

"How—"

"Doesn't matter," Lance said. "Don't hang up, I have something you'll want to hear."

"You have *nothing* I want to hear."

"Not even when it comes to exposing a worm in

your apple?"

Dominic stood very, very still.

"I thought that would get you," Lance murmured, triumph soaking his words. "There's a spy in your camp, Dominic, and I thought you might like to know that."

Dominic worked moisture into his mouth. "You —how do—"

"I have sources," Lance said. "Friends with sticky fingers in oh-so-many pies. I learn everything eventually."

"Who is it?" Dominic asked, dreading the answer, but it didn't come. He frowned. "You... you don't know."

"Yet," Lance said. "I don't know *yet*. But I will, believe me. And when I do, you're going to pay me for the information. Or I'll let whoever it is bring your little empire down around your ears."

The phone went silent, and Dominic stared straight ahead, unable to move.

A spy in his company. *Who*? It was a big company, it could be anyone.

Denise came around the corner, and her eyes lit up at the sight of him.

Dominic stiffened and gave her a quick nod before breaking into a near run to get back to his office. He needed to see Farid. He needed that calm strength to anchor himself to before his mind buffeted itself apart in the waves of anxiety currently drowning him.

Farid glanced up from his computer, and alarm flashed over his face. He stood up and rounded the desk as Dominic closed the door.

"What happened?"

"Nothing," Dominic said. He took a step toward

him but stopped himself, mindful of the glass walls.

Farid watched him carefully but didn't challenge the obvious lie. "Can I help?"

Dominic ran a hand through his hair, blowing out a frustrated breath. "Just… make sure no one bothers me until the interview, please?"

"You got it," Farid said. His smile was bewitching, like a half-forgotten song overheard or gossamer silk against Dominic's skin, and Dominic swallowed hard and spun for his office before he did something really stupid, like kissing Farid in the middle of Cory's fishbowl office for the whole building to see.

THE INTERVIEW WENT SMOOTHLY ENOUGH, with Dominic dodging only a few awkward questions about his love life. Otherwise, he managed to keep the reporter focused on the products they were about to roll out, flashing his best smile when she tried to change the subject back.

When he was done, they shook hands, and Dominic headed for his office again. Farid wasn't in there this time, so Dominic went straight through into his own sanctum.

Doors securely shut behind him, he sat down and dropped his head to his forearms on the desk. He was exhausted suddenly, limp and drained with no real reason for it, and he bit back a growl when he heard the door open.

"Go away," he said without looking up.

He heard rustling and then there was a warm hand on his head, stroking gently over his hair. Dominic closed his eyes.

"What is it now?" he finally said.

"You don't have anything else on your schedule," Farid said quietly. "I was thinking I could take you back to your place. If you want, you can work from home, or you can just let me take care of you for the afternoon."

That sounded like heaven. Dominic wrestled with his conscience for a minute and won.

"Yeah," he said, lifting his head. "I'd like that."

One side of Farid's mouth curved up, and he touched Dominic's lower lip with a gentle thumb. "I'll grab my things."

SOMETHING WAS BOTHERING DOMINIC, that much was obvious, but he just as clearly didn't want to talk about it, so Farid didn't push.

He waited until they were in the car and Dominic was buckled and then leaned forward to knock on the partition.

It rolled down, and Amber smiled brightly at him.

"How's it going?"

"Fine," Farid said. "Listen, could you take us to Trader Joe's first?"

"You got it!"

Farid sat back as Amber put the car in gear, and Dominic looked at him quizzically.

"Why are we going to a grocery store? What are you up to?"

Farid dropped him a wink and refused to answer. When Amber pulled up at the store, Farid unbuckled but held up a hand when Dominic made to follow.

"You're staying here. I'll be right back."

Dominic's brow furrowed, and Farid's hand twitched with the impulse to smooth away the wrinkle. Instead, he cleared his throat and stepped out.

It didn't take him long to pick up the items he needed, and he paid and set the bags in the trunk before sliding back in beside Dominic, who arched an eyebrow.

"Remember the meal service?" he said dryly.

"Oh, it's not for dinner," Farid said as Amber pulled away from the curb and merged with traffic, and hid his smile at the frustrated breath Dominic blew out.

———

HE REFUSED to let Dominic help carry the bags up when they arrived at the tower, insisting on hauling them in alone.

Thankfully Dominic didn't stop to talk to Jerry this time. In the elevator, he leaned back against the mirrored wall and looked thoughtfully at Farid.

"Are you going to clue me in or just let me wonder?"

Farid put a finger over his mouth, and Dominic narrowed his eyes but said nothing else.

Safely inside the apartment, Farid set the bags on the kitchen counter before turning. Dominic was by the door, facing him with hands at his sides and uncertainty on his face.

That wouldn't do. Farid closed the gap between them and caught the back of Dominic's neck to pull him down into a quick, hot kiss. He slid his fingers through silky curls and tugged gently, and Dominic rewarded him by stiffening with a gasp.

Farid broke away, breathless and still holding a handful of Dominic's hair. "I thought you didn't like your hair being pulled."

Dominic's throat worked, his eyes wide. "I'm—I don't."

Farid hummed and let go of Dominic's curls, smoothing them into place. He didn't miss the way Dominic leaned into his touch, eyes falling half-shut and body slackening, and the half-formed idea in Farid's head crystallized into focus.

"Here's what we're doing," he said, pulling away. "I'm in control for the rest of the afternoon. But I'm not going to do anything of my own volition."

Dominic's brow furrowed, and this time Farid gave in to the impulse, reached up, and smoothed the wrinkle out with his thumb, smiling.

"What I mean is, if you want something, you'll have to ask me for it. No judgment, no condemnation—whatever you need, just ask, and I'll give it to you."

Dominic tilted his head but said nothing, his eyes thoughtful.

Farid stroked the side of Dominic's face, skating his thumb down over the high cheekbone and along to his lips, which parted obligingly. His mouth was hot and wet, and he sucked on Farid's thumb with rapt attention to his task.

"You think—" Farid cleared his throat. "Think you can do that, pet?"

Dominic nodded fractionally.

"Good," Farid said. "There's one more thing."

He pulled his hand away and waited for Dominic's eyes to meet his before he spoke again.

"You're not to speak for the entire afternoon unless it's to safeword."

Dominic's lips parted, and he drew breath as if to protest.

"Ah—" Farid took a step back, putting distance between them, and Dominic's mouth snapped shut. "Good," Farid praised him. "Very good. Go in the bedroom, strip, and come back when you're done."

Dominic blinked and gathered himself as Farid turned away, taking his focus from him and giving him space to breathe.

He busied himself with putting away what he'd bought while Dominic was gone and didn't look up until he heard the soft scuff of bare feet on the hardwood floor.

Farid folded the last bag and lifted his head to see Dominic standing naked in front of him.

He'd seen this before, but Farid found he couldn't get enough of seeing Dominic stripped bare, the way his skin was a few shades lighter where shirt and pants usually covered him—a creamy tan instead of the darker brown of his hands and face—and his endlessly long limbs with their softly curling hairs, those high arched feet and elegant hands.

Farid took a step closer, trailing a finger along the countertop. Dominic watched him as if bespelled, eyes wide and wary, but there was no fear in his stance or the way he licked his lips as Farid drew near.

"You want me?" Farid asked.

Dominic's eyes widened a little more, and he shifted his weight.

"You can nod or shake your head," Farid said. He traced a line down Dominic's sternum. "You just can't speak, pet."

Dominic shivered and nodded.

Farid moved nearer, and Dominic leaned toward him, hunger in the tense cording of his shoulders.

"What do you want?" Farid asked.

Dominic's brow furrowed yet again, and Farid couldn't help the soundless laugh.

"Figure out how to tell me," he said, and waited, delighting in the way Dominic chewed his lip, concentration writ large on his expressive face. Whatever had been bothering him, it was put away, at least for now.

Finally, Dominic reached out and tugged on Farid's vest with finger and thumb.

"You want it off, take it off me," Farid said.

Dominic smiled then, making Farid catch his breath, and went to work. He pushed Farid's coat gently off his shoulders and folded it neatly before setting it on the counter and turning back to unbutton the vest.

Farid let him work, compliant with Dominic's hesitant directions, lifting his arms when needed to get his undershirt off and then dropping them to his sides again as Dominic turned his attention to Farid's pants.

His fingers were nimble and deft, and he had the belt unbuckled and the pants unzipped and pushed down in no time.

Farid stood unmoving, fabric puddled around his ankles, and waited until Dominic took his leg and guided each foot out of the trousers.

Dominic grinned in triumph when Farid was finally naked, and amusement flickered in Farid's chest, warm and affectionate.

"What now?" he asked.

Dominic captured one of Farid's hands with his own and led him toward the bedroom. Once there, he pointed at the bed, and Farid laughed and climbed on, Dominic right behind him.

Farid waited for Dominic to lie down before following his example, on their sides facing each other. They were close—Farid could feel Dominic's breath on his skin—but not touching.

They lay quietly, just looking. Farid didn't know what Dominic was seeing and didn't waste time wondering—he was too busy memorizing the tiny details of Dominic's face, the cowlick above his right temple, the smile lines around his eyes, the tiny scar above his lip.

"So beautiful," he murmured.

Dominic's eyes closed and his lips curved. He took Farid's hand and lifted it to his mouth, lips lingering warm and gentle on Farid's knuckles, and then put it on his ribcage.

Farid flexed his fingers, feeling the bumps of bone under Dominic's satin skin, and Dominic shivered and took Farid's wrist. He moved his hand back and forth, the unspoken request clear—*touch me*—until Farid nodded.

Only then did he let go, and Farid went to his knees.

"On your stomach," he ordered, and Dominic didn't even hesitate. He rolled facedown on the satin comforter, arms crossed under his cheek.

Farid straddled him, settling his weight gently across Dominic's hips, and Dominic stifled a gasp. Farid smoothed a hand across Dominic's back, running his fingers down the knobs of his spine. Muscles shifted and slid under silky skin as Dominic shifted position to get comfortable.

"You take my breath away," Farid said, hands still

busy exploring. "First time I saw you, I thought, 'God, what a dick, why's he so *handsome.*'"

Dominic shook with silent laughter, and Farid bent forward and pressed a kiss to his shoulder blade.

"You know what I want to do to you?" he asked, straightening.

Dominic slanted a curious glance over his shoulder, and Farid shook his head, unable to fight the smile creeping across his face.

"It's a *lot* more fun to show you." Farid dug his thumbs into a knot of muscle to the left of Dominic's spine.

Dominic made a curious noise—part groan, part whimper—and clapped a hand over his mouth, stricken horror in his eyes when they met Farid's.

Farid laughed soundlessly and bent forward to press their lips together. Dominic tasted like pomegranate juice but nothing else, and Farid frowned.

"Have you eaten today?"

Dominic hesitated and then shook his head. Apprehension flickered across his face and then disappointment as Farid swung a leg over and dismounted. He opened and closed his mouth, and Farid pointed at him.

"Kitchen, now." He strode that way without watching to see if Dominic was following. In the kitchen, he stooped and picked up his boxers, skimming them over his hips before turning to the groceries he'd bought.

Dominic trailed out of the bedroom, shoulders slumped and eyes unhappy.

"I brought you lunch at work," Farid said, pulling apples and the peanut butter from the bag. "I distinctly remember putting it on your desk. Put some clothes on and explain to me why you didn't eat it."

Dominic picked up his underwear and tugged them on. He chewed his lip, and Farid nodded.

"You may answer my question."

"I was busy," Dominic said, twining his fingers together. "I have to finish that code, and then Selene—and there were so many interviews, and they mess with my head, it's hard to *think* when I have to—I have to be… on."

Farid tilted his head. "On?"

"Like… when I'm alone, or with Cory, or—" Dominic stopped and swallowed. "I don't have to perform. I don't have to pretend I'm enjoying myself. I don't have to laugh at jokes that aren't funny. I don't have to be *on*. It's… it's unbearable. And when I'm already busy, food's the last thing I'm thinking about, I'm sorry I didn't eat but I *couldn't*—"

Farid rounded the counter and took hold of Dominic's shoulders. "I forget, sometimes, what an introvert you are," he said gently. "It's all right, pet. But you're eating now."

Dominic nodded, and Farid went up on tiptoe and kissed him, a quick, light brush of lips. "No more talking," he said. "Sit down, and let me pamper you."

He went through the drawers until he found a sharp knife. "I didn't really get nutritious food," he said ruefully. "Apples and peanut butter for now, and let's order in."

"What *did* you—" Dominic snapped his mouth shut and covered it with both hands as Farid spun toward him. His eyes were wide, and Farid couldn't help the laugh.

"Don't let it happen again," he warned. "I'm in the

mood for Korean barbeque." He made the call and placed the order without asking Dominic what he wanted, then set the phone on the counter. He sliced an apple, cored it, and filled it with a spoon of peanut butter, then came around it to stand between Dominic's knees. Dominic looked up at him silently, and Farid traced the line of his jaw with one finger. "What would you like to do while we wait for the food?"

Dominic's eyes sparkled with mischief, and he glanced at the bedroom, but Farid shook his head, smiling.

"No sex until after you've eaten." He put the apple to Dominic's mouth, and Dominic pouted but took a bite. Then he took Farid's hand, placing it on his ribcage.

"All right, pet," Farid said, stroking Dominic's side. "I'll give you a massage, as soon as you finish the apple. On the couch this time, so we don't get carried away."

Dominic wolfed the apple in three bites, bounced to his feet, and Farid followed him to the living room. Dominic stretched out facedown on the couch and Farid settled into place on top of him. Dominic sighed, pillowing his head on his arms.

Farid set to work, targeting each knotted muscle in Dominic's back and teasing out the tangles, stroking them smooth before moving on to the next. Dominic's eyes drooped lower with every rub of Farid's thumbs, his breathing slowing and deepening.

The faith Dominic put in him was terrifying. Farid worked on a particularly stubborn knot, lips tight, only half aware of his surroundings. Dominic had invited a viper into his nest; offered his body and trust and surrender to someone who was going to betray him, and asked for nothing in return.

Dominic jerked and made a noise that was definitely pain, twisting away from Farid's hands.

"Sorry," Farid said, remorse prickling his skin, and bent to kiss the spot he'd jabbed. "Sorry," he breathed against Dominic's spine. "I'm so sorry, pet, my beautiful boy—"

Dominic turned and reached up, catching the back of Farid's neck and pulling him into a kiss. Farid sighed, sliding sideways so that the angle was better and he could get deeper.

The doorbell rang and jolted them apart. Farid rubbed a hand over his mouth, and Dominic pressed his face into the pillow under his head, unsuccessfully trying to hide a smile.

The barbeque was still piping hot and delicious, and they ate cross-legged on the sofa in companionable silence.

Farid gathered the dishes and took them to the sink after while Dominic put away the leftovers. As he was rinsing a plate, Dominic came up behind him and wrapped his arms around Farid's waist, chin over his shoulder and cheeks pressed together.

They stood that way for several minutes as Farid finished the dishes but when he tried to turn, Dominic's arms tightened, keeping him in place. Farid got the hint and stopped moving, waiting to see what Dominic would do next.

One hand roved across Farid's chest, over the T-shirt he'd pulled on to pay the delivery driver, and the other slid lower, brushing his groin.

Farid caught his breath, leaning back into Dominic's bulk and letting him explore. Clever fingers slipped beneath the waistband of his boxers and coaxed him awake with quick, soft touches until Farid was fully hard, tenting the underwear and a damp patch forming.

He tried to turn again, but Dominic's arm was like an iron bar, holding him still. Farid huffed a breath and stopped trying as Dominic's hand closed around his shaft and stroked.

"Ah—*fuck*—"

Dominic's breath was hot on the back of his neck, and Farid reached up and tangled a hand in his silky hair as bliss rippled through his nerves.

Dominic's other hand slid down, around Farid's waist and back, and Farid stiffened as a questing finger pressed against his hole.

He rolled his head sideways to look at Dominic's face. There was a mixture of hope and lust painted across his mobile features.

"You wanna fuck me?" Farid whispered.

Dominic's nod was fervent, and Farid couldn't help his laugh, even though it came out breathy. Dominic bent and dropped a kiss on Farid's neck, then let go and stepped back.

Farid spread his hands. "What are you waiting for?"

Dominic's smile was radiant as he grabbed Farid's wrist and towed him toward the bedroom.

★

"LIE BACK AND DON'T MOVE," Farid said.

Dominic obeyed unwillingly, fingers twitching with the need to touch Farid's satin skin even as he arranged himself on the bed, flat on his back. His erection leaked slow, heavy drops on his stomach but he didn't touch it—he'd been told not to move. So he lay still, gripping the blanket under him in both hands, and watched as Farid slicked his fingers with lube and knelt forward, one hand on the bed by Dominic's shoulder and the other between his own legs.

Dominic's mouth was dry, and he couldn't figure out where to look. Farid's eyes were heavy-lidded, mouth red and wet, parted slightly. His neck was taut with strain, tendons in stark relief as he dropped his head back and drew a ragged breath. His cock hung hard and wanting, hand moving just out of sight, and Dominic shifted position.

Farid opened his eyes just enough to give him a warning look, and Dominic subsided.

Finally, *finally*, Farid withdrew his hand, leaning over to wipe it off with a tissue and retrieving a condom from the bedside table. Foil crinkled and then he bent over and dropped a quick kiss on Dominic's lips.

"All right?" he murmured.

Suddenly shy, all Dominic could do was nod.

Farid's eyes softened, and he kissed him again, sweet like honey in Dominic's mouth.

"Beautiful pet," he whispered when he lifted his head. He rolled the condom on in one smooth motion, making Dominic twitch and tighten his grip on the blanket.

Then Farid swung a leg over Dominic's hips, situating himself as Dominic forgot how to breathe. It was dark in the bedroom, the distant city noise a barely noticeable hum underlying the frantic beating of Dominic's heart in his ears. Farid bent, warm breath tickling Dominic's skin, and pressed a kiss to his breastbone.

"You're gonna like this," he breathed, and sat up, reaching behind him for Dominic's cock.

Dominic caught Farid's thighs, fingers digging into corded muscle as Farid sank down slowly, letting the head breach him.

Tight. Tight and hot and—Dominic couldn't help the noise in the back of his throat, wordlessly begging for more, but Farid would not be rushed. He circled his hips and slid another centimeter down, his body stretching to let Dominic's length inside. Farid's lower lip was caught between his teeth, eyes far off in concentration, and all Dominic could do was let the tight, slick heat take him in.

Farid slipped down another inch, then another, until Dominic was fully sheathed, Farid's ass resting in Dominic's pelvis.

"All right?" he repeated.

Dominic couldn't remember how to speak even if he'd been given permission, his mouth so dry words were impossible. All he could feel was the heat of Farid's body around him, silken walls twitching and fluttering against his dick, and he had no room in his head for anything else.

Farid lifted up and dropped back down, making Dominic gasp.

"Feels so good," Farid whispered, repeating the motion. "Feels—God, Dominic, I've wanted you inside me for so long—"

He leaned forward and pressed their mouths together briefly, hips still moving.

Dominic's fingers protested the death grip on Farid's thighs, and he loosened his hold slightly. Farid smiled against his mouth and sat up, never losing his rhythm.

He was beautiful, chasing his pleasure, head thrown back and long neck exposed in a clean, graceful line, and despite the ecstasy flooding Dominic's nerves, he suddenly wanted more. He wanted to drive Farid out of his mind, take and take until Farid fell apart in his arms.

He planted his feet on the bed and bucked his hips. Caught off-guard, Farid toppled forward, stopping his fall with a hand on Dominic's chest. His eyes widened, but Dominic drove up again before he could speak, and Farid's mouth fell open on a choked gasp.

There.

Dominic rolled them in one quick motion, ending with Farid flat on his back and Dominic between his legs. He'd slipped out in the move, and he didn't give Farid time to catch his breath, pushing back in in one swift motion.

Farid's spine arched, and he moaned. Dominic drove deep, again and again, bracing himself with an arm on either side of Farid's head. He was divided, pursuing the orgasm that hovered just out of sight but also intent on keeping Farid's eyes unfocused, his mouth open as he breathed in short, sharp gasps.

This was what he'd wanted since Farid had kissed him in the elevator. To take apart the neat, clever man who was never discomposed, pull down the walls he hid behind and see who he truly was beneath.

"Dom—" Farid's eyes were frantic, hands grasping at any part of Dominic he could reach. "I'm close, I'm—"

Dominic hooked an arm behind one of Farid's

knees and folded him in half so he could slam deeper, thrusting ever harder.

Farid thrashed, sobbing, held immobile in Dominic's grip, and then there was tight, shivery heat gripping Dominic's cock as he came, spasms rippling through him, and Dominic followed, the orgasm wracking his body until he collapsed on top of Farid's limp form, breathing harsh against his collarbone.

Dominic kissed the knob of bone beneath his lips, and Farid sighed and slipped a hand into his hair.

"What… the *fuck* was that?" he whispered.

Dominic said nothing, waiting for Farid to remember.

"Oh, right." Farid took a deep, steadying breath. "You may speak."

Instead, Dominic slid out, making Farid moan again. He trailed a hand through the mess on Farid's stomach, smiling. "You didn't even touch yourself."

"Didn't need to," Farid said. His hair was in his eyes, his lips bitten red, and he'd never been more beautiful. "Where did you learn to do that?"

Dominic shrugged. "Felt right." He hesitated, uncertainty taking over. "Was it—okay?"

"I think I demonstrated that it was *more* than okay, pet," Farid said, pushing his hair off his forehead.

"No, I mean… taking over like that. I know you like to be in control."

Farid sat up and pulled Dominic down into a quick kiss. "Sometimes it's nice to be fucked into oblivion. If I don't want it, I'll tell you. But was it as good for you?"

Dominic snorted rudely. "Shower?"

Farid followed, smiling. "Read my mind."

13

———

Farid opened his eyes, staring up at his ceiling. Above him he could hear his mother's nurse moving around, getting her ready for the day. Salma called a question to Nasim, whose answer was unintelligible but sounded groggy—he wasn't a morning person.

He had to take care of them. He was all they had.

Something small. Enough to satisfy Peggy's employers but not big enough to hurt Dominic's bottom line. Phantom. He had to get into the lab and steal Phantom. Wraith was too complex, too big a project, and from what Dominic had said about it, losing it could cripple him. Phantom was smaller, the bonus they were rolling out before Wraith's release, and all he needed to do was get his hands on the device Dominic had shown him.

Farid rolled over and buried his face in the pillow as self-hatred washed through him. *He's going to hate you too*, a tiny voice whispered.

He sat up. *Not yet.* He wasn't ready for what they had to be over. He needed more time. Phantom's release was in six weeks. If he played his cards right, he could have a month with Dominic before he tore it all down.

He pulled out his phone and called Peggy. "I need five weeks," he said without waiting.

"For *what?*"

"I'm going to get you something, something good. Something that will make all this worthwhile. But I need time. It's not ready to be released, it's hit several major snags, and if you want it as good as Dominic's gigantic brain can make it, you'll let him fix those snags before I take it. That means you give me five weeks, and I'll hand you a coder's wet dream."

Peggy blew out a frustrated breath. "They won't like this."

"I don't care," Farid said. "You know it's the best plan."

Peggy made a noise as if dubious, and something tapped—a fingernail, maybe. "You have a month," she said abruptly.

Farid throttled the triumph from his voice. "I'll be in touch."

He hung up, conflicting emotions tangling between his ribs. He had his month. He had time, time to learn Dominic from the inside out, see what made him tick, take him apart and put him back together. And then at the end of it—

He rolled off the bed and strode for the shower. He'd think about that later.

FARID SENT Dominic to visit Cory the minute she texted to say he was welcome. Dominic showed up with his arms full of gifts, feeling for the steps with his foot, and ringing the doorbell with an elbow.

The door swung wide, and Melissa smiled at him over the towering mound of presents. "Hello, Dom." She leaned in to kiss him on the cheek and then stepped aside so he could come in. "Cory's in the living room. Come on through." She led him into the house, and Dominic followed, praying he wouldn't trip on a rug.

"Did you buy out Babies R Us?" Cory demanded as he sidled into the room.

"I have no idea," Dominic said honestly. Melissa pointed at the couch, and Dominic put the presents down with relief. "I helped pick them out but honestly, there's more here than I remember us looking at, so I think Farid might have… contributed."

"Come over here and kiss me," Cory said. She was back in the same recliner, holding a small bundle wrapped in a blue blanket. She was glowing, her dark red hair sleek and her skin flushed with health, and Dominic bent and kissed her cheek and then pressed their foreheads together, letting her familiar presence comfort and ground him.

"I'm so glad you're okay," he whispered.

"There was never any doubt," Cory said, and patted his face. "You're just a panicky basketcase who automatically thinks the worst in any situation."

Dominic rolled his eyes and then focused on the bundle in Cory's arms. "How is she?"

"She's great," Cory said. Her smile was fond, and it made Dominic's heart ache a little.

Dominic touched the blanket. "Nice color choice. Smashing gender stereotypes at Wee Play already?"

"How the hell do you know what Wee Play is?" Cory demanded, and then shook her head. "Farid."

"Actually, I've been doing research into the odd phenomenon known as child-rearing in the modern era myself, thank you very much," Dominic retorted, and pulled the corner of the blanket aside.

Nicki blinked up at him, huge dark blue eyes heavily fringed with dark lashes above round, creamy brown cheeks. Her mouth was a perfect, tiny rosebud and she yawned and stretched as Dominic watched, fascinated.

"Do you want to hold her?"

"No," Dominic said immediately. "No, God! I'd— I'd drop her or break her or *something*."

"Sit down," Melissa said, coming back in the room. She sounded amused. "I'll hand her to you. Don't worry, you won't hurt her."

Dominic settled on the couch, heart in his throat, and watched as Melissa gently scooped Nicki from Cory's arms and turned to deposit her in Dominic's.

"Keep her head supported, and sit her up a bit. If you hold her on her back, she thinks she's going to eat." Melissa helped Dominic get his arms in the right position and laid the baby in them, then stepped back.

"Um." Dominic was terrified to breathe. He looked down without moving his head as Nicki squirmed in his arms, one chubby arm coming free of the blanket. "Her hair's so curly," he whispered. It clung to Nicki's head in wild whorls and stood up all over, making her look like she'd been dragged through a bush backward. He looked up at Cory. "And she's so quiet."

Cory snorted. "She could put a metal welder to shame with her volume, don't let her angelic face fool you. Melly, darling, hand me those presents, would you? I want to see what Dom and Farid got us." She ripped into each one, and both women oohed and aahed over what was revealed.

The first thing out was a plush lavender blanket. Cory quirked an eyebrow at Dominic, and then her mouth fell open as she stroked a hand across it. "Oh my God, that's the softest thing I've ever felt."

"The big package there is a matching one for you two," Dominic offered, most of his attention still on the warm bundle in his arms.

Melissa opened that and brought out a queen-sized dark purple blanket, flashing a smile at Dominic. "It's lovely, Dom, thank you."

Cory opened the next gift to discover a week's worth of baby outfits in soft spun cotton, printed with whimsical butterflies and unicorns frolicking with dragons.

Nicki opened her mouth, smacked her lips a few times, and flapped her arm. She frowned, tiny forehead puckering, and opened her mouth again.

Melissa stooped and whisked her out of Dominic's arms before she could make a noise. "She's hungry. I'll feed her and let you two catch up."

Cory went through the rest of the presents with delight written all over her expressive face and finally set them down beside her chair and got up to hug him.

"Thank you," she said as Dominic rose to meet her. She barely came to his chest. She wrapped her arms around his waist and pushed her face into his shirt. "I miss the fuck out of you."

Dominic hugged her back. "I miss you too. Is there anything you need?"

Cory shook her head and motioned for him to sit

down on the couch again before sitting beside him and drawing her ankles up to sit cross-legged facing him. "Tell me everything."

"Well, Debbie's still trying to get me into karaoke," Dominic began.

Cory rolled her eyes. "About Farid. There's something… different about you. You were a strung-up hot *mess* when I saw you last and now you look… almost relaxed. What happened?"

Damn her perceptive eyes. Dominic shifted his weight, debating what he should say.

"I *knew* it!" Cory exclaimed. "You kissed him. He kissed you? One of you kissed the other, it's written all over your face. Spill!"

Dominic sagged, admitting defeat. "I was… upset, when you were in labor. Having a panic attack. 'Rid couldn't get through to me, I was melting down in a fucking elevator, so, uh… he kissed me to snap me out of it."

Cory settled back, looking smug. "And? How was it?"

"Well, I was panicking, so it took a while for me to actually appreciate it," Dominic shot back. He rubbed his face.

"But once you did?"

Dominic sighed, half smiling at the memory. "It was good. It was… really good." He gave her a narrow look. "You're not going to lecture me about ethics?"

"Well, ideally I thought you might want to wait until after he left the company to make a move, but I get it, the heart wants what the heart wants." Cory shuddered. "I hate that saying. Besides, you're not fucking in the office, right?"

"Cory, *God!*" Dominic's face flamed with embarrassment, and he pulled at his shirt collar as Cory laughed. "No, only at my place."

The laughter slid off Cory's face, and she stared at him as if turned to stone. Dominic took a moment to enjoy her discomposure.

"You're not." Her voice was flat, unbelieving. "You *are*. Oh my God. Dom. Dom, you've had *sex* with him?"

Dominic spread his hands in a *guilty* gesture, and Cory slapped both hands over her mouth, eyes huge.

"Is he good to you? Did he take care of you the first time? If he hurts you I swear to God I'll rip his spine out through his *nose*—"

"Relax," Dominic said, laughing. "He didn't know, actually, the first time. I told him after. He wasn't… thrilled, but it was my decision. And yes. He is very good to me. He's… he's gentle. But he's also so strong, like rebar. He lets me turn my brain off."

"You. Turn your brain off. *Your* brain."

"He's managed to distract me from code for entire afternoons," Dominic said, his smile widening.

"How?" Cory waved a hand, forestalling Dominic's response. "I don't need physical details of what you do to each other. But… I mean, no offense, honey, you know how much I love you. But—"

"I'm neurotic, I know." Dominic traced a pattern on the couch with one finger.

"I've never seen you this calm, honestly," Cory said. She touched the back of his hand. "You're always tense, wound up like there's a goddamn coil in your chest just ready to blow. I don't know what to think."

"He sets me puzzles," Dominic said, looking back up at her. "He makes me use my head, but for other things than worrying about stuff I can't fix. He'll give me a task, and I have to figure out how to do what he wants. I'm—I don't know. It soothes me."

"So what's the problem?"

"Nothing!" Dominic said, startled. "Nothing's the problem, everything's fine!"

Cory arched an eyebrow and waited.

Dominic slumped against the sofa and blew out a breath, staring up at the ceiling. "He's going to get tired of it," he said finally, hating how small his voice was.

"It being you? Why would he?"

"Because...." Dominic groped for words. "Because I'm not sophisticated or smart or put-together like him. Because I trip over stuff and forget to eat and hate brushing my hair. Because he's clever and neat and handsome and patient, everything I'm not. Because I'm a fucking train wreck, Cory, and he's *going to get tired of it.*"

"Bullshit." Cory's voice was flat, but anger thrummed in it. Dominic turned his head to look at her. "First of all, how can you say you're not smart?"

"I know I can *code*," Dominic said. "I meant.... Farid is people-smart. He knows what to say and when to say it. He's... he's charming. People like him. They listen to him. I just get tongue-tied and run into doors a lot."

"There are different kinds of smart, and you know it." Cory took his hand. "So what if you're not... what'd you call it, neat and clever? You're also incredibly generous, thoughtful, and kind. Plus you're beautiful, with your stupid curly hair and those big gray eyes, and I'll bet Farid loves your height, doesn't he?"

Dominic shrugged, ducking his head.

"I don't know Farid very well, but I'll bet he

doesn't think about himself the way you do. All this shit about being graceful and coordinated and charming. He doesn't think of it that way, because it's a stupid comparison to draw."

"Thanks," Dominic muttered.

"I mean it," Cory insisted. "If you want to compare something, compare your… your hearts, or your senses of humor—does he have one?"

"Yeah," Dominic said, fighting the smile. "It's sneaky, but it's there."

"Compare the way you treat people," Cory continued. "Is he kind to people?"

"Very." Dominic sighed. "I don't think I've ever seen him lose his temper. I lose mine all the time."

Cory tapped his temple, making him glare. "You're doing it again. You're putting him up on this pedestal, and you're making him perfect, and you've decided that because he's—apparently—a god, and you but a mere mortal, then clearly things will never work out. And like I said, that is bullshit." Cory leaned in. "Farid is human, Dom. He's gonna fuck up. He's gonna do something wrong, and you're going to realize that he's not this mystical being; he's every bit as fallible as you. He sleeps, he breathes, he eats, he shits, just like you. So stop psyching yourself up to lose him over some stupid misconception that you're not *good* enough, and just… just *be* in the moment with him. He's with you for a reason, honey."

Dominic squirmed and rolled his head to look at her. "I miss you."

"And who can blame you?" Cory grinned. "But look at you, managing without me, just like I knew you would."

Dominic snorted a laugh and pushed himself sideways until he toppled into her lap. Cory stroked his hair off his face, smiling fondly down at him.

"Tell me about Phantom and Wraith. How are the rollouts coming?"

"Phantom is good. Wraith is fighting me."

"Are you going to make the rollout?"

"Phantom's, definitely. Not really sure about Wraith yet. I can't figure out where I'm going wrong, but I'll think I'm finally getting somewhere, and then the whole thing comes down around me." Dominic sat up, scowling. "The worst part is, I feel like I could get it, if I just had a chance to stay in the groove, but it seems like every time I turn around, someone else needs a meeting about something."

Cory frowned. "Farid should be keeping them off your back."

"He does, as much as he can. But you know how it goes—some meetings just can't be pushed or avoided. So it slows me down."

"I should be there," Cory muttered. "I can take those meetings for you. I hate that you have to do them."

Impulsively Dominic kissed her on the cheek. "You're wasted as my assistant. You should be running the damn place, not me."

Cory scoffed, but she looked pleased. "You're assuming I want to be that much in the spotlight."

"You *love* the spotlight," Dominic teased.

"Or maybe the spotlight loves me," Cory retorted, gently shoving his shoulder.

DOMINIC STAYED ANOTHER HOUR, until he got a text from Farid.

Board meeting at 2.

Dominic groaned. "Fuck me sideways, I have to talk to the board. *Alone.*" He turned and caught Cory's hands. "Come with me."

"Sure," Cory said tartly. "I'll just cram my swollen and still-healing body into my fanciest pinstripe suit and take care of the whole thing, shall I?"

Dominic hung his head, immediately regretting the words. "I'm such an asshole," he mumbled.

Cory patted his hand. "Not intentionally," she said. "You just don't think before you speak."

"Not helping," Dominic said, and sighed.

Cory's eyes were amused but sympathetic. "At some point you're going to have to do this yourself, honey. You can't hide behind me and Farid forever. Here's what you're going to do."

AMBER DROVE Dominic back to the building as he sorted through possible questions the board might have.

They'll want you off-balance, Cory had warned. *You're the boss. Don't let them see how nervous they make you. Keep your cool, give them that smile, and don't fidget, for Christ's sake.*

They were almost there when Dominic's phone rang. He answered, expecting Farid, and stiffened at the sound of Lance's cool voice.

"Have you made any progress?" Lance asked.

"Have *you?*" Dominic shot back. "You're the one

who came to me, why should I do your dirty work for you?"

"Of course, silly me for thinking you wouldn't want to have a traitor in your midst, selling secrets to your competitors. You have a lovely time with that, I'll talk to you—"

"*Wait*," Dominic said. Lance's laugh was dark and victorious and made Dominic grit his teeth. "I haven't… I don't know anything yet. Do you?"

"Maybe," Lance said. Dominic could almost see him, lean and elegant, resting one broad shoulder against the wall as he examined his perfect fingernails. Everything about him had always said, *aren't you the lucky one that I'm taking an interest in you?* Once, Dominic had found it flattering. "But I want something too."

Dominic's stomach sank. "What."

"Come now," Lance chided. "Honestly, you'd think I was out to take your company. All I want is an hour of your time, Dominic, is that really too much to ask?"

"Probably," Dominic snapped. "It depends on what you want it for."

"An interview," Lance said smoothly.

"Forget it."

"Really?" Lance said, sounding mock-surprised. "I'm going to all this work to find out who's selling your secrets and you can't even give me one tiny interview?"

Dominic pressed his forehead to the glass as Amber turned into the parking lot. "I won't answer personal questions," he said, knowing he'd lost.

"I'll be seeing you, sweets," Lance said, and hung up.

Dominic dropped his phone in his pocket and

clenched his fists, frustrated fury welling up his throat until he could barely breathe around it. He pushed the door open and slid out with a nod to Amber, and strode for the entrance.

Farid was in his office when Dominic stalked in. He glanced up, and his eyes widened, but Dominic was past before Farid could open his mouth.

Safely in his own office, Dominic stood very still, trying to breathe. He needed to install a punching bag, he thought vaguely. Something he could batter when the stress was tearing him apart.

The door opened and closed behind him, and Dominic turned to see Farid leaning against the frame, concern on his face.

"What happened?" he asked softly.

Dominic tensed. "Nothing." He couldn't tell Farid. He *couldn't*. He couldn't admit the potential breach, not to Farid, who did everything so perfectly the first time. It wasn't fair. Farid was so good at *life*, and Dominic was a walking disaster. He swallowed the rising resentment and straightened. "I want coffee."

Farid's eyebrows went up, but he nodded and left silently.

Dominic sat at his desk, opening and closing his hands, watching the tendons flex and slide under his skin. Lance's mocking laugh echoed in his head and he flattened his palms on the desk and squeezed his eyes shut as Farid came back in with a cup of coffee.

He set it on the desk and straightened. "Anything else?"

"Yeah," Dominic said abruptly. "I don't want *that* coffee. I want some from Fonté."

Farid said nothing, clasping his hands behind his

back, but his eyes were sharp and searching. Dominic tipped his chin up.

"Portofino, I think."

Farid opened his mouth, closed it, and nodded. Turning, he left the room, and Dominic waited until he heard the elevator ding before he punched his desk. The pain shocked him, a bright solar burst through his knuckles, and he caught his breath and did it again, then a third time. His skin split, and a trickle of blood slid down his fingers.

Dominic closed his eyes and leaned back in his chair. He was a nightmare, a neurotic tangled mess, and sooner or later Farid would stop trying to fix him.

He was staring at his screen, appearing to be engrossed in code when Farid came back, holding a cup of coffee with Fonté's distinctive label.

"I changed my mind," Dominic said.

Farid's eyes tightened.

He was on dangerous ground, Dominic knew, but he couldn't seem to *stop*. He lifted his chin again.

"I want the F2," he said. "It'll help me think."

Farid put the cup down, moving very carefully, and pivoted on his heel.

Fonté was twenty minutes away, and they usually had lines out the door, so Dominic had about an hour before Farid was back again, setting the cup down with slightly more force.

"Anything *else*, or can I get my own work done now?" he inquired, tone biting.

Dominic shrugged carelessly. *Whatever*, it said, *you don't matter to me and I don't care what you do.*

Farid's mouth flattened into a thin line, but he closed the door behind him quietly.

Dominic stared at the code a while longer. He

couldn't make sense of it, the symbols and letters blurring before his eyes. *You'll never be good at anything. Farid's already tired of you and it's your own fault.* And yet… and yet. If he pushed and Farid *didn't* go, did that mean Dominic was worth something? *He won't stay*, the voice whispered. *Make him go now so it hurts less.*

He wrote a quick note to Lily, put it in an envelope, and buzzed Farid, who came to the door.

"Take this down to Security, give it to Lily Annapurna."

Farid accepted the envelope without speaking, and Dominic swallowed shame. *He's not your errand boy.*

A few minutes later, his computer dinged. It was from Farid. *Board meeting in 15. Clean clothes in your closet.*

Dominic pushed away from his desk, seething with resentment. *Can't even be trusted to dress myself.* He stalked to the closet and changed, ignoring the pain in his split knuckles. He was almost ready when Farid knocked on the door, pushing his shirttails in and zipping the pants.

"Your hair," Farid said, but Dominic twisted away before Farid could touch him, keeping his injured hand out of sight.

"*Leave it*," he said, and found his neglected hairbrush in the bathroom. He hissed at the pain from the tangles, but kept brushing, avoiding his reflection in the mirror, until the brush slid through easily without catching on any snarls. Finally, he tossed the hairbrush back on the sink, shoved his hand in his pocket, and stomped out of the bathroom.

Farid was where Dominic had left him, his face unreadable.

Dominic didn't make eye contact. "Let's go."

They rode the elevator silently, Dominic staring at the doors and Farid a quiet, solid presence beside him. Dominic wanted to hurl himself against that steady strength, batter himself apart on it, let Farid catch and hold him and put him back together, but Farid wasn't looking at him, his mouth still a flat line.

You fucked up. Lance's laugh echoed through Dominic's head, light and mocking. *You always do, don't you? You find some way to torpedo everything that means anything to you. It's a gift, baby.*

Dominic didn't realize he'd closed his eyes until Farid touched his arm.

"We're here."

Dominic gulped and fought the urge to turn and drop to his knees, let Farid gather him in close, and hold him. But Farid would probably push him away, after the way Dominic had been treating him all afternoon.

"Cory texted me. Remember what she told you," Farid said quietly. His hand was still on Dominic's forearm, and Dominic pulled back before he lost his resolve. Farid's eyes tightened again, but he let his hand drop and followed Dominic out of the elevator.

THE BOARD of directors was waiting in Dominic's least favorite room, huge and open, with floor-to-ceiling windows that looked out over the city. It was too exposed, making Dominic feel like a butterfly pinned on a corkboard. The members of the board were grouped loosely around the table, and Dominic nodded vaguely in their direction as he took a seat at the head of the room, Farid behind his chair.

Don't let them see how nervous they make you.

Dominic summoned the calm that buoyed him up when Farid was focused on him, taking the control from him and letting Dominic just *be*, and crossed his legs.

"We'll keep this short," Laura Waites said. "We know how busy you are." She was short, stocky, iron-gray hair buzzed close to her scalp, and Dominic almost liked her no-nonsense attitude. "We need to know how close you are to completing Wraith and Phantom before their rollout dates."

Don't tell them Phantom's ready, Cory had said. *If you give them that, they'll push for more. They'll want a launch party immediately, with you headlining. They'll insist on letting the shareholders know. Keep them focused on Wraith.*

"Phantom's coming along," Dominic said aloud. "Wraith is slightly more problematic."

Laura frowned. "Problematic how? Like you won't make the release?"

Dominic smiled tightly, keeping himself from fidgeting with an effort. "Let's hope it doesn't come to that."

"What's wrong with it?" Ernest Rogelio wanted to know.

"Can you code?" Dominic said. "Because if not, whatever I tell you is going to be gibberish anyway."

Ernest glowered but sat back.

"We simply want to know that our investments are going to pay off," Ellie Cho said. "That you're on track to produce what you've promised to deliver. Our shareholders deserve that much, after all."

This was the hard part. "I'm going to need an extra month for Wraith," Dominic said.

The room erupted in noise, protests and angry voices tangling and overlapping. Dominic didn't move, summoning up an image of Farid, hands warm and strong on Dominic's ribs, breath sweet against his face.

When the uproar died down, Laura stood. "That's too much," she said flatly. "Our stocks will drop. We'll be seen as unreliable, unable to deliver."

"Three weeks, then," Dominic said. He put his hands in his lap, covering the bruised one. "If you want Wraith bug-free and reliable, you'll give me that."

A muscle jumped in Laura's jaw, and she glanced around the table. No one met her eye, and she finally looked back at Dominic and nodded sharply.

"Three weeks, not a second more."

Ellie Cho was next to speak. "The shareholders' meeting is next month. We need you there, Dominic. People want to meet you, get to know the mind behind these incredible products. And with Cory out on maternity leave, there's no one else."

Dominic let the silence draw out, looking at each face in turn. All these people, relying on him, demanding more than he could give—he wanted to scream his rage and frustration, to tell them they were asking too much, flee the room and never stop running—Farid shifted his weight, behind him, and Dominic drew in air.

"I'll be there," he said, tone clipped. "Are we done?"

Laura sighed and raised her hands in a defeated gesture.

"Ladies, gentlemen," Dominic said, and escaped.

He made it to the elevator and missed the button

his first try. He stabbed at it again, pressing it repeatedly until the doors slid silently open and he was able to stumble inside, Farid right behind him.

"Breathe," Farid said, the doors whooshing shut. They were alone, and Farid was close, his dark eyes sympathetic as Dominic fought to control the trembling. "You did well."

Dominic flinched backward when Farid touched his arm. "Don't—"

Farid backed up too. "I apologize." He stayed on the other side of the elevator until they got to their floor and waited for Dominic to step out first, maintaining a careful distance between them. "Are you going home now or staying to work some more?"

"I'm—" He should work, Dominic knew, but he couldn't *focus*, couldn't push through the fog of *traitor, neurotic mess, loser, asshole* that wouldn't stop swirling through his brain. He needed Farid's touch, to be taken out of his head, but he couldn't ask for that. "You can go home," he said, and went into his office.

Farid's office was empty when Dominic put his head out, about an hour later, and he told himself that was a good thing. He hadn't been hoping Farid would still be there, especially not after the way Dominic had treated him that day. He didn't *deserve* someone like Farid, and the sooner Farid realized that too, the better it would be for both of them.

Amber drove him home without speaking, and Dominic slipped an extra $20 into the cupholder for her in silent gratitude.

He nodded to his doorman and rode the elevator up to his apartment, hands in his pockets, where Farid was leaning against the door, looking as elegant and unruffled as ever.

Dominic gaped at him, and Farid straightened but said nothing, stepping aside to gesture at the lock.

It took him several tries, but Dominic finally got his key to work, far too aware of Farid beside him, his spicy cologne warm and bracing, eyes intent on Dominic's fumbling fingers.

The door finally swung open, and Dominic stepped through. Farid kicked the door shut behind them and caught a handful of Dominic's hair, dragging his head back.

"What the fuck," he hissed, "was that today?"

Fear gut-punched Dominic but he pushed it down, going limp. This was Farid. Farid would never hurt him, even as angry as he obviously was. This wasn't his father, and Dominic wasn't eight years old anymore.

Farid tightened his grip. "Answer me."

Dominic reached up involuntarily and caught Farid's arm. He wasn't trying to make him let go, just grasping for any sort of connection, but Farid released him immediately.

"Knees," he ordered, and Dominic fought back a sob of gratitude as he dropped to the floor. Farid bent, running a hand down Dominic's arm and bracketing his wrist, and too late, Dominic remembered his bloody knuckles. He tried to pull away, but Farid's grip was like iron. "What did you do?" he asked.

Dominic didn't answer, hunching his shoulders and staring at the floor.

Farid blew out an angry breath and let go. Turning on his heel, he stalked away toward Dominic's bedroom as Dominic waited, misery and grief and worry twisting his belly into knots.

Soon enough he was back, carrying the first aid kit

that stayed under Dominic's sink, and he knelt beside Dominic and opened it before gripping Dominic's wrist in one hand again.

"This is going to hurt," he said, and dumped antiseptic on the split skin.

Dominic choked on the pain, curling forward against it and pulling away, but Farid's hand didn't loosen, holding his arm steady with seemingly no effort.

"*Burns*," Dominic panted.

"Breathe through it," Farid said. He didn't sound sympathetic. If anything, he sounded even angrier.

Fucked it up, fucked it up, fucked—

Dominic closed his eyes so he wouldn't have to see the fury in Farid's eyes. He could feel Farid dabbing at the cuts and then a bandage being laid across his knuckles, taped into place with careful, methodical movements.

Then Farid let him go and stood. Dominic looked up as Farid took a step away and ran a hand through his hair until it fell over his forehead.

"You," he said, pointing at Dominic. "You are going to get naked, and you are going to kneel in front of the bed, with your forehead on the floor, until I'm not so fucking *angry*. Now."

Dominic scrambled to obey, shedding his clothes as he ran for the bedroom. He could hear Farid pacing behind him, but he didn't follow.

Alone in the bedroom, Dominic kicked his pants and underwear off and collapsed to the floor in front of the bed, folding forward over his knees to press his forehead to the plush carpet. It smelled like dust and polyester fiber, and all he could see was pale cream strands and a few specks of dirt that the housekeeper had missed.

Dominic flattened his hands against the floor. The penitent's pose. Praying for—what? Absolution, or simply forgiveness? He didn't deserve either. *Peace.* He didn't deserve that either, but oh, he longed for it, for the cessation of thought, the mantle of calm that draped across him when Farid touched him.

He pushed his forehead harder into the carpet as a memory floated up unbidden from the depths.

"Come on." Lance's voice was honey-sweet, cajoling with that note of laughter that always seemed to be just under the surface. "Just once?"

Dominic sighed, shifting his weight, and Lance, seeming to sense him weakening, pounced. He swung a leg over Dominic's lap and straddled him, grinning down into his face.

"You're gonna like this," he promised, and kissed him.

Dominic shook his head to dispel the memory but another took its place.

"Why won't you stop pushing? Why can't you be happy with what we have?"

"Because it's not enough!" Lance shouted. His tie hung loose around his neck, hair falling in his face and his eyes bloodshot. From the alcohol, Dominic supposed. "Because normal *people have sex, Dominic! Because I* want *sex! I want* you, *God only knows why, you're such a frigid* bitch—"

Forehead still on the floor, Dominic buried his face in his palms, rocking back and forth in place.

"I gave you everything! I was patient with you, I gave you 'space' or whatever, but all you ever do is talk about your stupid code. I'm sick of it! If the sex was good, maybe I could put up with it, but I don't even get a fucking

blowjob, *do I? Do you care at all about my needs? Do you ever think 'hey, maybe Lance would like to get something out of this relationship too?' I'm done! You're a whackjob with daddy issues and I've had* enough!"

Dominic didn't even realize he was crying until warm hands pulled him upright.

"Dom?" Farid knelt in front of him and wiped tears from Dominic's face. "Sweetheart, talk to me, what is it?"

"I'm s-sorry," Dominic choked out, and collapsed against him. Farid caught him, holding him effortlessly as Dominic sobbed into his white shirt. "I'm s-so sorry, 'Rid, I just—I f-fuck it all up, I always fuck it up, I can't stop, I c-can't, I'm—"

Farid eased them down onto the carpet until his back was to the bed and Dominic was in his lap, arms around Farid's slim waist. Farid stroked the hair off Dominic's forehead, saying nothing as Dominic wept.

Finally, the tears tapered off, leaving Dominic spent and exhausted. He tried to sit up, but Farid's hand on his shoulder kept him where he was. Dominic didn't fight it. Instead he pressed his face to Farid's abdomen and took a deep breath.

"What happened today?" Farid asked quietly.

Dominic shook his head minutely. "I can't—please don't—"

"So this afternoon," Farid said. "What was that?"

Shame flooded Dominic, and he buried his face in Farid's shirt.

"Something happened," Farid said, his tone thoughtful. "And you thought—what, were you punishing me?"

"*No*," Dominic said, tightening his grip. "I wasn't —it wasn't you, I—"

"So if you weren't punishing me, then…." Farid stroked Dominic's hair again. "You were punishing yourself, weren't you?"

Dominic said nothing.

Farid hummed, tracing the curve of Dominic's ear. "You need to be punished, you *want* to be, but you didn't know how to tell me, so you decided you'd *make* me punish you, is that it?"

Dominic burrowed in, hunching his shoulders, and Farid made a quiet noise.

"All you have to do is ask me for what you need, pet," he murmured.

"I'm sorry," Dominic managed, tears stinging his eyes again. "I can't… I can't get it right."

"Well, you haven't had much practice, have you?" Farid said. He caught a lock of Dominic's hair and gently pulled his head back until their eyes met. He was, impossibly, smiling, and Dominic was suddenly aware of what a wreck he was, nose running and eyes puffy, hair a mess. He ducked his head, pressing his face back to Farid's stomach, and Farid cupped the nape of his neck briefly and then let go and tapped his shoulder. "Get up. Facedown on the bed, hands on the rails."

Dominic froze, but Farid pushed against his shoulder until he scrambled upright. All trace of a smile was gone when Farid met his eyes this time.

"On the bed," he repeated. "You want to be punished, I'll punish you."

14

Dominic's legs were shaky and unreliable but somehow he managed to get into position, pushing the pillows aside and resting his cheek against the soft cotton sheet.

"Hands on the railings," Farid said. "Don't take them off or I'll stop, and I won't start again, do you understand?"

Dominic nodded jerkily and reached up, wrapping his hands around the metal posts directly in front of him. The bed dipped as Farid crawled on, but Dominic didn't look.

Farid's hand was warm, smoothing a line up Dominic's leg from his ankle to his thigh. He squeezed the muscle, fingers steady and reassuring. Dominic gulped and gripped the frame tighter.

"I'll give you what you need," Farid said. "Do you understand?"

Tears stung Dominic's eyes but he didn't say anything.

Farid patted Dominic's leg. "Up on your knees. Don't let go."

It took Dominic a minute to get himself into position, face still pressed to the mattress but on his knees, ass in the air, Farid still rubbing his thigh. Shame prickled Dominic's skin at the exposed position, and he squirmed.

Farid stopped touching him, and Dominic made a noise of protest in his throat.

"You don't like that?" Farid asked.

Dominic hesitated and then shook his head.

"Too bad," Farid said. "You don't get a say in what we're doing." He leaned over and patted Dominic's cheek. "Lift your head up."

Dominic obeyed, and Farid slipped his tie over Dominic's eyes, knotting it behind his head. The world went black, and Dominic tensed for a minute, looking for an escape. Dimly he was aware of Farid waiting for his reaction above him.

You don't get a say. Dominic forced himself to relax by increments, taking a deep breath and letting it out slowly and allowing the tension to drain from him like water through sand.

"*Good*, pet," Farid said, and warmth bloomed in Dominic's chest. Farid moved down the bed and settled between Dominic's spread knees. "There's only one rule," he said, petting Dominic's flank. "You're not allowed to come."

Before Dominic could parse the words, Farid bent and licked a stripe across Dominic's hole, wet and blistering hot. Dominic twisted and cried out, and Farid caught him and held him still with one hand curled around his hip, even as he buried his face and licked again and again, until Dominic's hole was dripping wet.

He traced around the muscle with one finger, pressing lightly but not penetrating, and then lowered his head and pointed his tongue, dipping just inside with the tip.

Dominic's nerves were on fire, his cock hardening so rapidly his head spun. Farid's hot breath, the faint rasp of his stubble on Dominic's sensitive skin, and his tongue probing inside Dominic's hole all combined so his senses were overwhelmed, world narrowing down to Farid's mouth and fingers. He tightened his grip on the bed frame again and pushed back, seeking friction.

Farid breathed a laugh. "Like that, do you?" He reached down and around and gave Dominic's cock several swift pulls, making his hips buck. "Remember what I said."

Dominic struggled to focus as Farid went back to work, licking and nibbling the edges of his hole. What had he said?

You're not allowed to come.

Dominic moaned out loud, and Farid's triumphant laugh shivered across him.

"Now you know why it's a punishment."

Dominic pulled on the bed frame, glad it was sturdy enough to withstand his strength, and pushed back into Farid's tongue again.

Farid's hum vibrated through Dominic's core, and he reached between Dominic's legs to cup his balls, rolling them with a featherlight touch between his fingers and pressing on the delicate skin just behind them.

"I'm not—I can't—"

"You can and you will," Farid said. "If you feel yourself getting close, you tell me, okay?"

Dominic pressed his face to the mattress and whimpered.

Farid pulled away. "Answer me."

"O-okay," Dominic managed.

"Okay what?" Farid's voice was implacable.

"I'll t-tell you," Dominic stuttered, tightening his grip. "I'll tell you, I'll tell you, *please—*"

Farid made a noise in the back of his throat as if dubious, but he lowered his head again.

Dominic lost track of time as Farid worked him over with light but merciless touches, drawing him right up to the brink over and over and keeping him there, suspended on a vibrating wire, until Dominic was sobbing and thrashing, and all too soon, he felt the familiar tightening in his balls.

"S-*stop*," he managed.

Farid backed off immediately, and Dominic pushed his face into the mattress, struggling to breathe. Finally, the tide receded and he lifted his head.

"Good," Farid murmured, and went back to work.

The second time, it was harder to get the word out, fighting the pleasure that rose inside him on an inexorable wave, but Farid stopped moving as Dominic panted against the mattress, fingers biting into the railings.

The third time, Dominic sobbed the word, balanced on the knife's edge, so close a gentle breeze would push him over. Somehow, Farid seemed to know that the slightest touch would undo him, and he stayed utterly still until Dominic's breathing had slowed, and then slid off the bed.

"Don't—" Dominic fought back the wave of irrational panic. "Don't leave—"

"I'm not going far," Farid said. "Stay like this, I'll be right back, I promise."

Dominic waited, ears tuned for the faintest whisper of movement, as Farid left the room. On his knees, ass in the air and face against the bed, he gripped the rails and told himself to trust. Trust that Farid would do what he said. Trust that he hadn't left him alone to ride this out. Trust that he would see Dominic through this. He closed his eyes, letting the waiting blackness rise up and fold him into its gentle arms. He was safe. The subspace seeped in, making his thoughts slow and syrupy, and he sighed, relaxing.

It was only a minute before Farid's footsteps came back and the mattress dipped again. His hand was warm against Dominic's flushed cheek.

"Lift your head and drink this," he said.

Dominic obeyed, sipping blindly at the bottle Farid put to his mouth, and cold water slid down his throat. After a few gulps, Farid took the bottle away.

"Face on the bed again."

Dominic obeyed, and Farid got between his knees. He seemed in no hurry to resume, though, stroking Dominic's thighs and ass in slow, gentle movements.

Half-soothed back to peace, Dominic's cock took an interest in proceedings again, but Farid would not be rushed. He pressed a thumb to Dominic's hole, pushing lightly, and then traced down and around his balls in slow, hypnotic motions until Dominic was fully erect again and breathing hard. Farid continued the featherlight caresses, leaning over Dominic's body to slip a hand around and splay it across his ribs, fingers reverent as if counting each in turn.

Then he moved down, circling Dominic's cock with a finger and thumb and sliding it up and down his shaft.

Even that was almost too much, the stoked fire in Dominic's belly growing with each pass of Farid's hand until his skin felt tight and stinging hot, like sparks burned into canvas.

"Stop," he gasped again, tears pricking his eyes.

Farid released him. "On your back."

Dominic waited a minute, until he was sure he wouldn't come and then obeyed, groaning as he worked his stiff fingers loose from the bed frame. Flat on his back, he reached up and gripped the rungs again without being told.

"Good," Farid said, stroking his inner thigh. "You're a natural, pet."

Dominic's mouth was too dry for him to respond. Farid held the bottle to his lips again and Dominic drank gratefully. Then Farid caught his knee and pushed, rolling his hips up and nearly folding him in half.

"One hand here," Farid said, patting the back of Dominic's knee. "Hold yourself like this."

Dominic swallowed the sob and obeyed, gripping his leg so that he was splayed wide, open and exposed and somehow safer than he'd ever been in his life, even as his cock fell against his belly and sent ripples of fire through him.

Farid just went back to working him open with his tongue, one hand exploring Dominic's cock while his tongue pressed ever deeper inside his hole, and then slipped one finger in alongside it.

It was too much and not enough, and it was going

to push him over the edge. Dominic shook his head, the sob ripping free. "*Please*—"

Farid withdrew. "Too much?"

"Not—not enough," Dominic managed. "Please, 'Rid, I need to come, please, it hurts—"

"What hurts?"

"Cock," Dominic moaned. "So hard… please…."

"We're not done," Farid said. He leaned across Dominic's body and a drawer opened and shut, then the bottle of lube clicked open. "If anything besides your cock hurts, safeword."

Dominic worked moisture into his mouth. "Are you—are you going to fuck me?" He didn't know if the thought terrified or excited him.

Farid pressed a kiss to Dominic's knee. "Darling, by the time I'm done, you're going to *wish* I'd fucked you."

It got difficult for Dominic to focus after that. All he could process were Farid's hands and mouth on him, pushing him closer with every breath, even as subspace pushed him deeper. Every touch was perfectly calculated to drive Dominic a little nearer the brink, but each time he thought he'd fall over the cliff, Farid backed off again.

"*Please*," Dominic begged. He was actually crying, he realized dimly, tears soaking the silk. Farid's hand on him was agony, ratcheting the bliss up with each relentless stroke. He let go of his leg and curled forward, blindly seeking Farid's warmth, the trembles rippling through him in unending waves. "Please, I—'Rid, *please*."

Farid leaned over him, the soft scrape of his clothes almost too much to bear on Dominic's oversensitized skin, and kissed his throat. Dominic caught his shirt with his free hand, pulling desperately, trying to bring Farid closer, but Farid stayed braced above him, mouth roving down Dominic's chest until he latched onto a nipple.

Dominic's back arched as lightning shot to his groin and he made a wounded noise. Farid licked and teased and nibbled until the nipple was an aching nub, stiff and sore, and then moved to the other one. His dress pants, silky polyester, brushed against Dominic's cock and he jerked and cried out at the touch.

Farid breathed warmth, life, *joy* into Dominic's gray existence. He brought color and dimension to a world that had been flat and dull. He was the piece to the puzzle Dominic hadn't known he was missing, and when he sat back, heat fading from Dominic's skin, Dominic protested wordlessly, groping for him.

"Don't leave," he whispered, turning his head in an effort to fix on Farid's location. "Please, 'Rid, don't—"

"Shh, I'm right here," Farid said. "How are you feeling?"

"Need t-to come," Dominic said.

"Tell me how you feel," Farid said, voice gentle but implacable.

"It h-hurts."

"I know, pet," Farid said. He scraped a nail lightly down Dominic's inner thigh. "What else?"

Dominic groped for words through the fog in his brain. "Skin feels... t-tight. Hot." He reached up and put his free hand back on the bed frame again. "When y-you touch me, it... it hurts but I want more, I n-need—"

"Doing good, pet," Farid crooned. He circled the head of Dominic's cock with one finger, gathering up the precome and spreading it over the crown as

Dominic twitched and moaned. "You're so beautiful like this, spread out for me, giving yourself up. Surrendering. You do it so perfectly, sweetheart." He pumped Dominic's cock lightly, once, twice, then lifted his hand.

"*'Rid.*"

Farid hummed. "You wanted to be punished. Are you being punished?" He clasped Dominic's cock and stroked again.

Dominic twisted, sobbing. "I'm sorry," he burst out. "I'm s-so sorry, 'Rid, I'm sorry, please forgive me, please—" Tears clogged his throat, swelling it until words wouldn't fit through, and he hiccupped as his breath caught.

Then Farid was there, pulling his hands away from the headboard and pushing the sodden blindfold off Dominic's eyes. He cupped Dominic's face, pressing their foreheads together as tears streamed down Dominic's cheeks and he grasped weakly at Farid's arms.

"I'm s-sorry," he repeated.

"You're forgiven," Farid whispered. He reached between them and began to stroke again, steady, toe-curling pumps that had Dominic arching off the bed, grabbing wildly at any part of Farid he could reach. "Come for me, sweetheart. It's okay, let me have it."

It felt, vaguely, like he was being turned inside out, the pleasure flooding and overstimulating every single nerve ending as his cock thickened and pulsed, jet after sticky, hot jet landing on too-sensitive skin, his entire body seizing up while Farid stroked him through it, murmuring softly in Dominic's ear with their cheeks pressed together.

When he collapsed back onto the bed, boneless

like a puppet with cut strings, Farid slid off the mattress. Dominic couldn't get a breath, heartbeat thundering in his ears, so he lay helplessly and stared at the ceiling until Farid came back with a warm washcloth.

His cock twitched feebly as Farid cleaned it and his stomach, and Dominic moaned a protest.

"Too much—"

Farid laughed quietly and leaned over to kiss him. He tasted like Dominic's mouthwash, sweet mint on Dominic's tongue.

"That was exquisite," he whispered. "*You* are exquisite."

Dominic didn't have the strength to muster a response. Farid went back to cleaning him up and then shook out the blanket on the end of the bed and draped it over him.

"Wait," Dominic said, pushing weakly at Farid's hand when he tried to tuck the blanket around his shoulders. "Wha' 'bout you?"

Farid stilled, surprise flickering over his face. "I'm fine, pet."

"No," Dominic insisted, struggling to his elbows. He felt almost *drunk*, lightheaded and dizzy, but he reached for—and missed—Farid's waistband. "No, you have to—" His arms gave out and he flopped back to the bed.

Farid huffed a laugh. "This was for you, Dom."

"But I *want* you to," Dominic protested. "Do you… not want…."

"More than you know," Farid said, leaning over and pressing a kiss to his mouth. "I want you, I *do*, God, more than I've wanted anything, but—"

Dominic threw the blanket back. "I want you." He silently dared Farid to argue. "Come on my chest."

Farid groaned and he slid off the bed again, this time to undress. Dominic moaned appreciatively as his cock sprang free, thick and leaking, and Farid took it in one hand, stroking himself slowly, eyes fixed on Dominic's form.

"This won't take long," he husked.

Dominic beckoned, and Farid smiled and crawled back onto the bed. Slinging a leg over Dominic's hips, he settled against his pelvis. Dominic ran his hands up and down Farid's lean muscled thighs and lifted his knees, planting his feet on the bed so Farid had something to brace against.

He was still dazed, like he was floating just outside his body, nerves tingling and mind blessedly silent, but he retained just enough coherent thought to appreciate the way Farid's eyes drooped as he fucked his fist, the way the tendons in his neck stood out and a flush crawled up his chest, hips rocking forward.

He was right. It was a matter of minutes before his hand sped up, breathing shortening, and he hunched over, catching himself on Dominic's arm as wetness splattered against his chest.

"Fuck, *fuck*, Dom, *fuck*—" Farid panted for air and folded forward, collapsing on Dominic's chest, face pressed to his throat and breath gusting sharp and heavy.

Satisfied, Dominic ran a hand up Farid's arm and fell asleep.

15

Farid lay on his back and stared up at the ceiling as Dominic slept beside him. Panic beat moth-soft wings in the base of his throat. *What are you doing? That wasn't just about sex.*

He turned his head and looked at Dominic, wrapped in a loose curve around Farid's body, one long arm draped over his stomach. He was angelic in sleep, that lush, lovely mouth soft and unguarded, lashes lying thick on his cheeks and curls tumbling over his forehead.

I gave him what he needed, Farid told himself. *It's what a good Dom does.*

Dominic reached out and pulled Farid closer, eyes still shut, pressing his nose into Farid's shoulder and snuffling a sigh.

It was too much to puzzle out, the exhaustion of the scene suddenly swamping him. Farid turned on his side and tucked Dominic up against his chest. He'd figure it out later.

He was alone in the bed when he woke up, but he could hear faint noises from the kitchen. Farid stretched and rolled out of bed to pad naked from the room. Dominic was at the counter, putting beef and broccoli on plates, and he looked up when Farid emerged. His smile was tentative, hopeful, and it made Farid's heart hurt just a little.

"Are you hungry?"

Farid rounded the counter and ignored the food, reaching up to pull Dominic down into a kiss. He went willingly, the spoon clattering on the counter, and wrapped both arms around Farid's waist, his mouth sweet and warm and wet as their tongues brushed.

When Farid pulled back, Dominic looked dazed.

"How do you feel?" Farid asked.

It took Dominic several tries to answer, throat working. "Um—better. I—" He ducked his head and glanced up, shame flitting across his face.

Farid didn't need to be a mind reader to know what was going on. He caught Dominic's chin and shook it gently.

"Don't do that."

"But—"

"You apologized," Farid interrupted. "I forgave you. Remember?"

Dominic nodded, Farid still holding his chin. "I was such an asshole, though," he whispered.

Farid almost laughed. "Over and done. Besides, I'm not always a bed of roses myself." He tugged Dominic's face down and pressed their mouths together again. "Now stop thinking about it. I mean it. I'm starving."

THEY ATE SITTING next to each other on the couch, Farid with his legs crossed, watching Dominic closely.

"Do you feel like you're dropping?"

Dominic shook his head, mouth bulging. He chewed and swallowed and gave Farid a sheepish grin. "No, I feel fine. I feel… good."

Relief crept over Farid. "Tell me if you do, okay?"

"Will," Dominic promised earnestly, and shoved another huge bite into his mouth.

Comfortably full, Farid set his plate on the coffee table and leaned back with a sigh. "Want to watch a movie?"

"Sure," Dominic mumbled, still eating.

Farid picked up the remote and scrolled through channels. "What kind of stuff do you like?"

"I don't care."

"Don't care or don't have an opinion?"

Dominic lifted one shoulder, eyes suddenly unsure. "I don't—I have a hard time sitting still for movies. So I don't watch a lot of them. Lance—" He clamped his mouth shut.

"Lance?" Farid waited, keeping his expression neutral.

"Ex. It drove him nuts," Dominic finally admitted. "He loved movies, especially action thrillers, and those are so boring to me. I could never manage to finish one, and then he'd complain about me fidgeting, and we'd end up fighting or he'd go off and sulk."

Farid breathed through the flush of fury that

prickled his skin. "He sounds like a dick," he said, managing to keep his voice calm. "Maybe you just haven't seen the *right* movies." He flicked through the options. "Aha! Seen this one?"

"*The Spanish Prisoner*," Dominic read aloud, and shook his head. "What's it about?"

Farid took Dominic's plate from him and set it on the table, then pulled until Dominic settled in beside him. "It's a puzzle movie," he said, twining their fingers together. "You have to pay close attention. The clues are all right there but if you don't see them, it won't make sense."

Dominic was warm and soft, tucked up against him, brow creased as the credits rolled and the movie started. Farid watched him more than the screen, enjoying the way Dominic followed every movement of the actors, trying to puzzle out their behavior.

"She's weird," he announced when the love interest was introduced.

"Is she?" Farid said mildly.

"Yeah, I mean…." Dominic gestured. "It's like… there's something sort of… off about her. Like she's playing a part." Farid raised his eyebrows and Dominic rolled his eyes. "I mean the *character* is playing a part, not the actress. Which if I'm right, I guess would mean the actress is playing the part of a character playing a part, which is…."

"Pretty damn good acting," Farid finished, and Dominic nodded.

Farid was delighted to see that Dominic grew more and more absorbed as the movie went on, offering up theories and conjecture on the ending, all of which Farid nodded along to with apparent gravity until Dominic wrinkled his nose at him and turned back to the screen. Farid laughed softly and pressed a kiss to his temple.

"I knew it, I *knew* it, I knew she was in on it!" Dominic said at the end.

Farid pretended to applaud, not trying to fight the smile. Dominic grinned back and bounced off the couch, rolling his shoulders and stretching his neck.

"That was fun," he said. "I want to work out. Come with?"

"Sure," Farid said.

The building had two gyms, Dominic explained to Farid as they stepped into the elevator. One for the first fifteen floors, and one for the last three.

"They never use it, though," he said, doing calf-lifts against the wall. "It's Mrs. Ferguson on seventeen—the only time you'll see her running is if Macy's is having a sale. Then there's some bank or hedge fund manager or something on sixteen—he's never met a donut he didn't like, so he's never here. And fifteen is shared by two families, but they have young kids, and I'm pretty sure they're too exhausted by the end of the day to ever bother. So it's just me."

Farid fiddled with the too-loose band of the shorts Dominic had loaned him. "If these fall down on me halfway through, you'd better promise to destroy the video evidence."

Dominic's laugh was loose and happy and made Farid want to kiss him breathless, but the elevator doors slid open before he could, so he settled for following him down the hall, appreciating the way Dominic's ass looked in his own shorts, his long, perfectly muscled legs and the small, curling hairs that Farid knew were as soft as they looked.

"I come here when I can't sleep," Dominic said,

holding open the door to the weight room. "Which is a lot." He stopped and reconsidered. "It was a lot, before, uh… you."

Farid grinned brightly at him. "Are you saying I put you to sleep?"

Dominic matched his smile. "You sure wear me out."

Farid bit back the urge to kiss him, far too aware of the cameras in the corners of the brightly lit, mirrored room.

They spent an hour working up a sweat, until endorphins coursed lazily through Farid's body and he was pleasantly exhausted, sweat dripping and muscles burning.

Back upstairs in Dominic's apartment, Farid pushed him into the bathroom and stripped him in quick, efficient movements, letting his fingers dance up Dominic's ribs until he squeaked and twisted away, laughing breathlessly, and then dragged him into the shower.

He loved going down on Dominic. The way Dominic never asked, but watched Farid with hungry, hopeful eyes when Farid went to his knees and nuzzled into the crease of Dominic's groin, smelling sweat and salt and Dominic's skin. The tiny noises he made when Farid took him in his mouth, his muscles tightening with the urge to thrust as his hands fluttered by his sides, like he couldn't figure out what to do with them.

Farid solved the problem for him by catching Dominic's wrist and guiding his hand to cup the back of his head and Dominic groaned out loud as Farid swallowed him down.

"I love the way you taste," Farid said, pulling off briefly.

Dominic shivered, fingers tightening in Farid's hair, and Farid went back to work, bobbing his head and using one hand to pump the length of shaft he couldn't take in. His knees ached distantly from the hard shower tiles, but he didn't care, too lost in driving Dominic out of his mind.

"I—'Rid, please—" Farid looked up at him, Dominic's cock still in his mouth, and Dominic groaned raggedly. "Please can I come, please, 'Rid—"

They weren't even scening, Farid thought. That was how thoroughly Dominic surrendered control, how joyfully he gave it to Farid and allowed him to dictate the terms of his pleasure, and if he wasn't very careful, it was going to prove Farid's undoing.

He patted Dominic's thigh in permission and took him deep, and Dominic curled forward, hands suddenly, brutally tight in Farid's hair as he came in throbs down his throat.

HE TUCKED Dominic into bed after, Dominic damp and rumpled and yawning, and couldn't resist bending to drop one more kiss on his mouth.

"Promise me you'll call if you drop."

Dominic made an assenting noise, fingers wrapping warm and soft around Farid's wrist, and yawned again. "Promise."

"See you tomorrow, pet," Farid said, and let himself out of the apartment.

Three weeks. Three more weeks before he had to walk away.

16

———

TWO WEEKS

Dominic hummed to himself as he stepped off the elevator. His heart lightened as he saw Farid frowning at his computer.

"Morning," Dominic said as he opened the door.

Farid glanced up, and the shadows in his eyes fled, replaced by genuine happiness to see him. Dominic's heart stuttered briefly and he tugged at his sleeves, suddenly unsure how to act.

"Good morning" was all Farid said, but the words were a caress, brushing along Dominic's skin and making him shiver. "Wait," Farid said before Dominic could escape into his office. "I have something for you." He held out a coffee cup, steam still curling from the vent, the Fonté label visible above his hand. "F2."

Dominic swallowed hard, guilt and shame and resentment warring for supremacy within him. "Are you—is this… punishment?"

"*No,*" Farid said sharply, rising. He stepped around

the desk and closed the distance between them as Dominic shifted his weight, feeling suddenly oversized and awkward again. "No, Dom, this is coffee. For you. Because I know you like the blend and because…." He hesitated, and finally lifted a shoulder. "Just because."

Dominic narrowed his eyes but Farid's expression was sincere, and finally he nodded and reached for the cup. Their fingers brushed and Dominic caught his breath. Farid's lips curved, but he just handed the cup over and went back to his seat.

"Product review meeting at ten," he said, straightening his cuffs.

Dominic winced and escaped into his office.

He did his best to immerse himself in code, managing several small victories but ever-aware of Farid's presence on the other side of the wall. His mind wouldn't let go of the way Farid had touched him, the last time they'd been together.

It had been so tender, so gentle, and yet somehow so merciless and uncompromising. *Safe.* That was the only way to describe it. Farid would catch him when Dominic stumbled, would always catch him, and keep him from breaking apart with his solid, steady faith that Dominic *wasn't* a fuck-up, that he was somehow worth—

Dominic flinched away from the word. *Aromantic,* he reminded himself, ignoring the pain that lanced through his heart. *He'll never love you. He* can't.

Against his better judgment, he turned to Google.

A person who experiences little to no romantic attraction to others, he read. *Aromantics do not feel the need for love or romantic relationships, being satisfied with friendship and strong platonic ties.*

It was true that Farid wasn't romantically inclined.

He didn't buy flowers or make grand gestures. There were no rose petals lining the way to the bedroom, no candles creating an "atmosphere." Something told Dominic the idea would make Farid laugh.

And yet. He touched Dominic with such devastating tenderness, like Dominic was something infinitely precious. Surely he felt *something* more than sexual attraction.

Dominic sighed and resisted the urge to bang his forehead against the desk.

THAT EVENING, they lay tangled in the sheets, Farid on his side and Dominic flat on his back, staring at the ceiling as he tried to catch his breath.

Farid rested a hand on Dominic's gently heaving ribs. "How are you doing?"

"Pretty great," Dominic said, the remains of his orgasm still curling slow and lazy through his belly. Farid's hand was hot as a brand against his skin. He rolled his head on the pillow to look at him. "Can I ask you something?"

Farid hummed assent, seemingly focused on Dominic's stomach.

"Are we... is there anything you'd like to do that we haven't done?"

Farid blinked. "How do you mean?"

"Well... you're the expert, right? You've had a lot of sex, so you know what you like and what you don't. So I guess... is there anything you want to do to me? Or with me? Or... I don't know." Embarrassment fired Dominic's cheeks but Farid caught his arm before he could roll away.

"I haven't had *that* much sex, pet. There's still plenty I haven't tried."

"It's not like I would think less of you if you'd slept with half the population of Seattle, as long as you were careful," Dominic said, and Farid huffed a laugh, amusement in his eyes.

"Not even a third, sorry to disappoint."

Dominic sat up and crossed his legs, and Farid followed suit so they were facing each other on the bed.

"What *have* you done?" Dominic asked. "Not who —I don't care about that. I just want to know *what*."

"Are we talking kink?" Farid said, eyes narrowed.

Dominic nodded.

"Why don't you ask, and I'll tell you if I've done it?"

"Uh…." Dominic struggled to gather his thoughts. "Penetrative—I guess you've done that."

Farid inclined his head, lips twitching.

"Pain, um… pain play, I guess? Have you done a lot of that?"

Farid took Dominic's hand, tracing his knuckles with a thumb. "I've done my share," he said, eyes steady on Dominic's. "Are you worried I miss it?"

Dominic ducked his head, focusing on their intertwined hands. "I just don't want to limit you," he whispered.

Farid squeezed gently. "I'm not a sadist," he said. "I find my pleasure from giving *you* pleasure. My friend San—I wish you could meet him, you'd like him—*he's* a sadist. He loves hurting people. With their consent, of course."

"And I'd like him?" Dominic said incredulously.

"That's only one part of him," Farid said. "There's

another part that loves art, and reading, and really boring opera music, and the part that adores his boyfriend, Fox, and the part that makes him want to take care of people after he's hurt them."

Dominic chewed that over. "I don't understand," he finally admitted. "But we're off-topic. Have you ever had sex with more than one person at a time?" He held his breath, waiting for Farid's answer.

Farid's eyes were shrewd. "Yes," he said bluntly. "Do you want details?"

Dominic shook his head. He'd been right; Farid, Sanyam, and Fox had definitely had sex. He pushed it aside and hurried on. "Have you ever had sex in a public place?"

"Define public," Farid said, smile widening.

"Holy shit," Dominic breathed.

"It was a dark booth at the far end of a club," Farid said. "Might as well have been behind locked doors."

"And that turned you on?"

"It was… fun," Farid said, lifting a shoulder. "Why, do you like the thought?"

"Um." Dominic shifted his weight. It was far too soon for him to be able to come again, but his cock gave an interested twitch, and Farid's eyebrows went up.

"You *do*. How very intriguing."

"I can't, though," Dominic said urgently. "I can't, you have to understand, I'm a public figure, like it or not. Maybe people on the street don't recognize me, but the paparazzi sure fucking do. I can't risk it. I *can't*. I'd be ruined. My company would—"

Farid put a finger to Dominic's lips. "You don't have to explain. What about group sex? Do you like the idea of that?"

Dominic turned the idea over in his head. "I'm—I don't know. I don't want to have sex with… um, anyone but you, but…."

Farid went to his knees and planted a soft kiss on Dominic's mouth. "But maybe you like the idea of other people having sex near us?" His breath was sweet and warm on Dominic's face, his dark eyes affectionate, and Dominic swallowed butterflies and nodded tentatively.

"Maybe? It doesn't… repulse me."

Farid laughed quietly and kissed him again. "You've given me some ideas, pet. Are you hungry?"

17

———

ONE WEEK

"What are you doing this weekend?"

Dominic blinked, trying to focus on Farid's slim form by the door but his eyes bleary. "Um. Working?"

"Oh, no," Farid said. There was excitement in his voice, and Dominic sat up straighter. "You're not working. You're coming with me."

"But—the launch party is next week," Dominic protested. "I *have* to—"

"You have to take a break," Farid interrupted. "And I know exactly how to turn off your brain."

"Sex?" Dominic said hopefully.

Farid's lips curved. "Wait and see. Be at the airport tomorrow morning, 5:00 a.m." He set a piece of paper on the desk and left the room before Dominic could ask questions.

Dominic picked up the paper. It was a ticket to Vancouver, BC. His heart surged in his chest. Was Farid—surely he wasn't.

Trust, he reminded himself, folding up the paper and tucking it into his pocket.

***

HE WASN'T sure what to pack, and Farid refused to elaborate when Dominic texted him, so Dominic finally shoved a few changes of casual clothing and one suit in his carry-on bag, grumbling about not-boyfriends who didn't answer *perfectly simple* questions. He fished a plain baseball cap out of his drawer and pulled it on, then rooted around for his favorite aviators and leather jacket. Sufficiently incognito, he arrived at the airport, tipped his cab driver, and walked into the huge main lobby, looking around for Farid, who was nowhere in sight.

His phone buzzed. *Just get on the plane. I like the Top Gun look, very sexy.*

Dominic turned in a circle, swearing under his breath. *Where are you?*

See you on the plane, gorgeous.

He settled into his seat, faintly grateful for first class and its ample leg room. The seat beside him was empty, another thing to be grateful for. Maybe he wouldn't have to make small talk with a stranger all the way to Vancouver. He couldn't help the nervous jiggling of his leg as the attendant came by, a pretty, dark-skinned young man with liquid eyes and a lovely smile.

"Welcome to Air Canada," he said. "My name is Parker, and if you need anything at all, I'm here to help. Can I offer you a mimosa?"

"It's, uh… five thirty in the morning," Dominic

said, and Parker grinned at him, making a dimple flash in his cheek.

"You'd be surprised," he said. "How about a bagel and some orange juice instead?"

"That sounds good," Dominic said. He looked around the plane, knee still bouncing, as Parker smiled again and left, and Farid slipped into the seat beside him.

Dominic's breath left him in an audible *whoosh*, and Farid put a hand on his knee, stilling the nervous tic.

"I thought—"

"You thought what?" Farid said. He looked tired, dark circles under his eyes again, but his hair was neatly brushed and his clothes—polo shirt and jeans that he somehow managed to make irresistible—were as impeccable as ever. "You thought I wouldn't come, maybe? That I'd put you on a flight to *Canada* and then leave you high and dry?"

Dominic hunched his shoulders. "It sounds stupid when you put it that way," he mumbled.

Farid tightened his grip on Dominic's leg. "Relax, pet," he said, and it sounded like an order. Dominic couldn't help the way his muscles loosened as he leaned into Farid's warmth. Farid was there. Farid would take care of him. His mind quieted, the anxiety tamping to a dull buzz in the back of his head.

"Where are we going?" he asked. He had an idea, but he wanted confirmation.

Farid just put a finger to his lips and leaned back in his seat, hand still warm on Dominic's thigh as if he'd forgotten it was there. Dominic would have died before reminding him. He settled for lifting the shade so he could watch the workers on the tarmac. He would be okay. He was with Farid, and that meant he was safe.

"Not a nervous flyer, are you?" Farid asked, head back and eyes closed as if it didn't bother him either way.

"Not—no," Dominic said. He fiddled with the seat controls until Farid clamped a hand over his.

"Doing a pretty good impression of one, pet."

Dominic fidgeted.

Farid waited, dark eyes calm and gently curious.

"I don't like uncertainty," Dominic finally whispered. "It makes me feel… um… when I was bad, my father used to lock me in my room and tell me I was going to be punished, but he wouldn't tell me *how*. I think he knew it drove me out of my head thinking about the various ways he might take it out on me."

Farid gripped Dominic's hand tighter, his eyes hardening.

"I don't know," Dominic said, staring at his lap. "Maybe that's *why* I have anxiety."

"Or maybe you already had it and he just made it that much worse," Farid said. His voice was gentle but there was fury in his eyes, and somehow it made Dominic feel better, knowing someone hurt for him, regretted the way he'd been raised. "I'm sorry I scared you, pet. We're going to Vancouver to see some friends of mine."

"Sanyam?" Dominic said, and immediately wished the word back.

Farid's eyebrows went up. "How did you know he's in Vancouver?"

"Give me some credit," Dominic said, relaxing a fraction more. "He's the first result for 'Sanyam' and 'BDSM' on Google."

Farid snorted a quiet laugh. "Fair enough. Yes, we're going to see him, and Fox. Who, by the way, will be a total asshole to you until he decides he can trust you with me, so be prepared."

Dominic gulped. "Asshole how?"

"He'll try to throw you off balance, say rude or outrageous things. I imagine he'll flirt with you, so if you can manage it, flirt back."

"His boyfriend won't care?"

"Sanyam's not the jealous type," Farid said, running a thumb over Dominic's knuckles. "He knows Fox loves him. Even when they have sex with other people, their focus is always each other. It's… sweet."

"I can't…." Dominic searched for words. "I can't imagine having sex with other—"

Farid squeezed his hand. "I know, pet. Maybe it's the demi thing, maybe just a *you* thing. But there's nothing wrong with wanting to be exclusive."

Dominic hunched his shoulders as Parker made his way back up the aisle. "So why do I like the thought of, um—"

"Public sex?" Farid said helpfully.

Dominic nodded, making a shushing motion with his free hand. "Like, obviously not full-on… banging it out or anything, but ever since we talked about it, I can't stop thinking about, um—"

Farid's eyes darkened with intent. "Blowing me in front of someone, maybe?"

"Oh God." Dominic crossed his legs as his cock hardened, and Farid grinned, sharp and predatory.

"Me blowing *you*?"

"Can we—" Dominic folded forward, trying to breathe and willing his body back to sleep. "Please… stop?"

Farid hummed. "No."

Arousal slammed into Dominic's chest like a hammer, and he made a choked noise, clutching his knees.

"We could call it testing the waters," Farid continued, leaning into Dominic's space just enough that their arms brushed. "See how much you can take without causing a scene?"

Dominic squeezed his eyes shut and counted his breaths. In, out, slow and steady, he could do this. He could do anything Farid wanted him to do. He straightened, although his fingers were still white-knuckled in the fabric of his pants, and met Farid's eyes.

"Well, well," Farid murmured, a smile flickering across his mouth. "I thought for sure you'd safeword."

Dominic's laugh was a little choked. "I still might," he warned. "Rules?"

"No touching," Farid said thoughtfully. "If I can't drive you out of your mind with just my voice and my words, then I don't deserve to call myself a Dominant. Also, no coming at all until tonight, not even going to the bathroom and rubbing one out." His smile was brilliant. "Turns out I like edging you."

Dominic wasn't sure what he said in reply, but Farid's smile just widened.

"Put the blanket over your lap and bunch it up a little bit," he ordered.

Dominic obeyed, his fingers numb and mind already beginning to fuzz around the edges. He was safe. No matter what happened, he could let go and Farid would handle it.

"Look at you." Farid sighed. "So beautiful when

you hit that headspace. God, I could do anything to you right now and you'd ask for more, wouldn't you?"

Dominic shifted his weight, fully hard and knowing a damp patch was forming on the front of his pants.

"Don't move," Farid said, a warning note in his voice, and Dominic subsided. His arms felt heavy and yet somehow floaty, like they weren't connected to him, and he leaned back in the seat, staring at the overhead bin above him.

Parker came past just then and asked Farid a question Dominic didn't try to understand.

"He's fine," Farid said. "Nervous flyer, he took a Xanax. He'll probably be pretty out of it for most of the flight."

Parker left and Farid laughed quietly. Dominic leaned toward him, wanting to hear him laugh more, to sink into him and let go completely. The fog was rolling over him, and he couldn't feel or hear anything except Farid's voice.

"Be still, pet," Farid said gently. "You're well and truly under, aren't you?"

"Mmhmm," Dominic agreed.

"God," Farid muttered. "Just a few words. How am I supposed to resist this? *You?*"

Dominic frowned, unease creeping in around the edges of his mind. Farid didn't sound happy. Farid should sound happy. Farid deserved happiness, and love, and—

"No, easy," Farid said, voice soothing again. "You're all right, pet. I'm here. What would you do, I wonder, if I touched you right now?"

"Please." Dominic didn't recognize his own voice,

it was so thick and slurred. "Please will you touch me, 'Rid, please—"

"Shh. We're in public, pet. Not only that, we're on an airplane filled with people who would definitely have a problem with us having sex in here." Farid sounded amused. "There's a lady across the aisle, two rows back, and she's got her eye on us. Maybe because I'm brown-skinned and therefore obviously a terrorist, or maybe because you're so completely out of it, I'm not sure. But if I touch you the way I *want* to touch you, we're going to get kicked off this plane, and you don't want that, right?"

Dominic shook his head because an answer seemed required. A heartbeat later, Farid took his hand, and Dominic caught his breath.

"If she reports us for holding hands, she's a homophobe," Farid murmured. "And our very pretty flight attendant will take our side. Now. Where were we?"

Dominic couldn't think. The fog had him well and truly in its grasp and all he could do was surrender to it, Farid's hand a lodestone, a beacon that shone to remind Dominic that he wasn't alone. He sank into it gratefully, and Farid groaned under his breath.

"God, you really are irresistible like this. Do you like imagining that I'm fucking you, pet, even though it's not something you want in real life?"

Dominic clamped his free hand over his mouth to stifle the moan.

"I'll take that as a yes," Farid whispered. His voice was dark with promise. "Do you think about me bending you over the arm of the couch or maybe your kitchen counter?"

Dominic squeezed his eyes shut, free hand

clutching the blanket in place. *Don't come, don't come, don't come.*

"I'd take my time, of course," Farid said, almost reflectively. "Open you up properly, make sure you're nice and stretched out. Hold you down with one hand while I fuck you with my fingers, until you're in tears begging me to fill you, wriggling and squirming and reaching for me, your legs all shaky and your asshole loose and ready for—"

"*Pomegranate.*" Dominic bent double, head between his knees. All he could focus on was holding his orgasm back by sheer force of will, breath thunderous in his own ears.

Farid put a palm between Dominic's shoulder blades, rubbing solicitously, but Dominic twisted away.

"Don't—"

Farid lifted his hand away. "Breathe through it," he said, a note of sympathy mixed with the triumph in his voice.

Dominic couldn't spare the brain cells necessary to glare at him, but he considered it, clutching his knees and thinking about the least sexy things he could imagine. *Cold showers. Football. Talking to the board. Sales and Legal.*

"Can you sit up?" Farid asked.

When Dominic obeyed, Farid was holding out a glass of orange juice. They were in the air, Dominic realized, the wisps of fog in his brain still making it difficult to hold a coherent thought. He accepted the juice dumbly and drank half the contents.

"How—" He gestured out the window, to the ground far below them now, and somehow Farid followed his thought.

"Well, you were a little preoccupied." His lips twitched, and he offered a plate with a cinnamon raisin bagel on it. "Eat some breakfast, pet."

Dominic eyed him. "No more?"

"For now," Farid said serenely, and Dominic gulped.

<hr>

THE REST of the flight was a blur, Dominic still half in the grip of subspace, and Farid taking merciless advantage of that by whispering filthy suggestions in his ear every time Dominic relaxed.

By the time the plane landed, Dominic was sweating, gripping the armrests, and praying he didn't embarrass himself. *More than you already have*, he thought. It was several minutes before he could stand up, still half-hard, arousal thrumming through him. Farid wisely stayed a foot away from him as Dominic groped for his luggage and dragged it out of the bin.

As he made his way down the narrow aisle, he caught the eye of a woman several seats back. Her frosted hair was shellacked into a careful helmet, heavy makeup applied in a vain attempt to hide her real age, and she was glaring at Dominic, blood-red nails digging into the armrests.

Dominic couldn't help it—he gave her a blinding smile and reached behind him to catch Farid's hand.

"Have a nice day," he told her, and Farid followed him off the plane, not even bothering to hide his laughter.

IN THE GLASS-AND-METAL BUILDING, Farid took the lead. They had no checked luggage, so they were through customs fairly quickly and from there into the main part of the airport.

"What are we going to do until tonight?" Dominic asked as Farid threaded his way through the crowds.

"Sightsee," Farid said, flashing a smile over his shoulder. "Have you ever been to Granville Market?"

"Never been to Vancouver at all," Dominic admitted. "Toronto a few times, for conferences, but not Vancouver. Always wanted to, though."

"Lots to see and do," Farid said. "I love it here. I'm gonna show you all my favorite places." He glanced back. "Are you tired? Do you want to go to the hotel and rest first?"

Dominic snorted. "A whole whopping hour in the air? No, I'm up for whatever you want to do."

———

FARID TOOK him to Granville Market, and they spent a few hours wandering the booths. Farid bought him ice cream—over Dominic's protests—and took a picture of him eating it. Dominic wrinkled his nose at him, but the ice cream was delicious, and the sun was warm, and Farid was laughing, his eyes crinkled, and Dominic was overwhelmed by the urge to kiss him.

And why not? They weren't in Seattle. No one knew who they were up here. He took a quick step forward, dodged a tourist, and wrapped an arm around Farid's waist.

Farid made a startled noise but melted against him, head tipping back to expose his throat as his eyes slipped shut. Dominic didn't bother trying to resist the temptation, pressing his mouth to the slender column as Farid sighed, a smile curving his lips and one arm going around Dominic's shoulders.

This is how it could be.

Dominic pushed that thought away. *He can't love you*, he reminded himself. *This will never happen.*

FARID TOOK him to Stanley Park next and they walked hand-in-hand along the seawall, looking over the bay. Dominic took a deep breath of the salt-and-seaweed scented air, feeling the tension draining from his shoulders.

"It's so pretty here," he said. The road curved along the seawall, a divide between the water and a forest that pushed right up against the tarmac. The sea was bright blue over the darker blue-gray of the water and a breeze ruffled Farid's hair.

Dominic pulled on Farid's hand and ducked in between the trees. Under the canopy of branches, it was dark and cool, a bird singing somewhere out of sight and fragmented rays of sunlight breaking through in faint streaks of light.

One fell across Farid's face as he tilted his head and smiled. "What's this?"

Dominic shrugged. "Felt like kissing you under the trees." He pulled Farid in, cupping his face in one hand and tipping his head so their mouths fit together, soft and warm and perfect. Farid hummed against his lips, arms wrapped around Dominic's neck as he went up on tiptoe to get a better angle.

"God," he said when they broke apart. "You should not be that good a kisser."

Dominic ducked his head, his cheeks heating. "Can we go back to the hotel and… practice some more?"

Farid laughed out loud. "Nice try, pet, but no."

"Dammit." Dominic allowed Farid to lead him out of the trees and back onto the path.

"Trust me, the wait will be worth it," Farid said, squeezing his hand.

Dominic cleared his throat. "What are we *doing* tonight?"

But Farid refused to elaborate, smiling cryptically and not answering no matter how much Dominic tried to pry details out of him.

"You'll enjoy it, I promise" was all he would say, and Dominic finally subsided.

After lunch, they toured the VanDusen Botanical Gardens and Farid bought Dominic a rose from a street vendor. Dominic tucked it into his lapel, unable to stop smiling.

"Want to rest?" Farid asked. "We still have a few hours before we're due at the Honeytrap and you'll need your strength."

Dominic perked up. "Any chance we can—"

"Nope," Farid said.

Dominic deflated. "You're so *mean*."

Farid laughed, the sound bright and happy.

THEY TOOK a helicopter ride over the city, the pilot pointing out sights through their headsets. By the time they were done, the sun was dipping over the horizon and the city's lights were blinking on by twos and threes and then in a wave that rolled across the skyline until it was lit up, twinkling in the early starlight. Dominic watched in awe as the pilot banked the helicopter and turned them toward the airport.

Beside him, Farid rubbed his knee. "Worth it?"

Dominic nodded, spellbound by the view. When he turned to Farid, he was struck dumb again, tracing Farid's features as they were backlit against the setting sun. The bold nose that would have been big and bony on anyone else, the sensitive lips that smiled so easily, and those almond eyes—God, those eyes. Dominic could get lost in them too easily, the serene, liquid depths that were so kind and expressive.

He turned away before he made a fool of himself, looking back out the window again.

BACK ON THE GROUND, Dominic shook his head when Farid suggested a taxi.

"Can we walk? It's a nice night."

They ambled along the sidewalk as cars zipped past, Dominic taking deep breaths of the cool evening air.

"Tell me about your family," he said abruptly.

Farid glanced sideways at him. "Really?"

"Why not? You know about mine."

"Not really," Farid said. "You've mentioned your dad, but only in passing and no real details. Do you have siblings? What's your relationship with your mom?"

Dominic narrowed his eyes. "You're not getting out of answering by asking *me* questions, and besides, I have your personal file, remember?"

Farid's smile flashed bright in the gathering gloom. "You first, then."

Dominic's sigh was theatrical and designed to make Farid laugh. It worked.

"Only child," Dominic said, taking Farid's hand as they walked. "I was actually—" He hesitated. "I grew up in a trailer park."

"Really?" Farid said.

"Yeah." Dominic hunched his shoulders. "We were on food stamps, SNAP or whatever it was called back then. My dad couldn't keep a job, and my mom worked her ass off but cleaning doctors' offices after-hours was never going to be enough to support us. As soon as I was old enough, I helped, but it was still—" The silence fell awkward and heavy between them. "Dad was an alcoholic, not that that excuses… anything. He hated noise. If I so much as lifted my voice to talk to my mom one room over, he'd start shouting. Having friends over was out of the question, not that I had many to begin with. My mom didn't do much to protect me, especially as I got older. As soon as I could, I moved out and didn't look back. When Spectral hit the big-time, I bought them a house and told them that was the last thing they were getting from me."

Farid squeezed his hand. "I have two siblings," he said after a minute. "Salma is my twin." He hesitated as if choosing his words. "My identical twin," he finally said.

Dominic just nodded. "I know."

Farid's laugh was slightly unnerved. "Of course you do."

"Has she transitioned?"

"Not yet," Farid said. He pulled his hand away,

wiping his sweaty palm against his pant leg. "There's just been so much, what with my mom, and Dad losing his job, and Nasim just graduated high school and says he doesn't want to go to college, and—"

"He *has* to go to college," Dominic interrupted. "He needs an education, and a good school that can give it to him, it'll open so many doors for him."

"I know," Farid said, sighing. He ran a hand over his hair. "Trust me, I know. But try telling the stubborn eighteen-year-old that."

"So your mom?" Dominic prompted gently.

"We don't know how much longer she has left," Farid said. The words hung in the air between them, bald and uncompromising.

"Are you two close?"

"Yeah," Farid whispered. "I'm the oldest. She relied on me when we were growing up. I kept the others together when she was having a bad day—this was before we knew what was wrong with her—and took care of her too. Made her eat. Helped her in and out of bed, stuff like that."

"What about your dad?"

Farid's laugh was sharp and brittle this time. "The only thing he can be relied on to do is misgender Salma, complain that we're costing him too much money even though *I* support us, and hole up in the den. He says he's looking for work—he got laid off from his job at the airport more than a year ago—but he never actually goes out for interviews or anything." His voice was tight, and Dominic took the hint.

"Tell me about Salma," he said.

"She's so smart," Farid said, lighting up. "I've never met anyone as smart as she is."

"Not even me?" Dominic said. He fought his grin.

Farid rolled his eyes. "You're smart, pet, but she could think circles around you."

"Wow," Dominic said. "So what you're saying is, I need to hire her."

Farid flashed a grin. "You can't afford her, baby."

That made Dominic laugh out loud, and Farid pulled them to a stop. "We're here," he said. "Time to go upstairs and change."

The hotel was small and quaint, lit with warm golden light from recessed alcoves. The entrance was a wide path carpeted in red, leading to a majordomo who waited behind a podium as Dominic and Farid climbed the steps.

"Good evening, sirs," he murmured with a shallow bow. "Your room is ready for you."

"Thank you, Carl," Farid said, and accepted the key that Carl held out. "We won't be here long, we'll be gone most of the evening. I'd like hot chocolate delivered to the room when we return, though."

"As sir wishes," Carl said, bowing again.

"There are only sixteen suites in this hotel," Farid said as they ventured farther into the building. "Privacy is of the utmost importance, and paparazzi are strictly forbidden from coming within a hundred yards of the premises."

"Is that legal?" Dominic asked, following him down a dimly lit hall with pictures of Nina Simone, Fats Domino, and Eartha Kitt gracing the walls.

"Don't know, don't care," Farid said over his shoulder. "This is us." He unlocked the door and stood aside for Dominic to enter.

The room was spacious and welcoming, tastefully decorated with more jazz legends—Dominic ran a finger along the frame of a picture of Billie Holiday, smiling. There was a jacuzzi in the corner of the room, up on a dais, and a king-sized bed right in front of him, with their bags neatly arranged on it.

"What should I wear? Something casual, right?" Dominic asked, reaching for his bag, but Farid got there first, pushing his hand away.

"I packed an outfit for you."

A tendril of unease wormed its way through Dominic's chest. "You what?"

Farid took his hands and stepped in close, until they were pressed together. "Do you trust me, pet?"

"Um." It was hard to think with Farid so warm and solid against him. "Maybe? Probably. I mean, I *do*, but—"

Farid's lips twitched, and he took a step away. "Well, here's the deal. You want this night to happen, you wear what I brought for you."

Dominic opened his mouth.

"*And* you agree without seeing it," Farid added.

Dominic snapped his mouth shut as horror crawled over his skin, leaving goosebumps behind. "You—that's—what if—"

"If you agree to this, I promise you the best night of your life so far," Farid said.

Dominic swallowed hard as lust and want and terror vied for supremacy in his chest.

"Trust me, pet," Farid said, his voice low and soft.

"I can't be recognized," Dominic managed.

"And you won't be." Farid bent to his suitcase and lifted out a length of sheer black fabric. "Look." He held it up to Dominic's head and then wrapped it around, covering his eyes and the tip of his nose.

Dominic blinked. He could still see, the gauzy fabric making his surroundings dark and blurred, Farid a familiar shape in front of him. He was holding something else up, and Dominic squinted, trying to see it as Farid settled it on his face.

A mask, Dominic realized as his belly surged with nerves. He felt the edges of it with his fingers, exploring it carefully. It was a half-mask, ending at his nose, with ribbons that tied behind his head.

Farid ran a thumb over Dominic's lips. "I might be using this mouth, but I promise, pet—no one will recognize you." He dropped his hand and stepped back, and it took Dominic a minute to realize he was waiting for something from him.

Dominic gulped. Did he trust Farid enough to do this? He was already half-hard in his pants at the thought of the night ahead of them, and somehow the mask only made it hotter. Finally he nodded jerkily.

Farid was there immediately, untying the mask and removing it and the fabric. His smile was radiant and he went up on tiptoe to kiss him as Dominic leaned into it.

"You're going to like this," he breathed against Dominic's mouth. "Strip."

When Dominic turned back to the bed, though, his heart stopped at what was laid out on it. "You're not—'Rid, tell me you're not going to make me wear that."

Farid cocked his head. "We can stop right now. Go back to Seattle. I won't be angry."

"I—" Dominic looked at the clothes on the bed. A sleeveless mesh shirt and a pair of bright blue shorts —*shorts*—that looked like Spandex and were no bigger than a postage stamp. He'd be exposed, laid bare for anyone who glanced in his direction. "I don't think I can," he said helplessly. *Help me*, he thought. *Help me do this.*

Farid studied him for a moment. "Put the shirt on, Dominic," he said, and the steel in his voice turned Dominic's knees to water.

He reached for the shirt and fumbled it over his head. He could feel himself sinking into the quiet space even as he found the armholes and got the shirt into place.

"Good," Farid said. "Now the shorts."

Dominic hesitated.

"*Now.*"

Dominic picked up the shorts with shaking hands. He missed the leg hole the first time and Farid steadied him with a hand on his arm as Dominic tried again.

The shorts were so tight they felt spray-painted on. *Everything* would be on display. Dominic could feel himself tensing again, breath coming short, and Farid's hand tightened on his arm.

"Easy, pet," he said. "You look so good. God, I could throw you on this bed and have you right now, fuck going out."

Part of Dominic wanted that, but the other part —*you promised.*

"I did," Farid said gently, and Dominic realized he'd spoken aloud. "I promised to take you out and give you this, and I will. Do you want the mask now?"

Dominic nodded. The odds of paparazzi being outside the hotel were slim, but he didn't want to risk it.

"Can we—back entrance?"

"I'd make a joke, but I think you're too nervous to appreciate it," Farid said. He scooped up the gauze and tied it around Dominic's head, making sure it was snug before reaching for the mask.

Dominic leaned into Farid's touch, wanting more, wanting his hands all over him, and Farid cupped his face briefly.

"Beautiful boy," he murmured. "I can't wait to show you off."

Dominic shivered.

"There's one more thing," Farid said. He bent to his suitcase and turned back with his palm flat out, a collar resting on it.

The air whooshed from the room, leaving Dominic in a vacuum, ears ringing so loudly he couldn't hear what Farid was saying. The collar was plain dark brown leather, about two inches wide, with a buckle closure. Dominic couldn't take his eyes off it.

Farid snapped his fingers, and Dominic jerked. Farid looked concerned but also amused. "I said, do you want this, pet?"

Dominic couldn't nod quickly enough. "Please, p-please, I—"

Farid reached up and buckled the collar in place. It fit snugly, feeling heavy and foreign. But the second it was on, the anxious buzzing in the back of Dominic's head stopped, leaving him feeling empty, raw, but somehow at peace.

Dominic took a shaky breath.

"All right?" Farid asked. "Tell me what you're thinking."

Dominic searched for the words. "I'm not—my mind… it's quiet."

Somehow Farid knew what he meant. "Your anxiety?"

Dominic nodded, feeling a smile tugging at his

mouth. "I'm not scared right now, Farid, I don't understand it but—"

Farid pulled him down into a hard kiss, lips and teeth and tongue, and Dominic sank into it with a moan.

He straightened when Farid let him go. "I'm still… freaked about tonight, of course."

"Of course," Farid said gravely.

"But I know you'll take care of me." Dominic touched the leather with two fingers, a solid reminder that he belonged to Farid, that he was safe and wanted.

Farid's voice was slightly unsteady. "I will, pet. Are you ready?"

Dominic nodded again.

18

———

THE CAB RIDE to the Honeytrap was a blur, mostly because Farid kept *touching* him, running a finger up and down Dominic's thighs, skating close to his groin, then up over his belly and across his chest.

Fire was kindling under Dominic's skin, following the path of Farid's touch, and he squirmed, feeling the leather shift against his throat.

"We're here," Farid said, handing cash to the driver. He had to nudge Dominic out of the vehicle, hands steady and firm.

On the sidewalk, Dominic wavered again, and Farid caught his arms, holding him still.

"There's going to be one difference about tonight," he said, and Dominic struggled to focus on him through the gauze. "There may be stuff that happens that you don't like, but maybe you don't want the play to stop. So we're going to use the traffic light system. If you're feeling good, want to keep going, like what's happening—you'll tell me green. If you're uncomfortable with a certain direction or person or activity, say yellow. And if you need to stop, I want to hear red."

"W-what about pomegranate?"

"Pomegranate will call off the entire thing," Farid said. His grip loosened, and he ran his hands up and down Dominic's bare arms. "But red means we'll stop what we're doing and reassess. Does that sound good?"

Dominic nodded.

"Recite the colors," Farid ordered.

"Green means good," Dominic said, fumbling for the words. "Yellow m-means slow down or stop to discuss, and r-red means stop immediately. Pome-granate shuts the scene down."

"Good, pet," Farid said, warm and approving, and Dominic leaned toward him, wanting to soak up that warmth, the quiet rising up and folding over him. "You're already halfway there, aren't you?"

Dominic made an agreeable noise, and Farid muttered something under his breath and tucked his hand into the crook of Dominic's arm.

At the door, Dominic balked briefly, tugging at his shorts as if somehow they would magically cover more of him.

"You're beautiful, pet," Farid said. "Let them see it. Let them envy me."

Dominic shuddered and straightened, and Farid opened the door.

There was a rush of cool air and golden light spilling from the opening as Farid guided him through. Inside, Dominic couldn't see much, but the music was a heavy, insistent thump in the back of his teeth. It smelled like peanuts and liquor and sweat. Farid kept his hand on Dominic's elbow and guided him between tables.

Even halfway to subspace, Dominic didn't miss the way conversation slowed or stopped as they passed, picking up again when they were by.

"Everyone's looking," Farid said in his ear. "I'm the luckiest son of a bitch in this place right now." Warm pleasure crawled up Dominic's throat, and Farid laughed quietly. "There's a step down here, careful."

The space they stepped into was more dimly lit, meaning Dominic could see even less, but it was also quieter, shielded somewhat from the heavy thudding music.

Farid maneuvered Dominic to a long, low couch and eased him onto it. "Stay here, I'll be right back."

Dominic tensed. Farid was leaving him alone?

"Right back," Farid repeated. "Color?"

"G-green," Dominic managed, lifting his chin.

Farid's hand touched his cheek briefly, and then he was gone, leaving Dominic by himself on the couch.

He sat quietly, his breathing loud in his own ears, and waited.

There were footsteps, and Dominic perked up. Was Farid back already?

But it wasn't Farid who sat down on the end of the couch, far enough away that they weren't touching.

"Hey there, gorgeous." The voice was deep and unfamiliar, and Dominic flinched. "Here all alone?"

You're an adult, Dominic told himself. *Handle this.* "My—" He faltered. "Um. Boyfriend… will be right back."

The man made a noise that sounded disappointed. "Are you here to play, beautiful?"

"Yes," Farid said, and Dominic sagged with relief, "but only with me." He sat down beside Dominic and pressed a drink into his hand.

"Is watching on the menu?" the man asked.

"Yes," Farid repeated, and Dominic shivered as he drained the martini glass. "As long as you keep your distance and respect his safewords."

"Of course," the man said, sounding insulted. "Is he new to this? He seems pretty tense."

"First time in public," Farid said, running a finger along Dominic's thigh. "He's not sure what he wants yet, so we're going to play it by ear. Spread your legs, sweetheart."

It took Dominic a minute to realize Farid meant him, and he gulped and sank down on the couch, letting his knees fall open.

Farid's hand was warm as he caressed Dominic's inner leg, sliding it up to his groin and slipping one finger under the hem of the shorts.

Dominic let his head fall back, staring up at the ceiling, as arousal surged in his blood. Was Farid going to jack him off right here, in front of a stranger? Farid palmed his erection through the fabric, and Dominic curled forward and moaned.

"Sensitive," the man remarked.

"You have no idea," Farid said. Dominic could hear the smile in his voice. "I've made him come with just my voice before."

The man groaned, and Dominic heard a zipper opening and fabric rustling. He was touching himself, Dominic realized.

Footsteps sounded on the stairs.

"Hey, Cane. Did you bring us a toy, 'Rid?" The newcomer's voice was light and careless, but Dominic stiffened. That was *his* nickname—

"I brought *my* toy, Fox," Farid said. "But you can watch, if you behave."

Fox. Dominic already disliked him. He tried to sit up, but Farid pushed him back into the cushions of the couch.

"Be still."

Dominic went limp, need zinging through him. He wanted Farid to touch him more, to get on top of him and hold him down as he took his pleasure. He made a noise in the back of his throat, wordlessly begging.

"Jesus fuck," Fox said, his voice hoarse suddenly. "Is he always so subby?"

Farid caressed Dominic's face. "In this headspace. Where's San?"

"Finishing up with a client."

Through the fabric, Dominic couldn't see details of Fox's face, just his shape as he sat down in the chair opposite them. He was slim and tall, almost Dominic's height but without his breadth. *I'm bigger*, he thought foggily, and turned his face into Farid's hand.

DOMINIC NUZZLED into Farid's palm as if looking for encouragement or comfort, and Farid couldn't help it —he bent and kissed him. Dominic sighed against his lips, opening willingly for him, and when Farid looked up, Sanyam was standing on the steps, one brow raised.

His cuffs were rolled up, shirt undone at the collar, almond eyes tired and black hair disheveled, and he was still one of the most beautiful men Farid had ever seen.

"Hello, Farid," he said. "I assume this is him?"

Farid nodded, putting a hand on Dominic's chest.

Cane was still on the other end of the couch, his eyes hungry. Farid had run into him a few times before at the club and never had a problem with him, but something possessive in his gut made him flatten his hand on Dominic's stomach and slide it under the waistband of his shorts. Dominic's hips bucked, and Cane grunted, palming his own cock.

Sanyam pulled Fox from his chair and sat down, then caught Fox's belt and tugged him down onto his lap. Fox slung an arm around Sanyam's neck and pressed his nose to his temple, but his eyes were still on Farid and Dominic.

Farid withdrew his hand, making Dominic moan in protest. "Knees, pet," he said, and Dominic nearly fell off the couch in his scramble to obey.

Sanyam's eyebrows rose, and he said something in a low tone to Fox, who tossed his head. Dominic clasped his hands behind his back, every line in his body tense. Like this, he faced away from Sanyam and Fox, presenting his profile to Cane, and he held very still, trembling.

"God, his mouth," Cane said, stroking himself faster. "I'll bet it feels so good."

"It does," Farid agreed.

"Wish I could try it," Cane rasped.

Dominic angled himself away from Cane, movement so subtle Farid almost missed it.

He frowned. "Color."

"Green," Dominic whispered, but his head was down, eyes averted.

Cane scooted a few inches closer, and Farid shot him a warning look. Turning back to Dominic, he tipped his head up, peering into his eyes through the flimsy fabric.

Dominic pulled his shoulders back, but he couldn't stop the tiny tremors running through his frame.

"Can I touch?" Cane husked.

Farid raised his eyebrows at Dominic. "Can he touch, pet?"

"Y-yellow," Dominic said, flinching away.

Cane immediately slid back to his original seat on the cushions. "Hey, no worries," he said, and Dominic's shoulders relaxed.

"You're doing so well," Farid told him. "Why don't you show our friends how you suck me?"

He'd been hard since the hotel, since commanding Dominic to put the clothes on and then buckling the collar in place, but he'd ignored it, focusing on Dominic's comfort. Now, though, lust swelled under his skin as Dominic reached for him, fingers clumsy but eager, and fumbled Farid's pants open.

This was good. This was right. Dominic on the floor between his knees, worshiping Farid's cock with hands and mouth as onlookers watched, hungry and envious.

Dominic's mouth was hot and wet, and Farid gasped as he was engulfed, Dominic dropping to the root until he gagged.

"Easy, easy," Farid said, catching a handful of Dominic's curls and pulling his head back. "It's not a race, pet."

Dominic twisted in Farid's grip, a whine falling from his mouth. "Please, I want—"

Farid let him go, and Dominic went back to it. It felt so good, *too* good, sparks gathering along his nerves, and Farid tilted his head to stare at the ceiling, holding off the orgasm through sheer will.

Dominic's hands were clasped behind his back

again, and Farid tapped his shoulder as an idea occurred to him.

"Touch yourself, pet."

Dominic jerked upright at that, red, wet mouth falling open. Farid raised an eyebrow.

"Take your cock out."

He expected Dominic to safeword, but Dominic seemed frozen in place, staring at him. Farid stroked himself slowly as he waited.

Finally, moving as if on autopilot, Dominic reached for his own waistband. His hard cock was clearly outlined against the straining spandex, and it fell free when Dominic pushed the shorts down around his thighs, heavy and leaking.

Cane made a guttural noise. "Jesus, he's gorgeous."

Dominic didn't seem to hear him, tilting his head to look up at Farid. There was hesitation in his movements, Farid realized. He didn't know what to do.

"Show me what you like," Farid ordered. He spared a glance for Sanyam, who had his hand inside Fox's pants, Fox's head thrown back against Sanyam's shoulder, but then Dominic reached for himself, and Farid forgot about everything else.

Dominic made an obscene noise as he slid his hand down his shaft, loose and almost tentative. Farid tightened his own grip as Dominic's head fell back, and he moaned, low and filthy.

"Like it—when you touch me better," Dominic gasped.

"Yeah? What do you like about me touching you, baby?"

"Everything, every—" Dominic's breath was coming short and sharp, his hand speeding up. "Feels so good, so—you touch me and my brain stops, all I can feel is you, I'm *safe*—" He hunched over and groaned. "Please, 'Rid, please can I—"

Farid glanced at Cane, who was leaning forward, mouth slightly open and face flushed red.

"Show him what he can't have, pet."

Dominic shot a glance at Cane, and then his head fell back and his spine arched as he came soundlessly over his fist.

Farid followed suit, catching it in his palm, as Dominic sprawled backward on the floor, chest heaving and limbs askew. Farid grabbed a tissue from the box on the table and cleaned himself up, then slid off the couch onto his knees next to Dominic's motionless body. He took a few minutes to clean him off with quick, gentle touches, and then pulled the shorts back into place. Finally he sat back on his heels and glanced at Sanyam.

"We need a private room."

Sanyam was silent for a minute, long enough that Farid looked back up. Fox was boneless against Sanyam's body, having evidently come as well, but Sanyam—his eyes were keen, and he was looking not at Dominic, but at Farid.

Dominic stirred.

"Room, San?" Farid said.

"Yes, of course." Sanyam maneuvered Fox off his lap as Cane stood up and shuffled out of the room. "You can use mine."

Somehow, Farid got Dominic to his feet, an arm around his waist and Dominic's draped across his shoulders. They wove a drunken path down the hall to Sanyam's private room, which he unlocked for them.

Farid steered Dominic for the couch and lowered him to the cushions, teeth gritted against the strain.

Dominic was nearly deadweight, barely conscious, but he reached for Farid's hand when he tried to straighten.

"Don't—please...."

"Take your time," Sanyam said, and closed the door, leaving them alone.

Farid crouched beside the couch, unfastening and removing the mask and then taking Dominic's hand in both of his. "How are you feeling, sweetheart?"

Somehow, Dominic summoned a smile. "Feel... good," he whispered.

"What do you need?"

"You," Dominic husked, eyes closing.

Farid felt the word like a hammer to his heart. *You.* He'd managed to put away the guilt for the weekend, pretend that nothing existed except him and Dominic, no agendas, no secrets, no deadlines, but now it all came rushing back.

He couldn't do it. He couldn't betray Dominic, not even for his family.

Farid bent forward and pressed his forehead to Dominic's as peace and a sense of fatality crept over him. When they got back to Seattle, he would call Peggy. She'd be angry. Maybe even try to bully or blackmail him into it. He was going to lose his job, his reputation, but Farid knew what he had to do. He had to protect Dominic, even if it meant *losing* Dominic.

"Scoot over," he said gently, and climbed onto the couch behind Dominic's limp form, gathering him up in his arms. "I'm here. You've got me."

Dominic snuffled a sigh against Farid's collarbone and fell asleep.

THey slept for about an hour until there was a quiet knock on the door. Farid disentangled himself gently and went to answer it.

Sanyam was standing there, two whiskeys in his hands. "Thought I'd see how you were doing." He held out a glass, and Farid took it gratefully.

"We're fine," he said once he'd drained it. "*He's* fine. Sleeping off the rest of the subspace. He'll probably drop tomorrow, but for now he's okay."

"Can we talk?" Sanyam asked.

Farid glanced at Dominic, still sound asleep, and stepped out into the hallway, pulling the door closed behind him. "What's up? How's Fox?"

"Fox is fine. Don't change the subject."

"What *is* the subject?" Farid asked, bewildered.

"You," Sanyam said quietly. His eyes were serious, troubled, and Farid fought a sudden surge of worry.

"What are you talking about?"

"You're in love with him."

Farid took a step back, feeling as though he'd been gut-punched. "I—what? *No.* I'm—San, you know I don't...."

"Baby," Sanyam said flatly, as if that explained everything, and Farid blinked at him. "You called him baby, while you were scening. In all the times we've played together, you've *never* done that, not even with that kid you dated for a while, what was his name—"

"Robert," Farid said numbly. "But I don't—I'm aro, remember? I don't fall in love."

"You never *have*," Sanyam corrected. "You know it's a spectrum. You told *me* it was a spectrum, remember? So why can't you be in the gray or demiromantic area yourself?"

Farid shook his head helplessly. "Even if I were,

San, I'm not a romantic *person*. I won't remember anniversaries or bring him flowers or make grand, stupid gestures for love, I—"

"You think that's what love is?" Sanyam interrupted. His eyes were angry now, as if Farid was deliberately misunderstanding him. "That's not love, Farid. That's infatuation. Love is taking care of each other. Love is wanting him safe and happy even when you're angry at him for doing something stupid. Love is putting the other person first. It's touching him and him knowing he's safe, because it's you. And you, Farid Qadir, you *fucking* idiot, you love that man in there, why can't you *see* that?"

Farid couldn't breathe. *Is this what an anxiety attack feels like?* And on the heels of that thought, another—*is this what Dominic deals with?* He bent double, struggling for air, as his vision dimmed and sparkles danced across it. "I can't, I can't, he deserves better—"

"He deserves *you*," Sanyam said. "He loves you too, anyone can see it. *Fox* saw it the second he walked in the room, and you know he's got the emotional intelligence of a mole rat."

Farid hiccupped a laugh, halfway to hysterical, and straightened. "It's true, he does. Are you sure he's okay? He looked pretty into it, back there."

"He was, and he is." Sanyam gripped Farid's shoulder. "Think about what I said, okay?"

Farid nodded dumbly. "San, I—"

"What?"

"I fucked up," Farid whispered.

"What'd you do, Farid?"

But Farid shook his head. He couldn't make the words come, couldn't explain how deeply and irretrievably he'd made things wrong, couldn't bear to see the judgment in Sanyam's eyes. "I have to get back to him. I don't want him to wake up with me gone." He fumbled for the doorknob and slipped back inside the room as Dominic stirred.

"'Rid?"

"Hey," Farid said, and helpless affection welled within him at the way Dominic's hair stood on end, his eyes sleepy and creases in his cheek. *Oh God, I am so truly fucked.*

19

———————

DOMINIC WOKE the next morning to Farid's mouth on his cock. He arched up into it and tangled his fingers in Farid's hair with a moan. He felt good, warm and relaxed and wrung out from the previous evening, although part of him was disappointed that he didn't remember more of the first night he and Farid had ever spent together.

Farid hummed, stroking Dominic's inner thigh and pressing a thumb just under his balls, and Dominic came groaning. When he collapsed back onto the bed, he tried to apologize, tongue thick and clumsy, but Farid crawled up his body and straddled him, kissing him to shut him up. Dominic could taste the bite of his own come in Farid's mouth, and it made him shiver and pull him closer, delving deeper inside.

"Good morning," Farid murmured, smiling against Dominic's lips.

"Your turn?" Dominic said, sliding a hand down Farid's ribs.

But Farid shook his head, dropped another kiss on

Dominic's mouth, and rolled off. "We need to get going. Fox and San are meeting us at the airport for breakfast before our flight."

Dominic propped himself up on his elbows. "Fox and—oh God. They saw me *naked*, 'Rid!"

Farid shot a grin at him over his shoulder as he picked a shirt up off the floor. "And now they'll see you dressed and civilized."

Dominic fell backward, covering his burning face. The mattress dipped as Farid sat next to him.

"Hey," he said, resting a hand on Dominic's stomach. "I can call them and cancel, if it bothers you that much."

Dominic shook his head and dropped his hands. Farid's eyes were concerned, the amusement gone.

"No, they're your friends," Dominic said. "I just —" He swallowed hard. "It's one thing, to… play. It's another to—"

"I know," Farid said, running a thumb over Dominic's ab. "I trust them with my life, if it helps. Neither one would ever breathe a word of our visit. Fox is an asshole, but I promise you can trust him."

"Okay." Dominic blew out a breath and sat up. "Okay. Shower?"

"I took one while you were asleep," Farid said, smiling at him. "Hop in while I get the bags packed."

Something about Farid was different, Dominic thought as he showered. Something in his eyes, a lightening of the shadows that always seemed to live there, but there was still tension in his shoulders. Dominic put his face under the water, eyes closed. Maybe he could figure it out on the plane.

Sanyam and Fox were waiting by the entrance to the airport when the taxi pulled up. Farid stepped out and hugged Sanyam as Dominic followed him from the car. As soon as Sanyam released him, Fox caught Farid's face in both hands and planted a kiss on his mouth.

Dominic stiffened.

Sanyam sighed.

Farid pulled away and pushed Fox a step back. "How have your manners gotten *worse?*"

Fox was grinning. Now that Dominic could see him in the daylight, he had to reluctantly admit that he was attractive, with olive-green eyes, a long, delicate throat, and dark hair that fell over a widow's peak.

Farid turned to Dominic. "Dom, I'd like you to meet Sanyam Desai, one of my best friends. San, Dominic Spector."

Dominic accepted the hand Sanyam held out. Sanyam was handsome, dark eyes kind and honest, with a short beard and curls brushed neatly in place.

"We didn't get a chance to talk last night," Sanyam said. "It's very nice to meet you properly, Dominic. I've heard a lot about you from Farid. Shall we go inside?"

"What, I don't get an introduction?" Fox interjected.

Sanyam shot him a look. "Maybe when you can behave like a person."

Fox scowled and turned to Dominic, one hand out and a broad smile replacing the frown. "Sterling Reynard. Everyone calls me Fox."

Dominic looked him up and down slowly, until Fox's smile faltered. Then he accepted the hand. "Dominic. Wish I could say it was nice to meet you,

Sterling, but I'm not crazy about people who kiss my boyfriend in front of me."

Farid's mouth fell open, and Sanyam's eyebrows went up.

Fox *laughed,* the bastard, head back and shoulders shaking. When he finally sobered, all three men were glaring at him, which sent him off into another round of giggles.

"Sorry," he gasped, wiping his eyes. "Just—oh my God, your *faces.* C'mon, Dom, I had to make sure you were gonna do right by my boy, didn't I?" He slung an arm around Dominic's shoulders and steered them toward the entrance.

Dominic went reluctantly, glancing back at Farid, who looked baffled and exasperated. "And the only way you could do that was by kissing him?"

"Worked, didn't it?" Fox shrugged. He pointed at a table for the nearest café, and Dominic reluctantly took a seat. Fox immediately flopped into the chair beside him, and Dominic grimaced as Farid and Sanyam joined them.

Dominic scanned the menu, trying to ignore Fox, who was saying something sotto voce to Farid across the table.

Orders placed and coffee brought out, Fox leaned back in his chair and looked Dominic up and down.

"Gotta say, you're not 'Rid's usual type."

"What type is that?" Dominic asked, curious in spite of himself, as Farid stiffened and alarm flashed across his face.

Fox lifted one elegant shoulder, toying with a spoon. "He likes a little more experience, usually. No offense, but you're pretty new to this whole thing." His grin flashed. "And he likes brats."

"Oh, *that's* why he likes you," Dominic said before he could stop himself.

Sanyam stifled a snort, and Farid laughed out loud.

"Yep," Fox said, preening. "I make him work for it." He glanced at Sanyam, and his eyes softened. "I make San work for it more, though."

Sanyam touched his hand, something unspoken passing between them.

Dominic glanced at Farid, who was watching him closely, eyes worried. Dominic shook his head minutely. *I'm okay.* And he was, he realized, somewhat surprised. Fox wasn't really after Farid—he even seemed to care about him, in his own way. Well, so did Dominic.

I love him. I love him even though he can't love me back, and it's okay, it's enough to know I love him. Dominic opened and closed his mouth, and Farid frowned.

"Will you excuse us for a minute?" he said, and stood, holding out a hand to Dominic. He led him out of the café and around the corner to a deserted hallway. "What is it?" he said, voice low and worried.

Dominic shook his head again. He couldn't tell him. It would put an immeasurable burden on Farid's shoulders. He'd feel guilty for not feeling the same way, and that would maybe even push them apart, when the guilt and resentment became too much to bear.

"*Talk* to me," Farid said, gripping Dominic's shoulders. "Are you dropping, pet? What's going on?"

"I'm fine," Dominic managed. Farid looked so *worried*, and it hurt Dominic to his core. "I am," he insisted. He touched Farid's face, smoothing out the wrinkle between his brows. "Fox has me off-balance, that's all it is. Do you—should I make you work for it more?"

Farid shook his head immediately. "*No*. God, I could smack Fox." He sighed. "It's true that in the past I've been… drawn to more, uh… challenging subs. And he's not wrong, you're not my usual type. But—" He glanced up, emotion raw on his face. "I've never had a sub like you, Dom. The way you submit for me —I told San once it was like poetry. It's the most beautiful thing I've ever seen."

Dominic swallowed hard against the lump in his throat.

"And Fox…. You know there's nothing… there, right?" Farid said. "He's very much in love with San, but he feels protective of me. He wants to make sure that you're—" He shrugged. "Worthy of me, I guess? It sounds stupid."

"It's not," Dominic said, leaning down to kiss him. "Your friends love you and look out for you. That's good. It's important."

Farid tugged lightly on one of Dominic's curls. "You didn't brush your hair after you showered."

"Forgot the brush," Dominic said, and turned his face to plant a kiss on Farid's wrist. "Besides, I like it better when you do it."

Farid's breath stuttered. "God, pet…. Hold still." He combed through Dominic's hair until it was tangle-free and curling softly behind his ears. "We should go back."

"Okay," Dominic agreed, and followed him back to the table.

"So how did you and Sanyam meet?" he asked Fox.

"I came to the bar one night, he fell madly in love with me and swept me off my feet," Fox said blithely, and took a sip of coffee.

Sanyam laughed outright at that. "Slightly more to the story than that, but yes, he was a patron and then a client of mine."

"And what do you do?" Dominic asked.

"He's a mosaicist," Farid said. "And he's really good. I'll show you some of his pieces when we get back to Seattle."

Fox squirmed in his seat, looking uncomfortable for the first time. "'S'not a big deal."

"He doesn't like it when we praise him," Sanyam said, voice warm and amused. "He has a show coming up, Dominic, perhaps you'd like to come up with Farid to see it?"

"I'd love to," Dominic said, surprised to realize it was true. He grinned at Farid, suddenly mischievous. "Maybe we can go back to the Honeytrap too."

Farid matched his smile.

Dominic glanced at Sanyam, who was looking at Farid, just as Farid glanced up and caught Sanyam's eye. Sanyam lifted an eyebrow. Farid, impossibly, *blushed*, looking away and suddenly finding his coffee cup fascinating.

What the hell was that about? Dominic set the puzzle aside to be worked at later and dug into his omelet.

Fox and Sanyam went with them as far as they could

and then waved goodbye, arms around each other's waists.

"You were right," Dominic said on the plane. "Fox is *awful*, but they're good people."

"He'll settle down now that he knows you," Farid said comfortingly. "Are you ready for the party tonight?"

"Fuck, that's *tonight*?" Dominic groaned, letting his head fall back against the seat. "Kill me."

"You'll be okay," Farid said. "I'll be there, and I'll run interference for you."

"Yeah, but I'll still have to talk to investors and press and be *charming* and this is my worst nightmare, why did I agree to do this?"

"Because the board would have pushed for more if you hadn't," Farid reminded him.

Dominic just groaned again.

———

WHEN THE PLANE LANDED, Farid hailed two taxis and put Dominic's bag in the first.

"Wait, you're not coming with me?"

Farid looked startled. "I have to go home, unpack, get cleaned up, and check in on my family, pet. I'll see you at the shareholder meeting."

"Right, of course." Dominic studied the ground, feeling like an idiot, and Farid stepped in closer, so they were almost touching.

"Hey."

Dominic looked up, and Farid smiled at him.

"It really is going to be okay, I promise. I would kiss you right now, but that guy has a camera and he's looking at us like he thinks he recognizes you." His voice heated, sending a thrill down Dominic's spine. "After the meeting tonight, you can take me home and fuck me over the couch, how's that?" Dominic bit back a groan and took a step away as Farid grinned with triumph. "See you tonight, pet."

Farid had his phone out before his taxi left the airport. The first thing he did was log into his mobile banking app. A few taps later, he closed it out and placed a call.

Peggy answered on the first ring. "You're ahead of schedule, Mr. Qadir. Can I assume you have good news for me?"

"No." Farid took a deep, centering breath. "I'm not doing it."

There was a beat of silence.

"I'm sorry?"

"You heard me," Farid said. "Find another lapdog to do your bidding. I won't betray Dominic."

"You took our money," Peggy said, her voice glacial. "We have records. You think every conversation we had wasn't recorded? You *will* do what we want, or I will hand Dominic your head on a plate *myself*."

"If you recorded them, I hope you're recording this too," Farid said, fury welling up and adrenaline crackling through him. "I'm in love with Dominic Spector, but even if I *wasn't*, I wouldn't do this. I never should have said yes in the first place. Dominic deserves better than this. I returned your money. It's over."

He hung up, hands trembling. The phone rang again immediately, and Farid silenced it.

Breathe. He leaned forward, putting his head between his knees and lacing his fingers over the nape of his neck. *Breathe, breathe, you did it, Dominic is safe.*

Peggy wouldn't let him go that easily, Farid knew. He'd just have to hope and pray that when it came down to it, Dominic would trust him.

20

———

Salma was in with their mother, sitting on the bed while they talked. Farid put his head in the door and Salma scrambled to her feet to hug him. Farid closed his eyes as she wrapped her arms around his neck. *I'm sorry, I'm so sorry, you'll have to wait a while longer.*

"How was your trip?"

"Fine," Farid said, managing to smile at her. "I have to get ready for the shareholder meeting tonight. Mama, how are you?"

His mother's eyes were sharp, but her skin was an ashy pale that Farid didn't like. She held out her hand, and Farid took it, swallowing another surge of guilt. He should have enough to retain the nurse for the rest of the month, but after that…. He bent and pressed his forehead to her hand.

"What is it, dear one?" his mother asked.

Tears prickled Farid's eyes but he shook his head. "It's nothing. I'm tired, all that traveling. I need to go shave and dress."

They both watched him, their eyes troubled, but Farid mustered a smile and escaped to his room.

In the bathroom, he stared at himself in the mirror. There were dark circles under his eyes and he looked… haunted. *Failing them, failing them, failing them. You love Dominic more than your own family, and now they'll suffer because of you. Stupid, selfish—*

Farid spun away from the mirror, going to his knees on the hard tile. "I'm sorry," he whispered, the tears welling up again. He didn't know who he was apologizing to. It didn't matter. "*I'm so sorry.*"

HIS KNEES HAD GONE numb before he was able to drag himself off the floor and get out his shaving kit. He avoided his eyes in the mirror as he shaved in mechanical motions, careful not to nick his skin. Everything had to be perfect for Dominic tonight, and that included him.

He dressed quickly, one eye on the time, and hesitated over which tie to wear. Finally he chose the dark gray shot with silver, and resolutely didn't think about how it was the color of Dominic's eyes.

Finally ready, he headed back upstairs, where Kevin was pulling a suitcase down the hall as Salma tried to talk to him.

"I'm sorry, Ms. Qadir," Kevin told her. "I *have* to go. I was told I no longer work here."

Farid jumped in front of him, hands out. "Wait, *wait*. Just… wait a second. What happened?"

"I got a call that my employment at this location had been terminated and I was needed across town,"

Kevin said. He looked bewildered, and Farid's chest ached.

"Look, Kevin. If I pay you double what you were making, will you stay until the end of the month?"

Kevin hesitated.

"*Please*," Salma said from behind him.

"Just two more weeks," Farid said. "Please, it would… be so helpful."

Kevin chewed his lip but finally nodded. "For double my rate."

"Thank you," Farid said, resisting the urge to hug him. "Seriously, thank you so much."

Kevin turned to take his bag back down the hall, and Salma looked at Farid.

"What's going on?"

"Nothing," Farid said, stiffening. "I have to go."

"Goddammit, Farid, you can't just run away from important conversations!"

"Gonna be late," Farid called over his shoulder. "Bye!"

HIS KNEE BOUNCED NERVOUSLY the whole way to the office, and he had a feeling he over-tipped the cab driver, but couldn't stop to check. People were already filing into the building. Farid recognized Harvey, Olivia, and Ryan, all of whom waved at him. Farid joined them, complimenting Olivia on her jewel-green gown.

"Have you seen Dominic yet?"

Harvey shook his head. "He's probably up in his office—he usually gets here early and hides out in there until Cory drags him down to the party."

Farid managed a grin. "I guess that's my cue, then."

He rode the elevator up to the top, but Dominic wasn't in his office. Frowning, Farid checked the break room and the R&D lab. Both were dark and still.

He took the elevator back down to the third floor, where the meeting was being held. As he waited, he went over possible scenarios in his mind. He'd hoped to find Dominic alone before the festivities, so he could tell him face-to-face then, but if he was already mingling with people, Farid was going to have to figure out how to get him alone.

The doors slid open, and Farid straightened his vest and stepped out into the crowd. A waiter offered him a flute of champagne, and Farid took it with a nod, searching the guests for Dominic's figure.

"'Rid!" That was unmistakably Dominic's voice, and Farid tensed, even as his traitorous body turned in Dominic's direction. "Over here, there's someone I want you to meet."

Farid made his way around people, murmuring apologies, and fetched up next to Dominic, who looked breathtakingly good in a perfectly fitted suit, with pants that hugged his long legs and a jacket open in front to reveal a mulberry-colored vest.

"You okay?" Dominic asked, sounding concerned, and Farid forced himself to attention.

"Fine," he said, summoning a smile.

"This is Peggy Jones," Dominic began, and a dull buzz began in Farid's ears, drowning out the rest of his sentence.

Peggy's eyes were glittering chips of ice, a malevolent smile curving her lips. "We've met," she said, and her voice was arctic, freezing Farid's blood in his veins.

"Dom, I need to speak to you *right now*," Farid said urgently.

"What is it?" Dominic said, clearly bewildered.

"*Now.*"

Peggy sipped her champagne, looking supremely unbothered. "I wouldn't worry, Mr. Qadir," she said. "As I was just telling Mr. Spector, we've suspected a mole in your company for some time now."

Farid managed to look up at Dominic, who looked furious and miserable. But not… heartbroken. Not yet. Farid turned back to Peggy.

"What are you talking about?"

"As Dominic's closest competitor in the facial recognition technology field, we felt duty-bound to let him know when we finally learned the identity of the infiltrator." Peggy took another sip of champagne, and Farid wanted to knock the glass from her hands, scream, and demand answers, but all he could do was stand in place, trembling, waiting for the ax to fall.

"Dom," he whispered.

Peggy sighed, the picture of sorrow. "I'm sorry to be the one to tell you that Farid came to us offering information about your company months ago."

Farid closed his eyes.

Dominic laughed.

Farid opened his eyes. Dominic looked *amused*, as if Peggy had told a hilarious joke.

"Pull the other one," he said. "Farid wouldn't do that."

"Wouldn't he?" Peggy murmured. "And yet I have recordings of us discussing what he would steal from you and what he wanted from us. Obviously I was never going to go through with it—I just wanted enough information to take him down, make sure he wouldn't be a threat to you or anyone else ever again."

"I didn't go to you," Farid flung at her. "*You* came to *me*. And I told you I wouldn't do it. Remember?"

Dominic blinked. Opened his mouth. Closed it again. Shook his head.

"No," he said.

"I'm sorry," Farid whispered, willing him to believe him.

"No," Dominic repeated. "*No*. It can't—what are you doing, 'Rid? Why are you doing this? Why would you say that?"

"Because it's all, sadly, true," Peggy said. She sounded sympathetic, and Farid wanted to strangle her. He reached for Dominic's arm instead, and something in his chest splintered when Dominic jerked away. "I have receipts of the money we deposited in Mr. Qadir's account, recordings of his verbal agreement on several different occasions, and plenty more evidence that he was indeed your spy, Mr. Spector. I'm very sorry to have to tell you like this."

"Do you have the recording of me saying I wouldn't do it?" Farid flung at her, and Dominic flinched like he'd been hit.

"You—" He shook his head as if clearing water from his ears. "But you—" He doubled over, hands on his knees, and Farid felt the first tear slide down his cheek, hot and stinging.

"I told them," he managed, voice cracking. "Dom, I told them today I couldn't go through with it, I said I wouldn't betray you, I *couldn't*—"

"But you were planning to this entire time," Dominic interrupted, straightening. There were tears on his cheeks too, and he wiped them away with the back of his hand, focused on Farid. "This whole time. While we—everything we did, everything we were to each other, and you were planning on stabbing me in the back."

Peggy made a sympathetic noise. "You were lovers? Oh dear, that just makes it so much worse."

"*Shut up!*" Farid shouted at her, and swung back to Dominic. If he could just make him *understand*—but Dominic was shaking his head and backing away.

"Get out," he rasped. "Get the *fuck* out and never come back." He turned and bolted as the spellbound crowd parted for him, leaving Farid standing alone on the polished wood floor, his heart a yawning pit in his chest.

Peggy set her champagne flute down. "Well, I must be going." She stepped around Farid's stone corpse and walked briskly toward the elevators.

Ryan worked his way through the milling crowd and ended up beside Farid.

"You need to go," he said, his voice pitched low.

Farid nodded dumbly. He stumbled for the stairs, and halfway down them his knees gave out. He sank to the concrete step, praying no one was following him, and rocked back and forth.

He'd ruined everything. Lost his job, his sister's best chance at transitioning, his mother's care, and his lover. Farid sobbed, covering his eyes, but he couldn't erase the betrayed look on Dominic's face as he'd pulled away and ran for the door.

It was a very long time before he was able to push himself back to his feet and stagger the rest of the way down the stairs.

21

"Welcome to the Schloss Hotel, Mr. Spector," the maître d' said, bowing shallowly. "Your room is ready for you."

Dominic nodded absently, rubbing a hand over his now closely-shorn head. It had become a habit in the last two weeks, one he couldn't seem to break. He pulled his hand away and followed the bellhop down a lushly appointed hallway and into an elevator.

"You have the North Room on the third floor," the bellhop told him in a thick Swiss accent as the car rose. "It has a lovely view of the lake. Anything you need, we are here to provide."

Dominic didn't say anything. He was numb, jetlagged, and exhausted, and all he wanted was to fall into bed and sleep for a year.

Cory had taken over everything when he showed up at her doorstep and broke down in her arms. She'd moved him into her guest bedroom and over two short weeks, made quick work of cleaning up the mess he'd left behind.

The first thing she'd discovered was that Peggy had been working without Lila Rathbone's knowledge, namely by storming into Lila's office and demanding to know what was going on. Lila had been stunned by Peggy's betrayal, and Cory had offered her two options —let Cory tell the world what Peggy had almost pulled off, or fire Peggy and allow her company to be merged with Spectral. Lila agreed to the second one, becoming CTO of the newly blended companies, and Cory had gone to the board of directors next.

The bellhop opened the door and ushered Dominic into the room, mahogany floors gleaming and the white quilt on the bed looking very inviting. Dominic pressed way too much money into his hand and nearly closed the door in his face.

He just got his shoes off before dropping onto the bed.

The board had been furious, of course. They'd almost ended up with egg on their faces, after all. But Cory brought them around just like she always did, pointing out that Spectral was twice the size now, the offending parties gone, and they had, in fact, come out on top.

Dominic shoved his face into the pillow and as always, his thoughts went to Farid. He hadn't pressed charges, even though Cory had wanted to. After all, he really *hadn't* done anything prosecutable. Accepted some money that he'd then given back? He hadn't given Wraith or Phantom to Peggy, hadn't actually done anything except lie to Dominic with every word, every touch, every *kiss* for three months.

He was crying again, Dominic realized in dim disgust, and he rolled onto his side and curled up in a ball, pulling a pillow to his chest.

He wanted it to stop hurting every time he saw dark eyes and a slim build. He wanted to go to sleep and wake up without dreaming about Farid's hands on him, soothing him out of a panic attack, talking to him, *listening* to him. He wanted it all to go away.

Cory had wanted to kill Farid, of course. She'd been incoherent with rage by the time Dominic managed to get the story out, in hiccupping fits and starts. But Dominic flatly refused to let her contact him for any reason.

"*He's out of my life,*" he told her. "*Just leave it alone.*" And then he'd gone home, pulled the covers over his head, and sobbed like a baby.

Dominic wiped a tear away with his thumb. In the end, he couldn't bear being around familiar faces, especially when they were full of love and pity and worry about his mental health. So he'd gone to Switzerland as Cory stepped temporarily into his position as CEO of Spectral. She'd promised to call him every day with news, and Dominic had gotten on a plane and literally run away from his problems.

He was going to hike in the mountains, ride the ski lift to the top of the nearest peak, even though it wasn't skiing season, take day-trips to every town and city worth visiting within range of his chalet, and sit by the lake.

What he *wasn't* going to do was waste another second of his time on the man who'd betrayed him.

Dominic closed his eyes and fell asleep.

HE MET Trick in the third week of his stay, by glancing over just in time to see him ogling the ass of the waiter who'd just served him in the small hotel restaurant.

Dominic raised an eyebrow and the man blushed, ducked his head, and grinned.

"Sorry," he offered. "I wasn't going to hit on him, if it helps? I just have an appreciation for fine art."

Dominic couldn't help the snort. "Well… you're not wrong."

Seemingly encouraged, the man stood up and joined him at his table.

"Do you mind? I hate eating alone."

"Uh—sure," Dominic said. He held out a hand. "Dominic Spector."

"Trick Monroe."

"Trick?"

Trick was a big man, taller than Dominic with muscles to match, light blue eyes, and fair hair that curled behind his ears. He grinned.

"Patrick, but I hate that name. And come on…. Pat sounds like someone's mother-in-law, and Rick is my dad's forty-year-old neighbor who has a barbeque every Saturday and wears dad sandals."

Dominic laughed out loud. "You make a compelling argument, but I hope you realize I'm going to make Cheap Trick jokes."

Trick's smile widened. "I *knew* I liked you. What are you doing in Switzerland, Dominic?"

"Vacation," Dominic said evasively, sipping his wine. "Needed a break. You?"

"Actually I'm studying the competition," Trick said. "My father's in hotels. I serve as his frontman for gathering intel on rival corporations and ways we can incorporate better service and hospitality to our guests." He spread his hands. "Free vacations for me pretty much year-round, so you won't hear me complaining. What are you doing tomorrow?"

"Not much," Dominic said. "Thought I'd read a book by the lake."

"Wanna come with me to Zurich?"

Dominic considered him. Trick's eyes gleamed in the dim light, his smile wide and uncomplicated. "Sure," Dominic heard himself saying.

"*Excellent*," Trick said, satisfied.

———

DOMINIC LIKED TRICK, he found. Trick was loud; he was messy; he laughed with his whole body and didn't care who heard him. He had a zest for life that Dominic envied, and he made everything he did look and feel easy, like life was uncomplicated, straight-forward.

They fell into a pattern within the first few days of knowing each other. Dominic, a habitual early-riser, would go down and get breakfast and bring it back up to Trick's room, where Trick would be sound asleep, his face buried in a dozen pillows.

It took him awhile to get going in the mornings, and Dominic learned quickly to bring him high-octane coffee to jumpstart the process. Trick would moan and paw at the cup Dominic held out, eyes still squeezed shut, and upend the contents into his mouth. He didn't care about taste, Dominic discovered early on—it was all about getting the caffeine into his system.

The best part about Trick was how completely different he was from Farid. Trick was never quiet, although he didn't expect Dominic to engage in his running commentary on anything and everything he deemed interesting—which was most things. He left his clothes everywhere and at least three times, Dominic had found him wearing mismatched shoes because he got dressed in the dark. He was rude and funny and outgoing, and Dominic was drawn to his light, finding comfort in Trick's careless warmth.

"You ever gonna tell me about your tragic past?" Trick asked lazily one night, two weeks after they met. He was on his bed, flat on his back with his head hanging off the edge so he could look at Dominic upside down across the room.

Dominic stiffened and put his book down.

Trick raised his eyebrows, which looked ridiculous from upside down.

"You're an idiot," Dominic said, but the words held no bite.

Trick grinned and flipped over onto his stomach to rest his chin on his fists. "C'mon, spill the juicy details. I need to practice my 'sincere and sympathetic' expression."

"Fuck you," Dominic said, laughing in spite of himself. He rubbed his head.

"You do that when you're nervous or upset," Trick observed.

"Don't psychoanalyze me," Dominic shot back. He sighed. "I run a fairly big software development firm in Seattle."

"Ooh, a genuine nerd! Do you keep a slide rule in your pocket?"

Dominic flipped him off, and Trick laughed.

Something loosened in Dominic's chest. "My assistant went on maternity leave a while back, and she hired someone to fill in. He was…." He hesitated. "Good. He was really good. He kept people off my back and let me do my work and somehow managed to keep my anxiety in check."

"And you fell for him." Trick's eyes were keen, but there was no pity in them.

That made it easier for Dominic to nod. "He was… gentle. When I needed him to be. And… not, other times."

Trick's eyebrows climbed. "Got a secret kinky side, do you?"

"Shut up, I'm telling a story."

Trick grinned but pretended to zip his mouth shut.

Dominic rubbed his head again, then pulled his hand away and glowered at it. "He confessed to taking money from my closest competitors on the market to steal information for them."

"Oh *shit*." Trick sat up fast. "Shit, Dom, what happened?"

Dominic shrugged helplessly. "I fired him. He hadn't managed to get hold of the data yet, so there really wasn't anything else I could do."

"Mother*fucker*," Trick breathed. "What a cock-sucking asshole. Did you punch him?"

"No!" Dominic said, startled. "I wouldn't—why would I punch him?"

"I'd have punched him," Trick said flatly. "Leading you along like that, making you think it was real, and then stabbing you in the back? Fuck yeah, I'd have decked him in a heartbeat."

Dominic shook his head. "He didn't—it wasn't like that."

"So why'd he do it?"

"I don't know," Dominic admitted. "His mom's sick, but I offer a really good insurance plan even for new employees, so she was covered as soon as he was hired."

"Greed, then? Or something else?"

"Not greed," Dominic said slowly. "He's…. Farid's not greedy."

"So he must have had a reason, then."

"*Stop*," Dominic snapped. Unease clawed at his guts. "It doesn't *matter*, okay? He took their money, he was planning to betray me, he *confessed* to betraying me, end of discussion!"

"Okay, but—"

"No," Dominic said, standing. "I'm done talking about it. I'll see you tomorrow."

"Got a better idea," Trick said. He let his legs splay wide against the bed as Dominic looked at him, and raised a lazy eyebrow. "We can fuck the bad feelings away."

Dominic spluttered. "You—*no*, we're not—you're *awful*, God."

Trick grinned at him and palmed his crotch. "You say that, but you're still here. C'mon, what's the harm? Have some fun? You know I think you're hot."

"You—what? You think I'm hot?"

Trick rolled his eyes and hopped off the bed, closing the distance between them as Dominic stood frozen in place and tried to figure out what to do.

"You've got cheekbones for days, man," Trick said, drawing a finger along one. "And this jaw could cut steel. Plus those pretty gray eyes? Please. I wanted you the second I saw you. I was only checking out the waiter to get you to notice me."

Trick's finger was warm as it trailed down Dominic's cheek, and the amusement in his eyes had fled, replaced by heat and invitation.

Dominic swallowed hard.

"If you don't feel the same…." Trick withdrew but Dominic grabbed his wrist.

"It's not that. I mean—I like you. I *do*. And you're hot as fuck."

"Yeah?" Trick smiled.

"Don't fish, it looks desperate," Dominic told him. "I just… I don't usually do… this."

"Friends with benefits, you mean?"

"Is that what you're proposing?"

Trick nodded. "I like you, man, but the truth is, I think we'd kill each other if we had to spend a month together. You're too quiet, and I'm too loud." He grinned. "That doesn't mean I can't think about the kind of noises you might make in bed, though."

Heat shot through Dominic's belly, and he considered. He didn't feel about Trick the way he had about Farid, but wasn't that the whole point? If he wanted to bury Farid's memories properly, so they wouldn't hurt him, maybe what he needed was Farid's polar opposite to help replace those memories.

He leaned forward to plant a kiss on Trick's mouth. His lips were warm, and they parted as Dominic took a step closer, flattening a hand on Trick's broad chest.

I can do this, he told himself. "Go slow?" he whispered.

Trick looked dazed, but he nodded, bringing a hand up to Dominic's waistband and unbuttoning his pants. "Slow. Sure. I can do slow."

Dominic kept the nervous giggle locked behind his

teeth as Trick pushed his pants and underwear down, then pulled his shirt off. Dominic stood naked, half-hard with nerves and anticipation, and Trick took a step back.

"Now *this* is art," he said, sighing in appreciation, and stripped his own clothes off in efficient movements. Then he gently pushed Dominic onto the edge of the bed. "Sit still. I've been wanting to get my mouth on your cock for a while."

Dominic stayed motionless, hands locked in his lap, as Trick rummaged for condoms in the drawer. He came up with one and made a triumphant noise.

"I'll do it," Dominic said, taking it from him. He still wasn't fully hard, but he managed to get it rolled on with shaking hands as Trick went to his knees in front of him and nuzzled along his inner thigh, his breath hot on the sensitive skin, and oh—oh yeah, that was nice, Trick's lips closing hot over the head of his cock and sucking him into his mouth, beginning to bob with experienced rhythm.

He pulled off briefly to say, "You can pull my hair, I like that," before going right back to it, and Dominic tangled one hesitant hand in Trick's fair hair. He made a fist and pulled tentatively, and Trick stiffened and moaned around Dominic's dick.

Guess he does *like that*. Dominic pulled again and closed his eyes.

Farid had pulled his hair a few times. Mostly when he was trying to get a point across. Dominic had liked it more than he'd thought possible, the way Farid's hand would catch in his curls and pull his head to one side, grip uncompromising and eyes hard.

Dominic hunched over and came, the orgasm

unrelenting but somehow unsatisfying as he filled the condom.

Trick pulled off and smiled up at him, lips wet and pink. "How was it?"

"Um. Yeah." Dominic caught himself before rubbing his head and reached for Trick's hand instead. "Get up here."

Trick sprawled on the bed, unabashed in his nudity, and Dominic steeled himself. He could do this.

He lowered his head, and Trick's hand caught him before he could make contact.

"You look like you're going to your execution," Trick said, concern on his brow. "Sit up and talk to me."

Dominic shook his head. "No. No, I can do this."

He tried to bend again, and Trick grabbed his shoulder and pushed him away. "*Can* do this or *want* to do it?" He looked angry, suddenly.

"I—" Dominic fumbled for words. "I want… to *want* to?"

"Fuck, man," Trick said, and sat up. "I don't want a pity blowjob, or one because you think you have to, since I gave you one."

"I'm s-sorry," Dominic whispered, curling in on himself.

"No." Trick shook his head. "I pushed you when you weren't ready. I'm an asshole, Dom, *I'm* sorry." He scooted away, putting distance between them. "You should go."

Dominic slid off the bed. "I—can I… bathroom?"

"Yeah, of course."

Dominic grabbed his clothes, shuffled to the bathroom, and cleaned himself up, avoiding looking in the mirror.

Dressed and neat, he stepped out to see Trick sitting on the end of the bed, fully clothed. He smiled like the last thirty minutes had never happened.

"Have a good night."

"What about…." Dominic gestured vaguely, and Trick laughed.

"I'm fully capable of jerking off, pal. Go on, get out of here."

Dominic reached slowly for the door, trying to figure out what to say. Had he ruined everything? He liked Trick, he didn't deserve this.

"Dom?"

Dominic turned. "Yeah?"

Trick's eyes creased in a smile. "Don't forget my coffee tomorrow."

Relief rushed through Dominic, and he smiled back. "I won't. Goodnight, Trick."

22

———

Cory called as Dominic was getting ready for bed. "Ready for your daily update?"

"Sure, distract me from the fact that I'm a giant socially inept moron who can't get out of his own way," Dominic said, flopping backward onto the mattress.

"What?"

"Nothing. What's new?"

"Bringing Lila on as CTO was a stroke of genius, if I do say it myself," Cory said, sounding complacent. "She's streamlined a dozen different procedures and improved workplace efficiency by 17 percent in the past month alone."

"Are the employees merging well?"

"Better than expected," Cory said. "We've had some turnover, of course, but morale is up. I've got Lily working on rooting out any of Peggy's followers or sympathizers."

"Have you heard anything from Lance?"

"Why would I?" Cory asked, tone sharp.

"He told me there was a mole in our camp a while ago." Dominic draped an arm over his eyes. "I promised him an interview if he found out who it was. But then everything… happened, and I guess he figured out he didn't have an angle anymore. I'm just curious how he knew."

"I'll do some digging," Cory promised. "How are you?"

"Fine," Dominic said, sighing.

"Sure, you sound it," Cory said. "Why Switzerland, again?"

"They have good chocolate," Dominic said, staring at the ceiling.

"You don't *like* chocolate," Cory pointed out.

Farid does. Dominic closed his eyes and didn't answer.

"Anyway, there's something else I wanted to talk to you about." Cory sounded hesitant, and Dominic opened his eyes.

"What is it?"

"Farid's mother died this morning."

Dominic sat up so fast his head spun.

"I didn't know if you'd want to know," Cory said, sounding unhappy. "I asked Lily to check on him."

"How—" Dominic cleared his throat. "How is he?"

"I don't think he's doing very well," Cory said. It sounded like she was shuffling papers, something she did when she was uncomfortable. "He can't find a job, because we blackballed him. He's been living off savings, it sounds like, and his mother's care wiped out most of it."

"Shit," Dominic whispered.

"You don't care, right?" Cory asked. "You know how I mean—you're over him, aren't you?"

Dominic hesitated a little too long.

"*Dom.*"

"I'm *mostly* over him," Dominic said, hunching his shoulders. "I just—look, this is new territory for me, okay? It's hard to just… stop."

"I know, but honey, he betrayed you."

"Technically he didn't," Dominic pointed out.

"*Technically.*" Cory sounded disbelieving. "Dom, he was planning to. You *know* that."

"I don't want to argue about this," Dominic said.

Cory made an irritated noise that promised she wasn't done but dropped the subject. "When are you coming home?"

Dominic sighed. "Is never good for you?"

"Unfortunately, no. I need you back here. The board is getting worried about your extended absence. They want to make sure their moneymaker hasn't slipped the leash."

"Nice way of putting it." Dominic draped an arm over his eyes. "You're right, I should come home."

"Great! I'll book you a flight for this evening."

Dominic coughed a laugh. "Efficient as ever. I'll see you soon."

HE WAS HALFWAY through packing when someone knocked on the door. Dominic opened it, and Trick grinned at him. The smile slipped a bit when he glanced past Dominic to the suitcase on the bed.

"Was it *that* bad?"

"I was going to tell you," Dominic said, hunching

his shoulders. "I—it's not you, I promise. I just—the company needs me. I have to go back."

"As long as you're not running away from me," Trick said, attempting a smile. "So are you going to talk to the guy who broke your heart?"

"*No*," Dominic said. "What? No! I'm not going back for him. I have a business to run."

"Sure, man," Trick said. He shut the door and sat on the mattress a foot away as Dominic sat down too. "And I'm going to marry a pretty blonde girl and make my parents happy."

"He betrayed me," Dominic insisted. "How can I ever trust him again?"

Trick shrugged. "Why don't you ask him?"

Dominic stared at him. "What?"

"Well, it's not like I can tell you what was going through his head," Trick pointed out. "But maybe he can."

"How am I supposed to believe anything he says?"

Trick shrugged again. "Maybe you can't. But I dunno, man. From what you've told me… I think you need to ask him that."

Dominic put his cheek on his knee and closed his eyes.

23

THE FLIGHT HOME took twelve hours, and Dominic felt each second passing as an eternity. He couldn't focus on anything. He jiggled his leg until his seatmate glared at him, then apologized and put on headphones, but the in-flight movie failed to entertain him. Eventually he crossed his arms and tried to nap, dropping into fitful sleep and dreaming of Farid saying his name.

Finally, *finally*, they were in Seattle airspace, circling the airport and preparing for their descent. Dominic's eyes were gritty and burning. Baggage claim seemed slower than usual, or maybe someone had a personal grudge against Dominic, but after another eternity, he was able to grab his luggage and stumble out into the Seattle evening air. It was nearly 6:00 p.m., which meant rush hour was going to be a bitch.

Nothing for it. Dominic hailed a taxi and crawled inside.

Halfway home, embroiled in traffic, his phone

rang. Dominic didn't recognize the number. He answered cautiously.

"This is Salma Qadir," a low, husky voice said, and Dominic froze.

"How did you get this number?" He already knew the answer. "Cory gave it to you, didn't she?"

"Yes." Salma didn't sound at all ashamed. "I need to talk to you. If you hang up, I'll keep calling. If you block my number, I'll show up at your office until you have to get a restraining order. It's going to be easier all the way around if you just let me say what I need to say."

Dominic could have laughed, if he'd been able to summon air. She sounded just like Farid. "So say it."

"Farid and I have done a lot of talking since everything went down," Salma said. Her voice was utterly composed. "I knew I wasn't a boy when I was five years old. Farid was the only one who believed me at first."

Dominic said nothing, staring out the window at the passing cars unseeingly.

"Mama… she came around. She didn't understand at first, but she loves—loved—me, and that's what matters most to her. So she supported me. She just wanted me to be happy. But Baba—he hates what I am." Salma's voice was tight. "Farid protected me. Growing up. When I first put on a skirt. When I decided to grow my hair out, when I finally came out to our father. He got between us every time, stopped Baba from—" Salma cut herself off. "He's always put me first. Taken care of me, and then Mama when she got sick."

"Is there a point to this?" Dominic asked.

Salma's silence was somehow as sharp as knives, and Dominic winced.

"You don't know what it's been like," she said. "You wouldn't. Everything's easy for you. You don't have to fight and claw for what you want, what you *need*."

Dominic couldn't help the bitter laugh. "You really have no idea what you're talking about."

"I know this much," Salma said. "Farid has never, not once in our lives together, been in love. Did you know that?"

"He *can't* love," Dominic snapped.

"Bullshit," Salma spat. "Farid loves harder and more deeply than anyone I've ever met. He's never been *in* love. Until you."

Dominic shook his head, sourness coating his tongue. "He didn't love me. If he did, he never would have even considered selling me out."

Salma made a derisive noise. "Because it's all about you."

Stung, Dominic opened his mouth to protest, but Salma didn't let him speak.

"He didn't know you when Peggy approached him. All he knew was he had a dying mother, a sister who needed hormone therapy and surgery, five people to support, and a difficult, neurotic, asshole boss making his life even more miserable. He didn't *want* to take her money. He told her no." Salma sucked in a ragged breath. "It's my fault any of this happened."

Dominic didn't challenge that.

"I wish you could have seen him, after," Salma whispered. "He was—broken."

Dominic closed his eyes. He didn't want to hear this.

"I've never seen him like that," Salma continued. "He'd compromised his morals, broken his own code, turned everything he believed in on its head to take care of us, and in the end it didn't even matter. He was in a terrible position, and he can't forgive himself."

"Good," Dominic managed. His throat was tight, and he had a horrible feeling he was going to start crying.

"I don't think you mean that," Salma whispered. She took an unsteady breath. "My brother still loves you," she said softly. "I think he'll never stop loving you. I know you don't want to hear it, but it's the truth."

The phone clicked in his ear, and Dominic pulled it away to stare at it. She'd hung up.

Dominic swore under his breath, clenching his fists. He wanted to punch something, to scream his frustration. He wanted *answers*.

He leaned forward and tapped the driver's seat. "Change of address," he said before he could change his mind.

It took nearly an hour to get through traffic to the north side of Seattle, where Farid and his family lived. Dominic hauled his bags out of the trunk, over-tipped the driver, and stared up at the house. It wasn't large, by Seattle's standards—narrow and tall, with three or four levels to it and a small yard that was carefully tended to.

Dominic climbed the steps and raised his hand to knock on the door as nerves welled up to choke him. What was he thinking? Would Farid even be willing to look at him? He should just… go, and leave them in peace to mourn.

Before he could turn away, the door opened and a

young man looked at him. He was a carbon copy of Farid, gangly and coltish with youth but with the same big nose and almond-shaped eyes.

"Who are you?" he said.

"I—um," Dominic said. "Is Farid here?"

The boy turned his head. "*Farid,* visitor!" He clattered out of the house and past Dominic, who sidestepped to avoid him.

When he looked up, Farid was standing in the doorway, staring at him.

Dominic's heart twisted in his chest. Farid looked *awful,* at least three days' worth of stubble on his cheeks, his skin sallow and hair unbrushed, and he'd lost weight he couldn't afford to lose, taking him from lean to gaunt.

"What are you doing here?" he whispered, folding his arms over his ratty T-shirt.

"I need—" Dominic swallowed hard. "I need to ask you a question. Please. Just one, and then I'll go forever if you want me to."

Farid just looked at him silently for an endless moment and then finally stepped aside and motioned for Dominic to enter.

DOMINIC FOLLOWED Farid down the hall to the basement steps without speaking. Farid nearly missed the first riser, catching himself on the railing. Dominic looked good, he thought as they went down the stairs. His skin was glowing, even with that awful haircut, he looked fit and healthy and—well, not relaxed, but then, Dominic never relaxed.

Next to him, Farid was ashamed of his own

disheveled appearance, but it was muffled, wrapped in the cotton wool that lived in his brain these days.

In his room, he gestured for Dominic to take the small recliner and sat down on the end of the bed.

Dominic folded himself into the chair, looking faintly ridiculous with his long arms and legs over-flowing it.

"So ask," Farid said. He was so tired, but he couldn't sleep. All his dreams ended the same way.

Dominic leaned forward. "What happened, the day Peggy approached you?"

Farid stiffened.

"You told her no," Dominic hurried on. "You said —you said you wouldn't betray your employer. And then an hour later you called her back, and you changed your mind."

Farid stared at him.

"What happened?" Dominic repeated.

"Does it matter?" Farid said, rubbing his arms. "I agreed to betray you. That's all there is to it."

"*No*," Dominic said. "I don't believe that's all there is to it. Please, 'Rid, just tell me?"

Farid fought tears at the unthinking use of his nickname and lifted his chin. "He—my father—he hit Salma. She was on the porch with a black eye when I got home. Called her an abomination and a sin in the eyes of God. I knew—" He stopped and swallowed. "I knew I had to get her out of here. Had to take care of —" His eyes burned. "Of Mama. I—" He shook his head. "I shouldn't have done it. I never should have said yes, I should have told Peggy to go fuck herself the very first time she contacted me."

Dominic slid off the chair onto his knees in front

of him. There were tears in his eyes. "I wish you'd told me," he whispered.

He was close enough to touch, and Farid's fingers twitched, but he pulled his hand back. "I didn't *know* you," he reminded him. "You were just some neurotic bigshot coder. And my family—" He clenched his fists. "My family needed me. Then by the time I realized—"

"Realized what?" Dominic asked, his voice low.

"It doesn't *matter*," Farid said.

"Do you want to know when I realized I was in love with you?" Dominic asked, and Farid's mouth fell open.

"You—*what?*"

"It was at the airport," Dominic said, ignoring that. "Fox was needling me, and you were worried, you looked at me and I thought, '*I love him*,' and that was that."

"But—" Farid couldn't make words form.

"I have one more question," Dominic said. His voice was unsteady.

Farid made a mute gesture.

"When did you fall in love with me?"

"I—" Farid rubbed his face. "I don't know when. But I figured it out in Vancouver. After the scene. You r-reached for me, and I knew—I knew I couldn't go through with it, that I was in love with you and even if I wasn't, that I couldn't do it."

Tears spilled down Dominic's cheeks. "How do I know I can trust you when you say that?" he managed.

Farid shook his head wildly, scooting backward away from the look in Dominic's eyes. "You can't, you can't trust me, not after what I did. You *can't*."

"Tell me why I *do*, then."

"You *shouldn't*," Farid said. "Dom, you can't—I'm no good for you."

"Don't I get a choice?" Dominic asked. "Don't I get to choose what and who I want in my own life?"

Farid covered his mouth with both trembling hands, hope welling inside him and threatening to overflow.

"It came down to a choice," Dominic continued. "And in the end, you chose to protect me at great personal cost to yourself and your family." He caught Farid's hand. "If you'd *told* me, there at the end—'Rid, I would have helped, you know I would have. I wish you could have trusted me, baby, I would have moved the world for you, can't you see that? I still would."

Farid sobbed out loud and hurled himself forward into Dominic's arms. "I'm so sorry," he choked, clinging to Dominic's rumpled shirt. "Dom, I'm so sorry, *please* forgive me, I know I don't deserve it but—"

Dominic put a finger to Farid's lips and then slid it down to his chin, tilting his head up. "I forgive you," he managed, and kissed him.

The kiss was soft and tentative, and Dominic tasted of salt, lips and tongue careful and questioning.

Farid couldn't breathe for the tears that choked him, but he somehow managed to get to his knees and wrap his arms around Dominic's neck, pressing himself desperately close, trying to merge with Dominic's body, unable to get enough of his taste and smell and the *feel* of him, intoxicatingly hard and strong against him.

"I love you," he said, tearing away. Dominic smiled, face tilted up to him. "I love you so m-much, and I didn't even *know*—San had to point it out. He told me I'm an idiot, and he was right, I am, I should have trusted you, I should have—"

Dominic covered his mouth again. "Stop," he said gently. "We were both idiots. It's behind us. I'm sure we'll find new and exciting ways to be idiots together in the future." He hesitated. "If—you want that?"

Farid hiccupped a laughing sob and grabbed Dominic's face to pull him into a hard, bruising kiss. "More than anything," he managed. He ran a hand over Dominic's cropped head. "Your hair, Dom, your beautiful hair—"

Dominic turned his head and caught Farid's wrist, planting a kiss to it. "I couldn't bear it. Every time it got a snag or tangle, I thought of you. But I'll grow it out again, okay? If you promise you'll be there to help me untangle it."

"I promise," Farid whispered, and buried his face in Dominic's throat, letting the tears flow freely.

"I'm so sorry about your mother," Dominic murmured after a few minutes, and Farid pressed in closer. "I'm sorry... I couldn't help, that I wasn't here for you."

"You're here now," Farid said, lifting his head to kiss him again. "That's all that matters."

24

<hr>

"PLEASE TELL me this is the last of it," Dominic panted, struggling to keep his end of the couch up.

Farid wasn't much better off, but he managed a grin, hands slipping as they maneuvered around the corner and through the door of Salma and Nasim's new apartment.

"Pretty sure," he said, only slightly winded. "And if not, they can get the rest themselves."

"Hear, hear," Dominic said, and let the couch drop to the floor. He leered at Farid over it. "Wanna christen it before they get here?"

Farid threw a pillow at him. "*Gross*. Come on, let's lock up and go upstairs."

Dominic followed him out, smiling. In the elevator, he eyed Farid.

"What?"

"Nothing," Dominic said hastily. "Just… do you think they'll be happy here?"

Farid took his hand. "They're going to be *so* happy, Dom. But I should warn you… they'll be up at your place all the time, day or night. And Nasim will eat you out of house and home."

Dominic grinned at him, happy and bright. "Our place. Guess I'd better start stocking my pantry with more than just snacks for you." He tugged Farid against him, and Farid went willingly. Dominic had been affectionate to the point of clingy since he'd gotten back, like he wasn't quite sure Farid was really there, and he needed to remind himself constantly.

That was fine by Farid, who was feeling much the same way, reaching for Dominic in the night and in quiet moments just to feel the warmth of his skin.

"So what did you do in Switzerland?" he asked idly, and was startled to feel Dominic tensing against him. Farid lifted his head. "Babe?"

Dominic blinked and dragged a smile into place, but he looked stiff. "Not much," he said. "Read books, played tourist."

Farid narrowed his eyes teasingly. "Why do you sound *guilty,* hmm? Were you off having lots of sex with beautiful men?"

Dominic hunched his shoulders and Farid's mouth fell open.

"You *were?*"

"Just one!" Dominic protested, and let him go to rub his face. "Fuck, I didn't want—Farid, I—"

Farid caught his hand and pulled on it until Dominic met his eyes. "Tell me about him?"

Dominic told the story of Trick as the elevator dinged and they stepped out on his floor.

"He was funny and nice and *fun,* and he made me laugh, and he was everything you aren't." That made Farid's eyebrows climb, and Dominic smacked himself in the head. "Not what I meant. He was… loud, and messy, and careless, he liked people and talked to everyone, he was tall and blond and… not you."

He fumbled the door open, and Farid followed him inside, where Dominic turned to face him, hands opening and closing by his sides.

"Everywhere I looked, I just saw you," he whispered. "I—it *hurt*, 'Rid, I wanted it to stop, I wanted to not feel that way anymore."

"You were trying to get over me," Farid said quietly, and Dominic nodded.

"I just wanted the pain to stop and I thought, maybe if I sleep with Trick, then I could put *you…* away." His eyes were miserable. "It didn't work. I just ended up feeling like I'd cheated on you."

Farid took a quick step forward. "But you didn't, love. You *didn't.* You were trying to fix your heart, the one *I* broke, by the way, and how could I ever condemn you for that?"

Dominic stared at the floor, and Farid closed the distance between them. He had to wipe those shadows off Dominic's face.

"So, this…. Trick. What's he look like?"

"Tall, blond, happy…." Dominic shrugged. "Sort of like an American Chris Hemsworth."

Farid didn't try to stifle the appreciative noise, and Dominic's eyes snapped up.

"You have good taste, pet." Farid tugged lightly on Dominic's earlobe. "Any chance he'll visit Seattle?"

Dominic sucked in a startled breath. "Are you —*'Rid.*"

Farid grinned at him. "Why, do you like the idea?"

Dominic actually gave that thought, while Farid traced the curve of his ear with a finger. But he shook his head.

"No. Trick is great, he is, but...." He wrapped his arms around Farid's waist. "I only want you." He frowned briefly. "Will that limit you? Because I know you like, uh… multiple partners?"

Farid laughed, leaning against him. "I like *you*. And if you ever want to play at the Honeytrap again, I'm more than willing, but don't ever think you're not enough for me, Dominic, because you are." He kissed him, quick and soft, as Dominic's phone buzzed.

Dominic made a face and pulled it out of his pocket. "Oh, it's just Cory, she wants to know what color scheme you'd like for your office."

Farid patted his pockets. "What did I do with my phone? Tell her I don't care, I trust her judgment, and I didn't need it redecorated in the first place."

"I think she's trying to make it up to you," Dominic said as he typed. "Or maybe just make you feel welcome." He glanced up. "You do, right?"

"Well, I imagine Cory's going to be very different to work for," Farid said. "But I'm looking forward to it. How does she feel about being the new face of the company?"

"She can't wait," Dominic said, smiling and putting his phone away. "Should have done it a long time ago."

"Did you ever find out how Lance knew about me?" Farid asked.

Dominic hummed and hooked a finger through Farid's belt loop. "Apparently he charmed it out of Peggy's secretary. He didn't even know what he was looking for—he got stupid-lucky and tripped over it while he was busy seducing the poor girl. At least he's smart enough to not try and pester me for that interview. Why are we still standing here? Let's go shower."

He pulled Farid laughing into the bathroom, and they shared lazy, soapy handjobs, arms around each other's necks. Farid bit down on Dominic's shoulder by accident as he came, shuddering through it, and opened his eyes to see Dominic looking wide-eyed and startled.

"Did I hurt you?" Farid said, touching the imprint of his teeth with a worried finger.

"No." Dominic cleared his throat. "I—uh… liked it. Maybe you could do that again? And I was thinking, um." He stalled out and Farid waited. "Maybe you could fuck me at some point?"

Farid sucked in a sharp breath. "*Pet.*"

"I know, I know, it didn't really go well last time," Dominic said quickly, "but I—I want you, 'Rid. I want you inside me, I want to feel you everywhere. I've been doing research, and it doesn't have to hurt, I was just too tense and freaked out. I want to try again. Please?"

Farid closed his eyes and swayed forward until his face was pressed against Dominic's throat. "You will be my undoing," he whispered.

Dominic curved his arms around him. "Well then, I'll just have to do you back up again, won't I?"

Farid laughed and released him. "Then what are we waiting for?"

"Now?" Dominic looked startled.

"Not up for it?" Farid challenged, and Dominic's eyes narrowed.

He didn't say anything, though. He just grabbed Farid's wrist and dragged him out of the shower. The dry-off was rough and perfunctory, making Farid laugh at how much of a hurry he was in. But when Dominic sank to his knees in front of him in the bedroom, Farid's laughter cut off like a switch.

Dominic's eyes gleamed up at him, and he leaned forward, nuzzling along the crease of Farid's hip. His breath was hot, and Farid's cock jumped. It was still too soon for him to come again, but Dominic didn't seem worried. He was taking his time, exploring Farid's body with his mouth, tongue flicking out to taste skin occasionally and making Farid jerk.

He put a hand on Dominic's head, tracing the curve of his skull, trailing it down and running a finger along his cheek.

DOMINIC TURNED his face into Farid's hand and closed his eyes briefly. *He's here, he's with me, he loves me.* It was too much, sometimes, the happiness that rose up and choked him when he looked over and saw Farid beside him on the couch, bare feet tucked under him as he read, or washing dishes in the kitchen. Dominic always had to stop and take a breath, calm his racing heart, and remind himself it was real.

Farid stroked his cheek with a thumb. "Okay, pet?"

Dominic nodded. "Glad you're here," he managed.

Farid's eyes softened. "So am I. Get on the bed for me, on your back."

Dominic scrambled to his feet and obeyed, putting his hands behind his head and arching his back as Farid watched, eyes full of heat.

"Showoff," he said affectionately.

"Only for you," Dominic said. "Are you joining me?"

Farid climbed on behind him and stroked a hand up Dominic's leg. "How do you want this?"

"Any way *you* want it," Dominic said. "Don't make me choose, please. I want to—please turn my brain off, 'Rid."

"Yeah, okay," Farid murmured. "I can do that. Turn over for me, sweetheart."

Dominic flipped to his stomach, and Farid rubbed his buttock, then pulled them apart gently. He blew on Dominic's hole, and Dominic twitched, hips already pushing back.

"Can I—" His thoughts were slowing, fragmenting as he gave up control, but Farid paused.

"Can you what?"

"Wanna… do this to you sometime," Dominic murmured, head pillowed on his arms.

Farid groaned. "I'll hold you to that, pet. Now be still." He dropped his head and licked once, then blew again. He resettled his grip on Dominic's ass, and then he was pressing inside and Dominic's core ignited, body going limp as Farid fucked gently in and out of him with his tongue, occasionally biting the rim just enough that Dominic tensed and quivered beneath him and then slipping back inside.

After an interminable few minutes, he pulled away. "What color, pet?"

"Green," Dominic slurred, rolling his hips so that his heavy cock dragged along the bedspread. "Green, 'Rid, please—"

Farid leaned across him and retrieved something from the bedside table. There was the click of a bottle-cap, and then something cold and wet landed on Dominic's ass. Before he could react, Farid slid one finger inside.

Dominic tensed briefly, dragged toward the surface by the intrusion. It didn't hurt, but it felt… *strange.*

"Breathe," Farid said, his voice sounding wrecked. "Push back into it."

Dominic obeyed, bearing down and gasping as Farid's finger slid deeper. The strangeness was evaporating, melting rapidly into pleasure that sparked outward in glimmering showers behind his eyes.

"Oh," he panted. "Oh, that feels *good.*"

Farid made a noise, and a second finger joined the first. Dominic groaned raggedly, hips jerking helplessly as he spiraled back down into the deep. Farid crooked a finger, and Dominic nearly shouted as his fingertip grazed a spot deep inside, making electricity ripple outward.

"Fuck, *fuck,*" he sobbed, struggling to get to his knees so he could rock back onto Farid's hand properly, but Farid caught his hip and pushed him back to the bed, holding him there effortlessly.

"Be still," he said, and there it was, that tone of command Dominic loved so much. He went limp again immediately, and Farid hissed. "God, the way you take it for me. I'll bet you can take more. Can you?"

"Yes," Dominic gasped against his forearm. He squeezed his eyes shut as Farid added a third finger but couldn't stop the moan that ripped free.

"Don't come until I give you permission," Farid said, fingers still an iron grip on Dominic's hip.

Dominic wasn't sure what he said in response, rocking in minute motions onto Farid's fingers, trying to draw him deeper.

"C-color," Farid managed, motionless.

Dominic was half-senseless with pleasure, drifting

in his safe place, but he struggled to find the word. "Green," he finally rasped.

"You're so good for me," Farid said, and added more lube before driving deep and rubbing his prostate again, hard.

Dominic came off the bed with a strangled scream, hips bucking. "'Rid, no—"

Farid backed off immediately, pulling his hand free. "What is it?"

"Too m-much," Dominic mumbled into the bedspread. "Wanna…." He closed his eyes again. "Wanna be good for you."

Farid said nothing, but his grip eased, and then there was a finger at Dominic's hole again, the slide easy and free as it dipped deeper.

This time, he moved slower, working Dominic open in smooth, easy motions, careful to avoid his prostate, as Dominic gripped the bedspread and whimpered curses and pleas into the fabric.

"C'mon," he said, pushing back again. "I'm ready, please—"

But Farid would not be rushed. He was up to three fingers again, adding more lube every few minutes, and Dominic was a writhing, begging mess beneath him.

Farid had the control. He set the pace, the rhythm, and Dominic was simply there to feel it, to fall into the water and let it close over him.

He went limp, surrendering completely, and the waves broke over his head as he sank beneath them. Hanging in the cool dark, he was only vaguely aware that Farid had pulled his hand out and replaced it with his cock, pressing home in one slow, smooth, agonizingly good slide. Fully sheathed, Farid lowered his chest to Dominic's back and kissed his ear and cheek, whispering words Dominic couldn't understand.

Then he began to move, and reality shattered in Dominic's grip. Farid's thrusts were strong and determined, filling Dominic's core, stretching him wide and taking him over so that conscious thought spun out of control, replaced with a growing pleasure that was too large for his skin to contain.

He tried, weakly, to push back into it, but Farid caught his hips and held him immoveable, still pounding home over and over. *Mine*, his thrusts said. *Mine*, his hot breath on Dominic's nape said. *Mine*, his fingers digging into Dominic's hipbones said.

Farid set his teeth in Dominic's spine and worked a hand beneath them. "You're so close, aren't you?" he said harshly against his skin. "You wanna come for me, baby?"

Dominic couldn't answer. He had no voice, no words. He was Farid's, body and soul, and he would come when Farid said he could come.

Farid tilted his hips, changing his angle, and drove deeper, hitting Dominic's prostate with every forceful thrust, and Dominic thrashed, pleading wordlessly, even as the pleasure swelled impossibly larger, threatening to split him open and spill out everywhere.

Farid closed a hand around Dominic's cock and bit his earlobe. "Come for me, Dominic," he ordered. "Come *now*."

Dominic's spine arched as Farid pulled the orgasm out of him, long, merciless throbs of ecstasy as he emptied soundlessly over Farid's fist, mouth falling open and every muscle tightening and clenching down on Farid's cock. Farid drove deep one last time, and heat bloomed in Dominic's core as Farid came in thick pulses inside him, groaning raggedly and falling forward onto Dominic's back.

Dominic sagged back to the bed, barely realizing that Farid had slipped free and was planting gentle kisses along his spine.

"So good, so perfect," he whispered. "My perfect, beautiful love. How are you feeling?"

Dominic managed a weak thumb's up and Farid choked on a laugh, pressing one more kiss to his shoulder and then sliding off the bed.

He came back with a warm cloth, and cleaned Dominic up with gentle motions. Then he rolled him out of the wet spot and gathered him into his arms.

Dominic yawned, squirming back against him. "Love you," he mumbled.

There was a smile in Farid's voice when he answered. "You know, it's the funniest thing; I think I love you too?" Dominic slapped weakly at him, and Farid laughed and kissed his hair. "Fine, fine, I definitely love you. Happy now?"

"Yeah," Dominic said. "Yeah, I am." Smiling, he closed his eyes and fell asleep.

Keep reading for a sneak peek of Broken Promises, the next book in the Beloved Scars series!

ACKNOWLEDGMENTS

Thank you to my betas—Aaliya, Rowan, Sarah, CJ, and Saumya. This book wouldn't be what it is without your input and suggestions. Special thanks to Rowan for That One Idea—you know the one.

Thank you to Sarah for all the incredible hard work she's put into helping me self-publish these novels. Check out www.purpledragondesigns.com if you'd like her to design a cover for you; I promise you'll get your money's worth. Sarah, I owe you more than I can ever express, and it's an honor to beta your books for you.

And lastly, thank you to my readers, who've stuck with me through the ups and downs, who read everything I give them and ask for more. You keep me writing.

ABOUT THE AUTHOR

Michaela Grey told stories to put herself to sleep since she was old enough to hold a conversation in her head. When she learned to write, she began putting those stories down on paper. She resides in the Texas Hill Country with her cats, and is perpetually on the hunt for peaceful writing time.

When she's not writing, she's watching hockey or blogging about writing and men on knife shoes chasing a frozen Oreo around the ice while trying to keep her cat off the keyboard.

Tumblr: greymichaela.tumblr.com
Twitter: @GreyMichaela
Facebook: www.facebook.com/GreyMichaela
E-mail: greymichaela@gmail.com

BROKEN PROMISES

"Safeword." The Dom's voice was gritty with exhaustion and something close to fear.

It took several long, agonizing moments for the command to filter through the haze in Kellen's brain, wrapped as he was in cotton wool. His tongue refused to cooperate, in any case, so he just shook his head mutely, the movement making the chain hanging from his nipples sway and sending sparks of agony through his chest.

"Goddammit," the Dom snarled, and threw the whip down. "Red, I'm done. You're too fucked up for me." He unbuckled the cuffs, letting Kellen's arms fall roughly, and Kellen bit back a whimper at the jarring of the clamps. He slumped forward, one weak hand catching himself before he went facedown on the whipping bench, as the Dom unbuckled his ankles with the same harsh touch, and then stood. "Find someone else to fulfill your death wish, boy," he grated, and stalked from the room.

Kellen sat still for a few minutes, coming back

from the edge in gradual stages, focusing on his breathing in slow, even repetitions, until the room swam back into focus, resolving in front of his tear-wet eyes. He looked around. *Five things I can see.* The black crushed velvet curtains hanging in a graceful arc at the end of the bed they hadn't even gotten to use. The whipping bench, marred with a streak of—Kellen touched it curiously and his finger came away red. Probably his. The picture on the wall, of a black-leather-suited Domme, bending over her sub and tracing a line up his ribs with the edge of her knife. Kellen glanced away. His clothes, folded neatly and set on the floor on top of his shoes. He couldn't remember how he'd gotten to the room, what time it was, or even the name of the Dom who'd brought him here.

He forced the panic down and looked for the last thing. His own reflection in a mirror on the wall caught his eye. Kellen saw haunted dark brown eyes in a pale face with a pointed chin, fair hair standing up in tufts as if it had been pulled. He jerked his gaze away.

Four things I can hear. His own breathing, ster-tuous in his ears. The thump of the bass from the club's main room, permeating the floor and walls with its insistent beat. Footsteps, walking past his room. And a man's voice, crying out in pleasure-soaked pain.

Kellen squeezed his eyes shut briefly. *Three things I can touch.* He smoothed a hand across the vinyl of the whipping bench, avoiding the bloodstain. Ran fingers through his own hair, concentrating on the way the strands curled against his skin as he tamed them. The movement disturbed the clamps again and Kellen gasped, jerked out of his routine. He had to take them off, and it was going to *hurt*.

Setting his jaw, he watched himself in the mirror,

fingers long and thin and streaked with blood, as he unscrewed the first clamp. The pain hit him in a fiery bolt as it fell free and he curled forward with a choked noise. The Dom—whose name he still couldn't remember—hadn't taken it easy on him. He'd wear these bruises for a week.

After a few minutes, Kellen sat up and fumbled for the other clamp. He let it and the chain tumble to the floor as he hunched in on himself, breathing harsh and fast through his nose as his abused nipples woke to angry, scorching life.

Two—he whimpered aloud and forced himself to concentrate. *Two things I can smell.* Blood, coppery and sharp in his nostrils, hit him first. Close behind was the smell of latex and leather and sweat, combined into one gut-punch of sensory overload.

Kellen fought the panic that threatened to drown him. *You're safe*, he told himself. "Safe," he said aloud, voice sounding croaky.

He breathed in through his nose and out through his mouth until the fear receded, leaving him drained and shaky but calmer.

One thing I can taste. Kellen licked his lips. Salt, his own tears and sweat mingled.

There was a knock on the door, and Kellen straightened, alarm zinging up his spine.

"Who—" He swallowed and tried again. "I'll be out in a minute."

"It's Martha," a concerned voice said.

Kellen didn't answer, focused on getting to his feet and staying there.

"The Dungeon Master?" Martha said. "I need to make sure you're okay. Can you open the door, please, Kellen?"

Kellen stiffened. "Just—just a minute." He reached his clothes and sat heavily on the end of the bed to pull his underwear and pants on as the doorknob turned. Kellen recoiled, clutching his shirt to his chest. "I *said* just a minute!"

Martha was a sturdy woman with a perfect Afro and high cheekbones, dressed head-to-toe in white leather, wide white wrist cuffs stark against dark satin skin. Her eyes were worried. "Philip blew out of here looking equal parts scared and angry. Took me awhile to calm him down or I'd've been here sooner." Her voice was musical and low, with a hint of a Southern accent in it. "I need to check your injuries, Kellen, and bandage anything that needs it."

"I'm fine," Kellen said automatically. "And how do you know my name?"

Martha narrowed her dark eyes. "You told me when you came in here. Do you not remember meeting me?"

I don't remember anything. Kellen stifled a slightly hysterical laugh. "I'm—look, let me just get dressed and I'll go and you'll never see me again."

"Doesn't work that way," Martha said. "You're under my protection and supervision when you're in this place, which means I'm responsible for your well-being. Stop being difficult and let me look you over, goddammit!"

Kellen opened and closed his mouth and sagged against the bedpost, suddenly so exhausted he couldn't muster the strength to argue.

"Facedown on the bed," Martha told him, her voice gentle but uncompromising, and Kellen rolled over in a sullen heap, ending up with his cheek pressed to the comforter. The satin was almost rough against his nipples and they flared to angry life again, but he couldn't find the strength to reposition himself.

Martha's fingers were gentle as she eased his pants back down and off his ankles. She sucked in a breath and Kellen wondered vaguely what she saw.

"Be right back," she said, and left the room.

Alone, Kellen drifted into a light doze. The room was warm and the bed was soft, and all too soon, he was going to be back out in the cold, praying it wouldn't rain so he could sleep in the park on the grass under his favorite tree, the one with the lacy fronds that let him see the stars in stolen glimpses when the wind stirred them. And then he'd have to go back to—

He didn't hear the door open again, but it must have, because someone was there beside him in the bed, hands icy cold on his burning back, and Kellen jackknifed away, flinging himself sideways off the mattress to land with a bone-jarring thump on the floor.

The impact sent ripples of agony through him but he ignored them, struggling to his feet to face his attacker—Martha, kneeling on the bed with her hands up, as if she was afraid to move.

"Kellen?" Her voice was tentative, as if she was *worried* about him.

Kellen swallowed hard and straightened, rolling his shoulders and pulling his air of bravado back into place. "Can I go yet?"

Martha shook her head, hair swaying. "Not until I dress your wounds."

"So I'm a prisoner?" Kellen flung at her.

"No," Martha said. "You can go, but—"

Kellen ignored her, scrambling for his clothes as his world dipped and swung dangerously. He was dressed in record time and out the door before Martha could say anything else to stop him.

"THE CROISSANTS ARE ABOUT TO BURN," Senna said without looking up from the dough she was shaping on the floury counter.

"Fuck, *shit*." Vee spun for the oven and yanked it open. "Hotpads, hotpads, where—" Senna threw one overhand at him and he caught it on the fly, grabbing the tray one-handed and dropping it on the granite countertop.

Senna leaned over, hands still buried to the wrists in dough, and wrinkled her nose.

"Melissa will make you throw them out."

"What? *Why?* I got to them before they burned!"

Senna gestured with her chin. "They dried out. She won't let us serve those to patrons."

Vee groaned, sagging against the counter.

"Oh, don't be so dramatic," Senna said. "Just toss them and start over. There's another batch proofing in the fridge."

Vee scowled at her but pushed upright and grabbed a bag. He shoved the hot pastries into them, muttering under his breath, and let the door to the alley slam behind him on his way to the dumpster. He was winding up to throw the bag when what he'd thought was a bundle of rags moved, and Vee lost his balance and nearly fell over.

A young man raised his head, dark brown eyes sharp and wary under hair so blond it was almost silver. There was a ring of bruises around his throat and matching ones on his skinny wrists. Vee opened his mouth to ask if he was okay, but the young man spoke first.

"Fuck off."

Vee's eyebrows went up. "Uh, you're in *my* alley."

The boy sneered. "You own it, huh?"

Vee bristled. "I have more right to be here than *you* do, since I work here."

The boy rolled his eyes and pushed himself to his feet. "I'm leaving, unbunch your panties."

"Wait," Vee said. He held out the bag of still-steaming croissants, but the boy just looked at them and back up at him. Vee hesitated and set it on the pavement. "There's nothing wrong with them," he said, knowing he sounded defensive, and turned to go back inside. He was nearly to the door when a croissant hit him between the shoulder blades.

Vee spun and the boy tipped his chin up defiantly, mouth set in a mulish line. Whatever angry words Vee was going to say died on his lips at the sight of the purple and green bruises mottling the young man's pale skin.

He cleared his throat and gestured vaguely. "You should… um. Get those looked at." He escaped inside before another croissant was hurled at him.

VEE SPENT the rest of the day on autopilot, thinking about the encounter and the stranger's dark brown eyes. He nearly burned the puff pastry, which made Senna yell at him, and then dropped a tray of scones halfway to the oven when he bounced off a wall, not paying attention to where he was going.

"My office," Melissa said, appearing in the doorway.

Vee looked up from where he was picking up scone triangles off the floor as Senna covered her face at the counter above him. "Um. Sure."

He sidled into her office, wiping his floury hands on his apron. Melissa was behind her desk, typing something. Her dark eyes gave nothing away as she folded her hands and nodded toward the empty chair.

Vee flopped into it gracelessly and something like amusement flickered through Melissa's eyes. She was tall even sitting down, dark-skinned with cheekbones that could cut glass, and she terrified Vee, although he'd die before admitting that.

"How's the baby?" he blurted.

Melissa almost smiled. "She took her first steps yesterday."

"Wow, that's great!" Vee hesitated. "Is it great? I mean, I don't know how old she is. Is she early or late or…?"

Melissa's lips twitched. "She's right on time. What's going on with you?"

Vee squirmed. "Like, in general?"

"I was thinking more today," Melissa said. "You seem distracted. Anything I can do to help?"

Vee thought about it for a minute. "Why do we throw away the burned food?" he finally said.

"Instead of—"

"Well, some of it's still perfectly edible, just not *perfect*, you know?" Vee said. "Why couldn't we give it to the homeless? People who need it? Wouldn't that be better than letting it go to waste?"

Melissa nodded. "Believe me, I'd love to do that. Unfortunately, the lawyers on Dominic's staff are sharks, and bloodthirsty ones at that. I'm specifically barred from giving away food from the bakery because they say it's a liability issue and I could open us up to a lawsuit."

Vee slumped, deflated.

"However." Melissa picked up a pen and spun it between long fingers, seemingly focused on it alone. "If someone were to buy the food from me, at a deeply discounted rate, perhaps, I would have no say in how that person distributed his baked goods, and the sharks would have no reason to complain."

Vee perked up and an actual smile flickered across Melissa's lips.

"Can I—um. I'd like to buy your overstock, ma'am," he finally said, and Melissa inclined her head.

"Get with Senna at the end of the day. She'll get it sorted out."

Vee nodded. Melissa was already turning back to her computer. Vee dithered and finally stood, nearly knocking the chair over, bobbed his head, and bolted.

When he got back to the kitchen, Senna was filling a basket.

"Order for the top floor," she said, adding croissants and sausage rolls. "I can't leave the brioche, so you're up."

Vee took his apron off, swiping at his face to remove any errant flour, and accepted the basket.

"It's for Dominic," Senna said, grabbing a pomegranate soda from the fridge and shoving it into Vee's arms next to the basket. "Farid called it in. *Do not embarrass me.*"

Vee scowled, affronted, and stalked for the elevators. He rode them up to the top floor and stepped out into lush carpet, wide hallways and huge paintings in muted swirls of blues, grays, and creams on the walls. Down the hall to the left—a small brass nameplate above a door proclaimed it Farid Qadir's office, in front of the inner sanctum that was Cory's domain, the holy ground no one set foot on without invitation. Which meant that to Vee's right, directly opposite, was Dominic's workroom.

He'd heard the wild rumors about what had gone down eight months ago, of course. Everyone had. They ranged from 'Farid had taken money to betray Dominic's secrets to a rival company but had backed out, giving himself up to keep Dominic safe', to 'Farid had been contracted to put a hit on Dominic and possibly Cory as well but had a change of heart at the last second'.

In any case, at the end of it all, Dominic had left the country, Farid had gone into seclusion, and everyone at Spectral had done their best to get on with life, buzzing with gossip whenever they met in the halls.

But then Dominic had come back, with Farid right beside him, and called an employee meeting where he'd told them that Cory was stepping into his position as CEO, Farid would be taking over as Cory's personal assistant, and Dominic was moving into a more behind-the-scenes position where he would be free to work on his code and not be bothered.

As Dominic had stood before them, his hands trembling before he shoved them in his pockets, Vee had remembered that Dominic hated public speaking. But Farid had stepped closer, as if offering his presence as reassurance, and Dominic's posture had eased, just a fraction. Vee had watched them, the way they looked at each other, the way they both seemed calmer next to each other, and had wondered what it would be like, to be someone's anchor that way, to trust someone that deeply.

Dominic's door opened and Farid looked at him, one eyebrow raised. He was a slim man, neatly built, with dark hair and eyes, a bold nose, and a distractingly sweet mouth.

"Planning on standing out there all day?" he inquired, his soft, husky voice amused.

"Sorry," Vee said, and shoved the basket at him just as Dominic appeared behind Farid.

Vee had never spoken to Dominic before. He'd been hired by Melissa, and kept in the bakery most of his time. Senna usually made the deliveries to the top floor.

Dominic was intimidatingly tall, with brown hair that fell in shining waves around his face and dark gray eyes. He looked politely interested but also somewhat irritated at being interrupted.

Vee gulped and held out the basket again.

"Oh, you must be Vee," Dominic said, as Farid took pity on Vee and accepted the baked goods. "I've heard a lot about you from Lily."

Despite himself, Vee groaned. "Whatever she told you, it's not true, I swear."

Dominic grinned. He had a nice smile, Vee thought helplessly. "So you didn't tell a police officer he was raised by a pig, which was why he made such a good cop?"

Vee winced. "I, um. That's not an exact translation, but...." He floundered as Dominic and Farid waited expectantly, matching looks of curiosity on their faces. "I don't keep halal?" Vee offered feebly.

Dominic burst out laughing as Farid rubbed his face, unable to hide the twitching of his mouth.

"I like you," Dominic said when he'd sobered. "It was nice to meet you, Vee. Tell Senna thanks for the pastries." He disappeared back into the office as Farid lingered, dark eyes amused.

Vee remembered the pomegranate soda and held it out hastily, kicking himself, but Farid just accepted it with a nod.

"Get in here, 'Rid," Dominic called, his voice dark with promise, and Farid gave Vee a smile and slipped back into the office, closing the door behind him.

Alone, Vee wondered briefly if he could die from embarrassment, or if retiring to become a monk in a secluded monastery was a more feasible alternative. He wandered back toward the elevator, thinking about the young man behind the dumpster again. Would he still be out there when Vee was off work? Probably not, and even if he was, Vee was likely to just get another pastry hurled at him for his efforts.

Sure enough, when he clocked out and stepped through the back door with a box of baked goods, the young man was nowhere in sight.

He walked around to the front of Spectral, a towering glass and steel structure, and stopped at the sight of a group of people gathered by the doors. They were holding up signs. One said "LEVITICUS 18:20", and Vee made a mental note to look it up later. Another said "KEEP QUEERS OUT OF OUR SOFTWARE." Vee scowled at that. A third sign simply said "SPECTRAL = SIN".

One of the protestors spotted Vee. "Excuse me, sir, do you work here?" he called. He was a tall man, thin and pale with blond hair fading to gray and stooped, rounded shoulders.

Vee tipped his chin up. "So what if I do?"

The man held out a pamphlet and Vee took it warily. "HOMOSEXUALITY IS SIN", it told him in bright, cheerful letters, and underneath, an address for the Church on the Hill.

Vee dropped the pamphlet on the ground and wiped his hand on his shirt. "You people are sick," he said, clutching the box of pastries to his chest.

"Oh no," the tall man said earnestly. "Gay people are the sick ones. We're trying to *save* them. That's our mission from God."

"They don't *need* 'saving'," Vee hissed. "*We* don't need saving. Take your hate elsewhere. Why are you even protesting here?"

The man's eyes clouded with anger and distaste and he took a step back. "One of the largest software development companies in north America, and it was founded by a pair of faggots," he spat.

Vee flinched. "Dominic and Cory are better people than you'll ever be," he said.

The man sneered and Vee shook himself. Why was he even engaging?

"This has been fun, but I have to go give food to the homeless and then have sex with my boyfriend," he said brightly, and relished the look of horror on the man's face as he spun and walked away. Safely out of sight around the corner, he hailed a taxi. "Nearest homeless shelter, please," he told the driver

Order Broken Promises now!.

www.ingramcontent.com/pod-product-compliance
Lightning Source LLC
Chambersburg PA
CBHW070827190726
48292CB00006B/2127